Koftas and

2

Warren Chapman

ISBN: 9798339633181

Independently published

© Warren Chapman

Warren Chapman asserts his moral right to be identified as the author of this work.

All rights reserved. No part of this publication may be reproduced, stored in a retrieval system, or transmitted in any form or by any means, electronic, mechanical, photocopying, recording, or otherwise, without the prior permission of the copyright owners.

All characters in this publication are fictious and any resemblance to real persons, living or dead, is purely coincidental.

Cover Design © Georgia Chapman

Koftas and Yellow Rice

by

Warren Chapman

TABLE OF CONTENTS

About The Author	vii
Dedication	xi
Yasmin. Bristol 1983	1
Funeral	3
Dad	10
Ronnie: Milktooth 1954	21
Ambulance	29
Yasmin. Bristol 1983	40
Nite Club	43
Mr Das	53
Miss Costello	65
Yasmin: Jakhoo Hill	71
The Punjab Paradise	74
The Legendary Fighting Cocks	84
Yasmin: The Gold Watch	95
Birmingham Polytechnic.	98
Koftas And Yellow Rice	107
Tommy Deathridge	117
Yasmin: Fire	126
Brockwell Park	128
Guitar	141
Yasmin: Partition	149
Turban	155

Mimi	169
Ronnie: Partition	178
The Social	184
Ronnie: Smoke	191
India	202
Ronnie: Lucas	211
The Red Lion	217
Whitey	223
Shame	235
Lenny	243
Accident Hospital	250
Burglary	258
Coffee At Gigi's 1984	268
Acknowledgments	279

ABOUT THE AUTHOR

Koftas and Yellow Rice is Warren Chapman's fiction debut. He previously worked as an advertising copywriter but now practises and writes as an Advanced Clinical Practitioner in Birmingham. He is widely published in healthcare journals. He also plays bass guitar in local Birmingham band, The Cadenzas. His family are mixed race Anglo Indians, an experience that has inspired this novel.

"Home was where the English came from and went back to, though I never could. Home was where they did not have a city and cantonment in every big town, so that the officers could laugh themselves sick at an Anglo-Indian who talked about how he was going 'Home to Southampton Cantonment'. Our house was Number 4 Collett Road, a bungalow sitting on a tied piece of land which Pater and everyone in the house repudiated."

John Masters. Bhowani Junction. 1954.

DEDICATION

This work is dedicated to my wife, Kaye, my children, Lewis, Callie and Bella, my mother, Sandra, my father Charles and his Anglo Indian family, who were nothing like the Merchants.

YASMIN. BRISTOL 1983

'At stroke of the midnight hour, when the world sleeps, India will awake to life and freedom,' came the scratchy voice through her red leather Roberts.

Yasmin Lal was chopping onions in her kitchen, and on hearing the Received Pronunciation of Jawaharlal Nehru froze, slicing her finger with the knife. Yasmin normally liked listening to Radio 4 when she cooked. But not today. Not that. Nehru's speech on the eve of that first day of Indian independence in 1947 marked a severing for her. A cutting from which she had never recovered.

Yasmin reached for a cloth to staunch the flow of blood dripping from her finger. Then she reached for the knob on the radio to stop the words, as if she could stop what had occurred on that night all those years ago. Finally, she reached for the gas, turned off the simmering lentils, and sat down, squeezing the cloth against her throbbing finger, feeling the pain reaching sharp into her chest.

Her eyes were streaming now, though whether from the onions, her finger, or the memories, she could not tell. She held her cloth-wrapped, bloodied hand against her breast. The hard lump she had found there felt like a knot, a physical manifestation of the deeper visceral canker inside her mind.

All her family but Yasmin died that night. She was all

that was left. Along with that wooden box and what laid within. And even that had been taken.

Yasmin looked out into the garden of her house in Bristol. The rhododendron had flowered spectacularly. Like her it was an exile from the Himalayas. A reminder of Shimla, the hill station town of her birth and home of her first family. Now it was time, if only her health would allow. Time to visit her hometown once again and try to retrieve that which had been taken from her.

FUNERAL

My father, Ronald Merchant, died in 1984. To me, Stephen Merchant, his funeral was much more interesting than my dad's apparently very ordinary life seemed to deserve. It was the unexpected appearance of two men that caused me no small amount of intrigue. For now, we will call the strange two, Red Kicker Man and Safari Suit Man.

Red Kicker Man stood over on the other side of the black, beckoning hole. I had no idea who he was. He was a little apart from the others, though there were only a few of us. He was a middle-aged man, but he had a shabby style that seemed to cost him little effort. Even as a seventeen-year-old I was impressed. He had long dark hair with streaks of grey, snapped back smartly in a ponytail. The cut of the fraying lapels and his long bony contours suggested his suit was one he had successfully dusted off for years. There was no tie, but he had a silk Paisley scarf with a dominant red pattern to match his shoes. A matching handkerchief puffed out of his breast pocket. The red Kickers, under the drainpipe trousers, appeared a more recent purchase. He looked good for his years, and I remember hoping I would be able to carry off a display like that when I reached his age.

I saw my mum squeezing her eyes at him like she did at me when I had done something really bad. She was also exchanging stabbing, look, look, glances with her sister, my Auntie Brenda, as the man took his turn to toss soil into the grave. They seemed to know him but not approve, and I suspected it was not just because he had worn red shoes to a funeral.

I looked at my sister, Susan, standing next to me. She had noticed him too. She made her dunno face. But then she made her look over there face and I saw another unknown man bobbing around behind some gravestones further back.

That was Safari Suit Man. He was short, slightly overweight and had darker skin and greying black hair. The safari suit was beige, and he wore large silver-framed sunglasses that put me in mind of Elvis. I was sure I had seen him before. In fact, I had been thinking of him only the previous evening. He was looking over at us, but then he seemed to slip, disappearing behind a tall gothic stone, before rising again, his sunglasses askew. As I watched him dust himself down, I was aware of Susan's shoulders quivering and I bit my lip hard. But then I made the mistake of looking at her. That was when we both started spluttering and quickly walked away together to escape the disapproving looks. No one else seemed to have noticed the Safari Suit Man, who I saw was now quickly departing, patches of adhered mud on his trousers and suit jacket.

I know it was wrong to laugh at my father's funeral, but that was a nice moment for me. Susan is two years older, and when we were growing up it was rare that we weren't having a dispute about something or other. But we were close too, and we got on well. At the time my dad died though she was away in Leeds, at University, so we had drifted apart. That fit of mutual giggles was a return to the closeness we had once shared, and it felt good amongst all the bleakness of the burial.

Red Kickers Man came to the gathering after at The Robin Hood, a large pub on the edge of south Birmingham, not far from the cemetery and near my mum and dad's house. Safari Suit Man did not attend. I suppose his outfit was in no fit state for a social occasion after sliding around in cemetery mud. But he had not really joined in at the burial in any case. He had only stood on the periphery, reflecting his place perhaps in my father's life. I had no idea and was more confused as the funeral went on.

Red Kickers Man seemed the sort of bloke at home in a pub with a pint. I saw him chatting to Brenda's husband, my uncle Derek. Brenda kept looking over at them and Derek seemed uncomfortable, stepping back as if to try and get away, but each time the man stepped forward and re-closed the gap. I was sitting with my mum, Susan, and the elderly couple who lived next door to us. I wasn't paying attention to what they were saying, though, I was too engrossed in RKM.

In the end, Derek successfully left the man and returned to Brenda. She had her back to me, so I couldn't see her facial expression, Derek's smile quickly disappeared though as he looked at her.

The Red Kicker Man caught my eye and nodded towards an empty chair and table, it seemed he wanted to speak. I was intrigued. I wanted to know more about him. Why had he come to my father's funeral? I managed to creep away from Susan and my mum without them noticing. But that would not last long.

'Clench your buttocks, Stephen,' he said as I took a seat.

'What?' I wondered what he was going on about.

'When you get the giggles, you should clench your buttocks.' He reached down, pulling a tin out of his pocket, then opened it. I could smell the warm fug of the tobacco inside. 'An actor told me that,' he continued, pulling cigarette papers out of a Rizla packet and starting to place tobacco inside. 'If you clench your buttocks, it will stop you laughing when you shouldn't be. I had to do a lot of buttock-clenching listening to what was said about your father during that service.' He picked up the open tobacco-filled cigarette paper and deftly rolled it into a neat cylinder. Licking the edge, he placed it into his mouth. I was fascinated by this sleight of hand. I had never seen a cigarette rolled. More than that I was still wondering what he was doing at this funeral.

He lit the cigarette and went on speaking. 'I don't blame you for laughing, Stephen. Sometimes we do that when we're nervous or upset. It helps us take our mind off things. Have you been to a funeral before?' He nodded as I shook my head. 'I thought not. And then the first funeral is your father's.' He blew out a perfect smoke ring, as if to punctuate his statement.

His words were welcome to me. Finally, there was

someone who understood what I was feeling. After our graveside giggling exploit, Susan and I were in disgrace. My mum had not said anything, but you could tell she was upset with us. Her silence made it worse, I would have preferred it if she'd had a go at us in the car back from the cemetery, instead of the injured taciturnity we were subjected to.

'Who are you?' I asked.

'I knew your father,' he said simply, blowing cigarette smoke to one side, to avoid it going in my face. 'We went back a long way.'

I was interested. My dad had not, to my knowledge, had any friends. There was Ken, who worked for him at the factory. And dad seemed to get on well with Derek when we all met up, but other than that my father was a very solitary man. The funeral reflected that. Ken had come, and we had Brenda and Derek, a few neighbours, this old man who said he knew dad from the allotment, and then a couple of nurses from the hospice where dad had spent his final days. If the number of people who attend a funeral is an indicator of what you achieved in life, the amount of humanity you leave an impact on, then my dad's life appeared to be a failure. I was not even sure how I felt about dad's death myself. We had not had a good relationship and my teenage years did nothing to improve that. In fact, I feel more grief at my father's passing now I am in my 50s than I did back then when I was seventeen. I guess I know and understand a lot more about him, can imagine the way mine and my dad's relationship might have developed as I reached adulthood.

'What the priest said about your dad was wrong,' said Red Kicker Man. 'There were whole aspects of his life missed out.'

This made sense to me. I knew very little about my father. He didn't speak about his childhood or anything like that. He had hardly spoken to me at all, except to complain about something or other.

'Even the music was wrong,' said Red Kicker Man. 'I don't mind a bit of classical myself. But your dad used to be mad on the Everly Brothers and Eddie Cochran. All that old rock 'n' roll.'

I thought, well maybe he was, but his tastes definitely changed as he got older. My dad would not countenance any other music but classical played in the house as long as I'd known him. So this revelation into another facet of my father was intriguing. It made me want to learn more about him. The funeral up to this point had not provided enlightenment. At the service, the priest said a few words about dad's apprenticeship at Lucas and then him setting up his own business. There was his love of Aston Villa. Then his marriage to mum and the arrival of Susan and later me, but nothing else. I knew absolutely zero about his childhood or his parents – they had seemingly died before I was on the scene. Dad never even mentioned them and I was keen to learn more. I had the bits and pieces I found at dad's factory unit but had yet to go through, and I was hungry to find out what this man knew about my father.

But I was not likely to find out on that day.

'I don't think I'm wanted here. That's a shame as I need to talk to you about something,' said the Red Kicker Man, looking past me.

I turned. Brenda and Derek were approaching. Brenda looked annoyed. Derek looked nervous and was hurrying to keep up. Mum was watching us all, her eyes doing that squeezing thing again.

'Will you go to your mum,' said Auntie Brenda to me. It wasn't phrased as a question, if you know what I mean.

I moved quickly, nodding apologies at the man.

As I walked away, I heard Derek speaking. 'Look Lenny, it's probably best if you just go.'

Susan was sitting by the bar, a glass of Coke before her, reading the Guardian: an article about coalminers, judging by the picture.

'Did you speak to him?' She looked up, then took a sip from the straw poking out amongst the ice cubes.

'Well, I was hardly given a chance,' I replied, wondering why she had a newspaper at her father's funeral.

'They don't like him. Ken was just telling me. Dad caught him burgling the house once.' She looked down at the paper, turned a page and then looked back up briefly. 'Apparently he's our uncle.'

DAD

The current trend at funerals is for people to get up and talk about their loved ones. They play their favourite music. Celebrate their lives. There was not much of that at my dad's funeral, though we were allowed to play a piece of music. The night before, mum and I sat in the living room while Susan went through dad's records. She placed the disc on the turntable, examined the sleeve notes and then carefully counted the patterns of the grooves to get to the track she wanted. It seemed Susan had insider knowledge regarding our dad's collection of vinyl. The music meant nothing to me, it just sounded like the usual boring noise when he'd played his classical records. Nowadays, my tastes have changed. I know that Susan was playing the wonderful Nimrod, from Elgar's Enigma Variations. I don't know whether Susan meant it, but the choice of that work seems apt as I reflect on what a mystery my dad was to me back then. But these days, dad is less of an enigma, and I find nothing boring about Elgar. But was I right about Elgar in 1984, or am I right now? Have I just become like my father because that was the only flawed template I had to follow?

Earlier that day, Susan and I had gone to dad's factory unit to sort through his things. Mum couldn't face it and wasn't keen on us going either, but Susan was adamant.

'We need to go through his belongings,' she said. 'We need to look to see if there were any insurance policies or anything.'

'But you can't go through his things. They're his. They're private,' said mum.

'He's dead, Mum,' replied Susan flatly.

I remember how shocked I felt at Susan's bluntness. Mum looked upset, confused and small. I can still see her, sat there, leaning forward on that horrible brown Dralon sofa we had, blinking her eyes at Susan, as if she had been just told of her husband's death for the very first time.

'You'll have to go through them if you don't want us to.' Susan was heedless of mum's reaction. 'He should have told you all about that sort of thing anyway.'

Mum just sat there, her mouth slightly open, though whether she was looking for words or a breath, I had no idea.

My dad had dealt with all the business side of things in their marriage. The bills. The mortgage. Insurance etc. But then when the lung cancer was diagnosed, he went into denial. At first, he didn't even tell us what was wrong; that he was going to die. It was the consultant at the hospital who told my mum. Dad was really annoyed about that.

So, he did not prepare us for any of the things we were supposed to do. The only person he did speak to was the Catholic priest at the hospice. Father O'Shea visited him every day and dad gave him all the details of how he wanted the funeral, with the burial and a full mass and everything, and then Father O'Shea told us later. Even the Funeral Directors had already been paid and instructed. But we had been in the dark. We didn't even know dad was Catholic, baptised and everything, according to the priest. Even mum hadn't known that.

'We were married at St James' Church in Handsworth,' mum told us, bewildered. 'That's C of E. He didn't tell me he was Roman Catholic. He never, ever showed any interest in religion.'

So, mum would not, could not, deal with looking through dad's things, but Susan was insistent.

'Mum, we've got to manage on our own now,' she said. 'How are you going to pay for things? How are we going to live? You've got your job at the bank, and I have my grant, but that isn't enough. We need to see whether there's any insurance and what's going on with dad's business.' Susan turned to me. 'Stephen, we need to get all the paperwork together and sort it out for her.'

There was nothing at home, so that's how we ended up going to the factory to check dad's office. As it turned out, everything was all neatly laid out and in its place, ready for us. There was a will, a life insurance policy and it seemed the mortgage was paid off. I won't bore you with the details. Suffice to say, we were all taken care of well enough. I don't know why he couldn't have just told us and saved us a lot of worry, but that was my father.

While we were there, Susan went to speak with Ken, and I was left alone. I sat down at dad's desk and looked about me. The office was very neat and tidy. There was an Esso poster with a picture of a tiger on it. At some point it had been torn and a once neat, but now peeling, strip of Sellotape had been applied. I idly pulled out the drawer in dad's desk, looking at the tidy array of stapler, packet of paper clips and Bic biros. I saw a wooden box pushed to the back and pulled the drawer out further to get at it. Too hard. The weight of its contents sent it crashing to the floor, scattering stationery everywhere.

'What are you doing, Stephen?' Susan rushed back in, staring at me and shaking her head as I squatted on the floor amongst a sea of paper clips. 'Well, don't expect me to help you, you clumsy idiot.' She went back out again.

I was happy to be left alone because I wanted to take a look at the wooden box without anyone else there. It was about the same size as a tobacco tin and inlaid with different colours of wood to form a beautiful pattern. I shook it gently and could hear something inside, sliding against the wooden casing. I tried to open the box but it was stuck fast. After trying for a while I noticed one of the inlays could slide out, revealing a keyhole.

I gathered up the paperclips and other drawer contents, looking for the key. The drawer was upturned and I picked it up to set it right. As I did so, the bottom fell out and a sheaf of papers and envelopes drifted across the floor. The drawer had a false base, which was really well made. When it was placed back in, it was very difficult to notice that it existed. It looked like my dad's work. He was good with tools and well able to turn his hand to jobs like this.

'What are those papers?' Susan came back in again and started to gather them up. There were several closely-written sheets of A4 paper, written in faint pencil, along with some old typed letters. 'It's dad's writing,' she said, squinting as she started to read. 'Seems like some story he was writing.' Susan folded the sheets in half and put them in the rubbish bin.

I picked up one of the envelopes. It was addressed to dad and had been opened. The letterhead was a company called Das Pickles, in Tyseley, and the typed letter very simple:

```
Dear Mr Merchant,

Please contact me at your convenience
to pursue a matter that will be to your
pecuniary advantage.
```

The letter was signed with a spectacular signature above the typed name:

```
Chandra Das, Managing Director.
```

There were several envelopes, all dated at various times and all with the same typed letter.

Susan and I looked at them.

'This is strange,' she said. 'Maybe we should get in touch with this Mr Das.'

I took the A4 papers out of the bin and put them in my rucksack, along with the wooden box and the letters. Then I continued putting the scattered stationery back into the drawer, still looking for the key to the little wooden box. I searched all over the floor, under the desk and the other furniture in the office, but I found nothing.

I showed mum and Susan the box, paper and envelopes, while we were sitting around listening to Elgar.

'I thought I threw those in the bin,' said Susan, referring to the handwritten sheets.

'Let's have a look.' Mum squinted at the faint writing. 'My reading glasses are upstairs, and I can't be bothered to get them.' She tried again, then put the sheets down on the coffee table. 'I'm too tired now, anyway. I'll read them another time.'

She shook her head blankly at the letters from Mr Das and was only marginally interested in the wooden box. 'No, there's no key that I know of,' she said. 'He had that old Oxo tin full of bits – you could look in there. There's nowhere else I can think of that he would keep something like that.'

I knew the tin she meant, and got it, along with mum's reading glasses. When I got back into the room Susan was gently shaking the wooden box.

'Well, knowing dad, it's probably something completely boring. Is there a key?' she asked.

I looked inside the tin. There was an old electric razor, a few pencils and some foreign coins, but not much else, certainly not a key.

'We could force it open,' I suggested, thinking of dad's tools in the garage.

Mum examined the box then. 'It's beautiful. It would

be such a shame to damage it. Let's see if the key turns up.'

I gave mum her reading glasses so she could look at what dad had been writing. I felt unsure about reading the words myself. I was so used to knowing nothing about my dad, I was apprehensive seeing something apparently so personal he had taken trouble to keep it hidden away.

Mum didn't seem to want to read it either, though. 'I told you, I'm too tired to read now.' She waved away the glasses' case, looked at the clock, and turned to Susan, who was pulling out another of dad's LPs. 'That's enough now. Can we have the telly on? It's time for the news.' Mum picked up the remote control. She stood up, jerking her hand in an exaggerated manner towards the TV as she pressed buttons. Nothing happened.

I reached up snatched it from her. 'You don't do it like that, Mum.' I turned the television on.

'I just can't get used to it.' Mum sat down again, defeated.

On the news, coal miners had walked out on strike from a colliery in Yorkshire. They were protesting over proposed pit closures, and they wanted increased pay. The reporter talked about the possibility of a national miners' strike and potential power cuts.

'Remember the last miners' strike in the seventies?' Mum brightened. She looked at the lampshade in the centre of the ceiling. 'Your dad fixed up lights powered by car batteries to cope with the power cuts. He was always very resourceful.' She sighed and looked at his photograph on the mantelpiece. 'He would be shouting at the television by now over this strike.' She shook her head. 'He said the unions have destroyed this country. He thought Maggie Thatcher was a godsend.'

'She's an evil woman.' Susan looked up. 'She's trying to break the miners. She hates them for bringing down the last Conservative government.' Susan put back the record she was holding. 'And I'm sorry to say this, but much as I love him, dad was deluded by that woman.' She pointed at the photograph of him. 'Forgive me, but he was exactly the sort of small-minded petty bourgeoisie Thatcher was fooling to get into power in the first place.' She stood up and held her hands in front of herself, fists clenched. 'And then... and then...' She dropped her hands. 'You idiots voted her in again last year.'

'You're so much like your dad.' Mum smiled and carried on watching the news.

Susan stared at mum, but whatever she might have been going to say she kept to herself. She left the room, slamming the door.

Mum looked round at me. 'She's been getting some funny ideas since she went to university.'

I quickly left the room too and went up to my bedroom, taking the wooden box and the papers with me. I did not want to be left alone with mum. I thought again of how Susan's knowledge of dad's record collection was a complete surprise to me. The music had always been like an irritant, and I had never discussed any of it with him. Susan seemed to have had a relationship with him completely different to mine. She spent a lot of time with dad at his work, though, helping out and earning extra money when she was between university terms.

I remember a day two months after dad was diagnosed with lung cancer. The years of smoking twenty Player's Number Six had seeded a lump of chaos and his decline was fast. He had been at home for a while and was then admitted to a hospice. I took my turn to sit by his bedside but struggled to know what to say. Dad was unable to converse for very long in any event, his breathing was too laboured and rapid and just saying a few words seemed to exhaust him. He'd called one of the nurses over and slowly, reaching his wasted hand under his pillow, he brought out a letter.

'Would you post this for me, love?' he asked her.

I caught a brief glance of a stamp, but then he turned the envelope so I couldn't see whom it was addressed to. Of course, I know now. Back then, I said, 'I could post that for you, Dad. There's a pillar box on the way out. I can drop it in.'

'No.' Dad was emphatic. He nodded slowly, finding a smile for the nurse. 'Jane?'

The nurse smiled back. 'Anything for you, Ronnie.'

Dad grinned, winked at the nurse, and then slowly nodded, his skeletal chest heaving to find air. I was intrigued at the charm he managed to display for the nurses looking after him. I had never witnessed such charisma at any other time. He looked at me. 'Don't tell your mum.'

I nodded, wondering whether I was not supposed to tell mum about him flirting with the nursing staff or sending someone a letter. Regardless, those were pretty much the last words I heard from dad.

His was the first dead body I ever saw. I clearly remember standing by it with mum and Susan. It haunted me for ages afterwards, seeing my dad lying there lifeless, the breath sucked out of his cheeks. It was especially haunting that night before the funeral, after I had retreated to my room with the wooden box and dad's writing that no-one seemed interested in but me. I went to look at the papers, and as I did so, I found a photograph that must have got caught up with the sheets when they were placed on the coffee table. Mum had been going through lots of old photos. She seemed to get some comfort from them.

The photograph was of all of us: mum, dad, Susan and me. In it, we were walking down a road on a caravan site in Wales; I could see the caravans behind us, framed by a green, fern-covered hillside in the background. Dad was as inscrutable as ever.

I looked at the face in the picture and compared it to the one I'd watched sucking its last breath out of the air. I had known dad would die, and in the end, I felt that final breath could not come soon enough, an end to the suffering we were all going through. But now, lying on my bed, the sweet smell of dad's decay lingered in my thoughts like a rebuke. I could not believe he was dead, at all, and I regretted – still regret – not finding out who and what dad was while he was alive.

Before we left the hospice, the staff nurse spoke to us. 'He was a lovely man.' She patted mum's hand and swabbed a tear herself. This comment from a stranger warmed me and would prove both a comfort and an enigma. Was my dad really a lovely man? Was that how other people saw him? I had seen him turn the charm on with the nurses. But that was not my own experience.

The photograph had been taken as we walked to the caravan site's social club. A photographer took pictures of families as they wandered down and they were all displayed the next day. Mum bought a copy. But it was not a nice photograph. Mum had complained because I got my trousers dirty climbing a wall, so dad slapped me hard against my head. Mum then transferred her anger from me to dad and, despite her smile for the photographer, I could still see the rage in her face. There was also the pain of injustice in my younger self's eyes, and I could still feel the hurt even after so long. I still feel it now, to tell the truth, even though all I have is just have a memory of a memory.

Our family had dressed up to go out; we were always well turned out, mum insisted on it. Hence the trauma with the dirtied trousers. Dad would have washed, shaved, and changed his shirt. He had long hair he tried to comb over to hide a bald patch, but the wind was blowing it out of place. Susan was holding one of his hands. In his other, dad had the ubiquitous cigarette.

There was some kind of entertainment on at the club

– a singer, or a band, I can't remember. There was one man, though, who looked and sounded Indian, and he seemed to know Dad. He called him by his name: Ronnie. But dad just told him, 'You've got the wrong man, mate. I don't know you at all.' He was even more bad tempered throughout the holiday after that. And we didn't go to the social club again.

The next time I saw the Indian-looking man from the social club was at dad's funeral. He was wearing a safari suit and sliding around in the cemetery mud.

RONNIE: MILKTOOTH 1954

I went out of the house and into the yard. There was what they called a brewhouse there, where mother and the court's other women tried to keep our clothes clean. It was an impossible job, what with all the filth everywhere – even in the air. Next to the brewhouse was the outside lav, which we shared with the neighbours. It always stank. It was worse in the summer, but even on that cool, wet, autumn night it stank like something was dead. I stifled a retch, and put my hand in my wind-cheater pockets, wishing I'd put on something warmer, but it was too late now. I didn't want to be late. I cut down the entry, then wound my way out through the shiny streets amongst the back-to-backs and factories.

That was the night I met Milktooth.

I was off to collect my mother from The Palladium, where she was working as an usherette. Once she'd expected to carry on teaching when we arrived in England. Just like she had in India. But that was a joke. They wouldn't recognise her qualification here, and of course there was no money spare for her to stop working and go back to college – assuming she could have got into college in the first place. Getting a job that wasn't in a factory had been hard enough. She was too dark-skinned for many jobs, you see. And of course, she had an accent. But after many attempts mother had managed.

I remember her face when she came back from the interview. She had slowly sat down on the armchair by the kitchen range, easing off her shoes and grimacing as she massaged her bunions. You had to sit down carefully on that chair and then lean to the right. The left armrest was loose, and you would end up toppling out if you weren't careful. That was the standard of the furniture we had, and father didn't have a clue about fixing anything like that. The dim gaslight sent shadows over her face, and I remember how old she was starting to look.

'How did it go?' asked father.

She looked up at him. She looked angry. Her eyes were shining.

'Oh well, don't worry,' my father said. 'There are plenty of other jobs.' He winced as a loud crash and shouting came from next door. That was always going on. Fighting and arguing from the neighbours.

'They offered me the job,' said mother, dabbing at her eyes with a handkerchief.

'Well, what's the matter, then?' Father lit up a Woodbine.

She shook her head and looked down at the cracked hearth. 'When I arrived, I had to go to the ticket booth to report for the interview.' She traced her toe along a threadbare section of rug. 'The lady there looked at me like I was nothing.' Mother pointed at her best dress. 'And I'd made such an effort for the occasion.' She took a deep breath. 'That lady left me standing there and went into the manager's office…' The tears were running black from her eye makeup. 'She said, "There's a coloured lady here".' Mother stared at father, looking for his response.

Father sat down at the dining table, lit the cigarette and, grimacing from smoke as he gripped the fag in his mouth, he poured a cup of tea for mother, adding two spoons of sugar and then milk. He took it over to her.

She nodded a thanks and continued staring. Waiting for him to say something.

He started to smile, but on seeing her face he stopped.

I watched father sit back down again slowly at the table and pour his own tea. I knew how he'd struggled. Carrying on as an engine driver had been impossible. He had only managed to get work as a platelayer: long, hard days in all weathers, maintaining the railway tracks. He had seen other inexperienced drivers recruited and trained, so could only assume he was being prejudiced against because of his darker skin and accent.

Mother was looking around the room. 'What have we come to, Bill? We're living like paupers. There is damp on the walls and rats in the yard. Lenny's got a cough that will not go away... ' Lenny coughed in response '...and we have to share an outside lav with four other families. Why are we living in a place like this?'

'It's all we can afford, Mary,' countered Bill.

'Yes, I know that.' She closed her eyes and shook her head. 'That's the problem. We would have been better off staying in India.'

'But you were the one who wanted to leave.'

'Yes, but I did not think it would be like this.

The conversation was all too familiar. Moving from India had been difficult. Lenny and I were sad to say goodbye to what we knew in Simla. But then lots of the Anglo-Indians were leaving. Since Independence seven years earlier, the India of our people was disappearing, and all our friends and relatives were packing up. Many went to Canada and Australia. Mother wanted to go to England though, to be near her sister, Elizabeth. We had been so excited to go to the mother country. But then we had to live with Auntie Betty and though she had made us welcome, her daughters and husband had been cold and unfriendly. Even the joy of reunion for the sisters Mary and Elizabeth had been short lived; the tension of our two families living together led to arguments. So, father had managed to find a house we could afford in Winson Green, a deprived Birmingham area, home to a prison, a mental asylum and an old workhouse and its infirmary. They said if you lived in Winson Green you would end up in either one or all of them.

Mother took the job at The Palladium. It was just on the end of the Soho Road, where Handsworth met Hockley. There was no direct bus service, but it was about half an hour's walk from our house. Mother was scared to walk home alone in the dark, though, so one of us had to meet her at the end of the evening shift.

Making my way to The Palladium, this evening, I cut down South Road. As I walked, I made out the shapes of youths under a streetlamp: Teddy Boys. Trouble. I crossed the road, wondering whether I should have turned back, but it was too far round going up past the church, and I worried I'd be late for mother. I should have gone back though, because as I continued, one of the Teddy Boys crossed over towards me.

'Leave him alone, Milktooth,' shouted one of the gang tiredly from over the road.

Milktooth raised a hand dismissively and strode closer. His feet were clad in thick crepe shoes, his hair greased forwards into a thick roll. He carried chips wrapped in newspaper, open in his left hand. As he got close, he smiled. I thought he was being friendly, and I relaxed a little. I noticed one of his teeth was gold.

'Hello mate. What's your name?'

'R... R... Ronald.' My voice came out higher than normal and my stutter kicked in. It had improved over the years but showed up whenever I felt unsure of myself.

'Rararonald,' repeated this Milktooth, affecting a falsetto voice. 'Where are you from, Rararonald? You're not from round here.'

I felt my hands beginning to shake; the initial friendly greeting followed by this mockery was disorientating and chilling. I could not speak. Saying anything more would just humiliate me further. It was not just the stutter and the tight, high voice, it was my accent, too. I still had an Anglo-Indian twang then, you see.

Milktooth brought his face close to mine until I could smell the chips on his breath.

'I asked you a question. Where are you from?'

'Devonshire Street,' I answered, regretting my reply almost immediately. For one, I had told him where I lived. And secondly, he didn't mean my address in

Birmingham.

Milktooth looked irritated. 'I mean where are you from, before?' And then repeated. 'You're not from round here?'

'I... I... I... India,' I answered, finally.

In reply, Milktooth held out the newspaper-wrapped packet he held in his hand. 'Would you like a chip?'

I was confused. I didn't want to take food from this stranger but then I was reluctant to cause offence. I decided it would be best to take a chip so I put my hand forward, tentatively. As I did so, Milktooth screwed the chip wrapper up in his left hand and drove his right fist hard into my face. Flashes lit up in my brain as I staggered back. My lip split and I bit into my tongue. Blood came thick into my mouth.

'Have a taste of that.' Milktooth's face changed, his eyes had grown wide, his head tilted back and cocked to one side. He spoke again. 'What are you doing on my street?'

I said nothing, uncertain, unable to find words. My silence earned me another solid, driving blow. This time to my left eye. I felt my legs slacken and collapse. I fell to the ground, watching Milktooth massage his fist. Then a kick to the abdomen left me sucking for air. Tears came to my eyes, and strangely I noticed how they created beautiful sparkles in the streetlamps.

'Leave him alone, Milktooth,' someone shouted again from over the road. The other youths were walking off now. I lay there, wounded. In our brief encounter – the smile and greeting; even in the violence – I felt a bond with Milktooth. It was completely disorientating, just like entering a mother country that did not want me.

I was aware of him kneeling beside me now, gently patting my pockets, like a caress. Then I felt a hand in my wind-cheater pocket; there was a half crown in there, but I wasn't worried about that. The hand went inside the trouser pocket, and I felt sick. I heard a low whistle as he emptied it.

'Very nice,' said Milktooth and softly stroked my cheek.

He stood up. He unwrapped the chip packet and slowly released the remaining chips from their Daily Sketch covering. They fell over me like petals. Then Milktooth swung his foot and kicked me again, this time in the ribs. 'Go home, you're not wanted here.' He crossed over the road, laughing, and following his friends, who were already walking off.

After a while, once I was sure they had gone, I got up. I found it difficult to walk. My lip and tongue were bleeding, and I felt a black eye coming on. But mother would be waiting for me. I held on to a garden wall, dusted off my clothes and tried to wipe the blood from around my mouth with a handkerchief. Then I started walking.

When I got to The Palladium, the doors were already locked, and I could see mother waiting inside.

'Oh, my God. What has happened, Ronnie? Who has done this to you?' Mother pulled me into the cinema and took me into the ticket office, sitting me down on a chair. 'Mr Murray, Mr Murray, can I have the first aid box.' She knocked on the manager's office door.

Mr Murray came out, looked at me and then disappeared back into his office. He came out slowly with the box. 'Here you are, Mrs Merchant.' He looked at me with disapproval. 'It looks like he's been in a fight.'

Mother took out a bottle of iodine and some gauze and started dabbing the cuts and abrasions on my face. 'My boys don't get into fights. What happened, Ronnie?'

I reluctantly related the night's events, missing out the theft. Mother turned to her manager. 'I need to call the police, Mr Murray. Can I use the telephone?'

'Please don't call the police, Mother,' I begged, wincing as she pushed a damp cloth against my eye. 'It's not worth it.'

'The lad is right,' Mr Murray agreed. 'The police won't do anything. It doesn't sound like there were any reliable witnesses.' He looked at the clock on the wall and took his coat from the stand. 'That lad needs to get home. Come on, I'll give you a lift.'

As we drove through the streets, I looked out of the car window, wondering what to do. But then the theft and the terror of my meeting with Milktooth were to pale into insignificance with what awaited us when we arrived back home

.

AMBULANCE

As inevitable as death is the inevitability of guilt for those left behind. My own particular guilt regarding the loss of my father included my first reaction as the storm clouds of his death started gathering. When I first came home to see an ambulance on the drive and the uniformed men manoeuvring dad down the stairs, I felt an exhilaration in the change of the weather. It was as if I could smell something different and exciting in the wind. A storm was coming, and things might never be the same again.

They were bringing him down on some kind of collapsible chair. He had lost a lot of weight recently, but he was still a large man, and the ambulance men were struggling.

Mum backed out of the cupboard under the stairs, pulling with her a suitcase. It was one of those battered old cases she would pack for our rare holidays to Cornwall or Wales. Her face was strained, and she opened her mouth to say something, but as usual she was interrupted by dad.

'Rose, get him in the living room.' Dad waved towards me as if I was some kind of inanimate obstacle.

I went through to the back room, threw my rucksack on the sofa, and stared at the blank TV screen. I wanted to put it on, but I knew it was best to wait until he was out of the way. I could still hear him barking instructions at mum and the ambulance men.

'Rose, have you packed my shaving gear? Where are

my cigarettes and lighter? Careful, lads, watch the paintwork.'

I placed my hands over my ears and looked at my rucksack, heavy with books and folders.

As if he knew what I was thinking, dad's voice came through from the hallway. 'Make sure he gets on with his reviewing.' He was speaking to mum, but his voice was pitched so I would hear.

My 'A' levels were coming up in May. It was already March, and I knew I was not making enough progress with my revision. Now all this was going on.

Mum came into the room. She looked really scared.

'What's going on, Mum?' I asked.

'He coughed up blood,' she said. 'It was all around the wash basin.' She pushed her hand through her hair. 'I found him sitting on the bathroom floor. I think he must have fainted. There's a bruise coming up on his head. But you know what he's like. He doesn't want any fuss and he says nothing is wrong with him.'

Dad had seemed unwell for a while now. He was coughing continuously. He looked incredibly pale and he had lost a lot of weight. Mum kept asking him to go to the doctor's, but he wouldn't go. In fact, he got angry at any suggestion of it.

'I called the ambulance without telling him.' The worry on her face broke for a second as she gave a quick, almost imperceptible, mischievous grin. 'He was furious when they arrived. But the ambulance men were so good, and they've managed to persuade him to go to the hospital.' She looked away from me towards the back garden as she spoke, her voice breaking. 'He couldn't even stand up; that's why they've had to carry him down the stairs.'

Getting up, I passed her tissues and put an arm around her.

Mum wiped her face and sniffed. 'I need to go in the ambulance with him. I better hurry.' She looked towards the kitchen. 'There's a casserole in the oven, you'll need to give it another twenty minutes. Is that alright?'

I waved her on, telling her I could cope, and followed her to the front door. I tried to grab the suitcase for her, but she gently pushed me away. 'Just stay by the door, Stephen. He's ashamed for you to see him. I'll call you from the hospital.'

I watched mum get into the ambulance. She briefly lost her footing as she climbed up the steps; the ambulance man had to steady her. She looked so small and vulnerable, and I wished I could go with them to support her. Instead, I went back to my rucksack and emptied the contents on to the sofa beside me. There was a worn copy of George Orwell's Nineteen Eighty-Four that I put to one side. The rest was all the stuff for my 'A' levels: maths, physics and chemistry. But I could not work up any enthusiasm for the subjects. They were dad's choices, not mine. He had pushed me to study for and apply to do Mechanical Engineering at University. I had been looking at Leeds. But the only real attraction for me was getting away from home. In reality, I was more interested in thinking about books like Nineteen Eighty-Four.

My friend Jay was studying the novel for his 'A' level English. It seemed the examination board had thought it very appropriate to set Nineteen Eighty-Four for the exams taking place in the same year. Once, rather than hanging around waiting for Jay, I joined him for a revision session, held by the English teacher, Miss Costello. She had given me a spare copy because I had been so interested. I had actually joined in more of the discussion than the others, enjoying reading about a dystopian future. It was awakening questions. Not only about the society we lived in, but also the views of my father, which I had never questioned before. The fact that the book was set in the year we were living in, chilled me and I could see the examination board's point. At the revision session, Miss Costello compared the future Orwell had imagined when he wrote the book in 1948, with the 1980s we were living in. Some of the comparisons she drew out were so interesting and frightening that I spent more time discussing 1984 with Jay than I did going over Newton's laws and the Periodic Table of Elements.

It confirmed to me that I was taking the wrong path. My mum and dad, especially dad, constantly told me that I should work hard because of the impact on the rest of my life: unemployment was high; school leavers were going straight from school to the dole queue. Despite the otherwise appearances of indifference, I realise now that dad genuinely cared about my future. But his scope of life's opportunities was limited, pushing me into 'A' levels in the only field he could make sense of. But I didn't even want to do mechanical engineering,

I could not revise. Dad was going into hospital, and I felt overwhelmed and confused. However, at the forefront was a sense of release. An oppression lifted, and I decided to make the most of it.

I went upstairs and got my cassette player from underneath the bed. Hidden in my wardrobe were some illicit tapes. One was Black Sabbath, Paranoid. Dad did not like either me or Susan listening to what he disparagingly called pop music – though I wouldn't call Black Sabbath pop. In fact, he would not allow us to play our music in the house at all. Downstairs was an expensive array of HiFi equipment but no-one, including mum, was allowed to touch it. Dad's extensive collection of classical music and his intolerance of any other musical genre meant he had even adjusted the inner workings of the radio so that only Radio 3 could be tuned into.

I amassed my secret selection of music thanks to Jay. His older brother, Bal, had a big record collection and Jay would do recordings for me. He had taped the Black Sabbath album as well as Pink Floyd's The Wall and Led Zeppelin IV. But Bal was also into the Beatles. Consequently, I was getting into them too, and every night, when I went to bed, I listened covertly to my secret music collection via an earphone plugged into the cassette player Jay had leant me. I always prayed dad wouldn't come in and catch me.

Now he was out of the house, I could dispense with the earphone and put the volume up high. But then, as I pushed the button and the cassette housing rose from the machine, I had a better idea. I shut the cassette player and took the tape downstairs. I turned on dad's HiFi and slid the cassette into his player, turned up his amplifier and felt that first distorted guitar chord reverberate through the living room.

The enjoyment I felt at hearing this music in such clarity was tempered by knowing it wasn't allowed, bringing my resentment of my father into greater focus, dad had not even addressed me properly as he was being taken out by the ambulance men. That was typical of him. I felt like he had given up on me, that I hadn't turned out to be the sort of son he expected. He never praised me. Even when I passed my 'O' levels with 8 Bs, dad wanted to know why I didn't get any As.

And I hadn't just failed dad on the academic side. One of his few interests was football. He talked about how he played football as a youth, how he had been in trials for West Brom and played in Sunday League football. But he never got out a football with me; I had never even seen him kick a ball. Yet dad was disappointed I didn't get picked for the school football team. It was a joke that he even thought that I could – I could barely get picked for a kick-about in the school playground, always the last to get chosen. The best I could do was feign an interest and had even gone to a few Villa matches with him.

As a young child, I learnt not to go crying to dad when

I was bullied by other boys at school. I remember how angry he had been when I talked about being punched by an older lad at school. I was only six.

'Why didn't you punch him back?' Dad asked. 'You let them get away with it once and they'll always be at you.'

A lesson in punching had followed, with me having to reluctantly punch dad's hand.

I didn't bother to complain about any injustices at all. I knew he would be not only unsympathetic, but also angry. So, when I was fifteen and came up against Shane Spooner, it naturally followed that I would earn more of dad's disapproval.

Spooner was a skinhead from Brookfields, the comprehensive I attended. I was in the top stream of classes, where the higher achieving students were taught. Spooner was in one of the lower streams. It was a big school and though Spooner didn't know me, I knew him. Spooner was notorious. Kids at school were scared of him. He didn't even have a gang around him. He didn't need one, he worked alone.

I did a paper round at that time. After school I delivered fifty-six Birmingham Evening Mails on Hurst Lane. On Mondays, the papers were thin, making the job simple. By Thursday, the papers would be full of classified ads, making them thick, dense and heavy. I remember the cutting pain in my shoulders from the newsprint-stained bag's thin strap.

Hurst Lane consisted of massive early twentieth

century houses, the inhabitants of which were notorious amongst the other paperboys and girls for giving small tips at Christmas. The preferred round was on the nearby council estate where the morning papers were lightweight tabloids rather than heavy broadsheets and the yuletide tips were far more generous. I learnt a lot about life working the paper round.

On the Hurst Lane round there was a haven, a little cul-de-sac of more modest, friendly houses, built where one of the mansions had been pulled down. On this road an elderly couple were in the habit of looking out for me. The old man would leave the front door open and, as I walked up the drive with their paper, he'd run up from the kitchen, his wife clattering a Zimmer frame behind him, smiling as she struggled up to the door to see their paperboy. There was always something for me to eat. Some days a Penguin Bar or a Wagon Wheel, but on others it would be a piece.

'He's eaten all the Penguins, the greedy pig,' the old lady might say, nudging her head sharply at her husband as she grimaced up the hallway with her frame. 'So, I've had to make you a piece.'

The old man would grin sheepishly, wink and hand it to me, laid out on a sheet of kitchen roll. A slice of bread with a thick slab of butter and a generous spread of strawberry jam. I would balance it in one hand and eat as I continued the round, trying not to get my nose in the jam. It was easily my favourite over a Wagon Wheel or Penguin.

It was a heavy bag Thursday when I met Spooner.

'Alright, mate,' Spooner said, spitting spectacularly on the floor and staring intently at me. 'Can you borrow me 10p?'

'I don't have any money,' I lied, automatically patting my back pocket containing the neatly folded one pound note my mum had given me. It was to buy lamb chops for tea.

Spooner punched me on the cheek. It was not a hard punch. It was a testing of the water, like firing a gun over my head as a warning. I recovered quickly, and continued walking. Spooner followed.

'What's your name?' He took a half-smoked cigarette from behind his ear, placed it in the side of his mouth and lit it from a box of Swan Vesta.

I told him, my voice tight and high. The sulphurous odour of the match was tempered by the sweet smell of the tobacco, as I watched Spooner inhale, screwing his eyes up from the smoke.

Suddenly, Spooner pushed me hard. He timed the attack perfectly. The weight of the paper bag added to the momentum and took me over a low wall into a front garden. I landed heavily, crushing a geometric arrangement of flowers. I picked up and reassembled scattered newspapers, then brushed dirt and marigold petals off my school uniform. Spooner stood patiently waiting, drawing on his cigarette and staring blankly into the distance. On another occasion, the push and the fall into the garden might have been comical. High jinks.

Schoolboy fun. With Spooner it was pure malice; the fact that he appeared to take no pleasure in the act viscerally chilled me.

Spooner accompanied me for the rest of the round. The violence and humiliation continued in small and rising increments. Of course, he found and took the pound note. But the worst part of the experience was my relationship with the elderly couple. I could not walk up to their house with Spooner in tow. Spooner's malignant universe and their world seemed so far apart that I could not bear for them to meet. I certainly did not want them to see me in his company. And I did not want Spooner to witness my relationship with them. So, they did not get their newspaper delivered that day and, as Spooner and I left the cul-de-sac, I caught a distant glimpse of the old man, standing at the top of his drive, hand shading his eyes, staring, bewildered.

The door was never open after that. I was fined by the paper shop owner for missing a delivery and I pushed papers through the letterbox. No more Wagon Wheels, Penguins or pieces. If the old man or lady happened to see me, I was pointedly ignored.

That first day, after the last paper had been delivered, I saw dad's Rover pulled up by the end of the road. As we drew up to it, dad rolled down the window.

'Hello, son.' He looked long at Spooner and then back to me. 'Is everything alright?'

Spooner stared at dad, drew a long rattle at the back of his throat, spat, and then walked away.

'G... g... get in,' said dad.

His stutter had kicked in, which meant he was angry. I got in slowly; I wasn't sure what was worse. Being with Spooner or my dad.

Dad started the car and drew away. 'What's going on?'

'He's just a friend.'

'He didn't look very friendly. He didn't look like the type of friend I want for you.'

Suddenly, I felt an ache in my throat, and I could not stop the tears.

'What are you c... crying for?'

I told him what had happened. How the pound had been stolen. How I had been bullied by Spooner. But dad was not sympathetic, seemingly angrier with me than with Spooner.

'You've got to learn to stand up for yourself. Once you let people like that take advantage of you, they keep on coming back for more.' He looked at me with disgust. 'And wipe your face. You're like a girl.' It was the same refrain as he drove around looking for Spooner. I was praying we would not find him.

In the end, dad gave up, and we went to the butcher. He bought the chops and warned me not to say anything to mum about what had happened. He never mentioned the event again. But I felt it had marked a tipping point in dad's disgust for me. For months after, I continued to be terrorised by Spooner and I gave up the paper round in the end. But there was no way I could speak to my dad about it.

YASMIN. BRISTOL 1983

She was led into the consulting room by a nurse.

A pinstriped, suited figure sat with his back to her. 'Take a seat,' he said, head hunched in deep concentration as he wrote. After a while he turned, swivelling in his chair. A round-faced, middle-aged man with greying hair and erythematous complexion peered at her through small circular gold-framed glasses. He had a porcine air.

His actions put Yasmin in mind of a small boy, playing at being a doctor.

He screwed the lid on a gleaming, black fountain pen, scanning his eyes over her.

'Speak English?' The three syllables came out in a slow, steady staccato, each punctuated by a nod of his head.

'I have a modicum of understanding.' said Yasmin. 'I work as professor of linguistics at the university, I think I'll get by without an interpreter.'

Yasmin recalled with some satisfaction how the consultant coughed and dropped his Mont Blanc. But she also felt annoyance with herself at her attempt to impress the man. He thinks I'm some peasant fresh from the village. Wearing the salwar kameez didn't help. Since arriving in the UK as a child she had worn Western clothes, but more recently she had started dressing in Punjabi attire. This was primarily a political act. A reassertion of her identity and past, an assertion she felt that with her academic status, it was essential to make. But there were other reasons too. With its baggy trousers, loose top and matching scarf Yasmin found the salwar kameez very comfortable. She also liked the different colour combinations. Most of all, she liked visiting the Asian clothes shops on the Stapleton Road in Bristol. The visits took her back to her distant childhood in India, and her home before they burnt it down.

'So, why are you here?' the consultant asked her, straightening a bright red bow tie that put her in mind of the vaudeville.

Yasmin talked about her problems, the sudden weight loss and fatigue. The lump. The consultant then asked various questions. until he came to the one that had taken her straight back to India.

'Family history?' He inked an F and an H onto her notes and looked up at her expectantly.

Yasmin started searching in her handbag at that point, with no idea what she was looking for. She wondered if the doctor wanted the history of her family.

'Do you have any illnesses that run in the family? Have your parents or siblings had any cancers?' he clarified, pen hovering.

'I don't know, I'm afraid,' Yasmin finally replied, pulling her scarf, which was forever slipping, back over her head. 'I was orphaned when I was eleven years old.'

'I notice you have a Muslim first name and a Hindu surname.' The consultant placed his pen down and led her to the examination couch.

Yasmin was impressed at his knowledge. In spite of her initial antipathy towards the doctor, she was sensing the humanity beyond the bluster and pomposity. Yasmin thought of her name. She had essentially become a Lal following that first day of independence. She had lost her original Muslim surname and she could barely remember what it had been. As Muslim and Hindu India had been torn apart her new name was literally a coming together: the more typically Muslim Yasmin and the Hindu Lal. 'I was adopted by a Hindu doctor and his wife in India,' she replied finally, as he carried out the examination.

'They brought you to England?' The consultant was palpating where she had found the lump.

'Yes, we came in 1949. I was thirteen,' Yasmin told him. She remembered how cold and grim it all seemed when she arrived, the frosty welcome she received at the boarding school she was sent to. Now, as she re-dressed, she thought of her life in the UK. University had followed that boarding school, then a life in academia.

But all her achievements were now overshadowed by this lump.

Yasmin had to get back to Shimla.

NITE CLUB

Waiting for dad's funeral was hard enough. The last thing I needed was to meet up with Shane Spooner again.

It was customary practice for sixth formers to celebrate their eighteenth birthday at one of the Birmingham nightclubs. The clubs must have had databases with all our details. I don't know how they got them, and I didn't care at the time, but it could have been another parallel to draw with Nineteen Eighty-Four. They would send tickets out to the celebrant for a 'party' on or around their birthday date. It was not really a personal party; the club would be full of other sixth formers from around the city celebrating other students' birthdays. I had never been to a nightclub before. Clubs would go on until, two o'clock in the morning and dad would not allow me to stay out so late; there was no point in going only to leave early. But now dad was dead and, when I received an invite from one of the girls at school, Mum was more easily won around to the idea. She must have thought it would do me good to get out.

The party was to be held at Tommy's, a club at Five Ways in Edgbaston. The clubs had a strict dress code. If you were male, you had to wear a shirt, tie and shoes to get in. My wardrobe was limited in all respects and the only suitable attire I had was a suit I had worn to my mum's cousin's wedding the year before. The trouble was I had grown since then.

I put it on and went downstairs.

My mum looked me up and down, grinning. 'Are you wearing that?'

'Yes,' I replied, looking in the hall mirror and then back to her, wondering why she seemed to be questioning my outfit.

She put her hand over her mouth and turned away. 'You'll need to get a new suit for the funeral.'

I looked in the mirror again. The suit was a bit tight in parts, but it would have to do.

'Haven't you got anything else you could wear? I could help you sort something out,' Mum offered, moving to go upstairs.

'No, it's OK.' I was adamant now and getting annoyed.

'OK, suit yourself.' Mum smiled and then repeated the line to herself, emphasising the words. 'Suit yourself.' She seemed pleased with the pun. 'Do you want something to eat before you go out?'

'No, I'm having dinner at Jay's.'

'OK, suit yourself,' she repeated, stressing the words once again and laughing to herself.

I looked in the mirror once more. I thought I looked fine. I left the house quickly and walked down to the bus stop.

Jay's house was a large Victorian terrace with stainless steel windows and porch and a 1970s faux stone-clad exterior.

Jay's mum answered the door. She looked suspicious at first, but then her face relaxed. 'Stephen. So sorry.

Your daddy.' She gave me a sympathetic sad face and I knew she meant it. She was a nice lady. 'Come in.'

I followed her to the kitchen, where the swirly orange carpet was covered in plastic. Jay was sitting at the kitchen table with his grandfather. His mum spoke a few words in Punjabi and Jay started laughing.

'She didn't recognise you at first, in all your finery.' He pretended to knot an imaginary tie. Jay's mum grinned sheepishly and tapped Jay softly across his head.

'Nice trousers,' said Jay. 'Is it a new fashion to have them halfway up your calves? The jacket looks a bit snug too.'

'It's not that bad.' I looked down at my suit. I was starting to have misgivings about it now. Perhaps I should have listened to my mum. I looked at Jay. He was wearing a very nice suit and tie with a matching turban. The whole ensemble was spoiled, though, by a pair of tartan carpet slippers. 'Are you going in those?' I pointed at the slippers.

'Yeah, I'm going to wear slippers,' he said sarcastically. 'Actually, we don't wear shoes in the house.'

I looked down guiltily at my shoes. 'I'm sorry, shall I take them off?'

'No, no. Don't worry, you've already trodden dog shit everywhere.'

I looked back, worried, at the route I had taken to come in.

Jay's grandfather spoke angrily to Jay in Punjabi and then turned to me. 'Ignore him. You're a guest, please sit down.' He sat back in his chair and stared at Jay. 'Where are you going?'

'To a party, Baba,' said Jay.

As Jay's mum left the room, his grandfather looked down the hallway after her and lowered his voice. 'Are you going out drinking?' He smiled conspiratorially. 'Be careful, boys. Don't get drunk.'

Jay's mum turned back. Her English was limited but she had overhead and got the gist of what was being said. 'No drinking,' she insisted. 'Where are you going?'

'To a party,' Jay repeated.

'OK, no drinking. You be good boys.' She left the kitchen again.

Jay's grandfather winked at us and then turned to me, getting serious and putting his hand to his heart. 'I'm so sorry about your father, Stephen.'

I knew it had been five years since his son, Jay's father, had died in an accident at the foundry where he worked. I had found it so difficult to know what to say to Jay and his family at the time. Today, I was grateful for the fact that Jay's grandfather and mother had acknowledged my loss, but I was keen to move on to another subject.

The old man must have sensed this. 'How are you getting on with your studies, Stephen?'

'OK, thanks, Mr Virdee,' I replied. 'I'm just trying to keep up with the revision for my exams.'

'Very good,' said the old man. He gestured to Jay. 'I'm trying to make sure this rascal keeps up with his revision too. You are lucky to have the opportunity to get to university.'

Jay's grandfather was wearing a tweed jacket, light brown trousers and green military tie with a repeated red cannon motif. His hair was neatly combed and cut short on the sides and back. He had a thick, tightly-groomed moustache. He had been working on the crossword in The Guardian, and now he unfolded the newspaper and turned to the front page. The headline was about the miners' strike: "BLOCKADE AT THE PITS". He showed it to us.

'This is a key moment. The Conservatives are taking on the miners. But the miners brought the Conservatives down in 1974. Maybe they can do it again. Sometimes you must stand up for what you believe in. You have to stand up for yourself. Like we did against the British in India. Now the working classes need to stand up to Mrs Thatcher. If the miners lose this, then the left-wing in Britain will never be the same again. We will have lost the fight.'

Jay stood up. 'Yes, Baba.' He turned to me. 'We do need to do something about this. We need to act.'

I was wondering what we could do about it? It wasn't as if we were coal miners.

Jay seemed to lose interest, though, and started looking in the various gleaming aluminium pans sitting on the stove. 'Shall we eat?'

His grandfather shook his head and turned back to the crossword.

I loved eating at Jay's. His mum was a good cook. That

time we ate saag paneer, a Punjabi dish made with spinach and an Indian cheese. We also had some chickpeas, flatbreads called roti, and rice.

As usual, Jay served me the food without giving me cutlery: his family ate with their fingers. I started to eat, struggling to mix the rice with the curries and scoop it with my own fingers. I was getting it everywhere.

'The boy needs some tools,' said his grandfather, getting up. He handed me a spoon and fork and then sat down again with his newspaper.

'No, Baba,' said Jay. 'He eats like that even when he's got cutlery.'

Once we had eaten, we left to catch the bus into town.

At the bus stop, I looked at Jay's feet. 'Those are trainers.' He was wearing all black Adidas trainers. I could see the raised three stripes and a logo.

Jay looked down. 'Sort of.'

'It says on the ticket: no trainers.' I was annoyed. I had been looking forward to the evening. I hoped I might get together with a girl. I had no particular one in mind, just any nice girl. Now we might not even be able to get in.

'They're all black,' said Jay, still looking down. 'They look like shoes. Why would they have a problem with these?'

'Why couldn't you just wear shoes?'

'I don't like my shoes.'

The arrival of the bus ended the conversation. We sat in silence for a while as we drove past the shops on the Stratford Road. Eventually Jay spoke.

'My grandad makes a lot of sense when he talks about politics. He reads The Guardian every day. He watches the news. He never stops complaining about Margaret Thatcher.'

'Yeah,' I replied. Unsure what to add, I thought for a while. 'I'm not into politics. I heard enough of my dad going on. He loved Margaret Thatcher. I think they're all as bad as each other.'

Jay shook his head. 'That's not true. They're not all the same. My grandad is right about the Tories. And I think he's right about this miners' strike – it's time more people stood up against what's going on.'

I felt unable to contribute further to this. 'What was your grandad's job?'

'He used to work at Longbridge. But in India, when he was younger, he was in the Army. He's very proud of that. Later on, he became involved in politics and was part of the Independence movement. He got interested in literature and reading, that's why he's encouraged me to do English literature. My mum wanted me to be a doctor. Obviously.' He laughed and then stopped and lowered his voice. 'Probably, if my dad was still alive, he would have made me do medicine.'

The bus arrived in town. Getting to Tommy's involved riding another bus down Broad Street and to Five Ways. Tommy's was situated underneath a 1960s office block, which also housed a small shopping centre. There was already a queue of teenagers snaking by the shuttered shops. We recognised a few fellow sixth formers. I could see Katy Carter, a girl I had asked out for a date a few weeks ago. It had taken me months to work up the courage and she turned me down. And not in a nice way either. 'Why would I want to go out with someone like you?' had been her crushing response to my suggestion we go ice-skating together.

Jay straightened his gold-threaded tie. 'Tracey Turnball is here,' he said, looking over to the group. 'I think she fancies me. And,' he pointed at his red button down collar shirt, 'I've got my pulling shirt on.'

I looked at it. 'The only pulling you'll be doing in that is when you get home.'

Jay gave me a hard shove. 'She offered to revise with me.'

'There's an offer,' I said with sarcasm. But still, I was impressed Jay had got as far as that with any girl. It was better than I could do myself.

We reached the front of the queue. Two muscular-looking bouncers were checking tickets and frisking the entrants. They looked us up and down.

'We've got a right pair of beau Brummies here, ain't we?' The taller of the two looked at me. 'It's time you bought a new suit, mate. Looks like your trousers have fallen out with your feet. Anyway...' He pointed to me. 'You can go in.' He looked at Jay. 'But you can't.'

'Why not?' Jay was affronted.

The bouncer pointed at Jay's feet. 'Trainers.'

'What!' Jay squared up angry.

The bouncer stood firm, looking down at Jay, 'Come

on,' he said calmly. 'You,' he pointed at me, 'get inside. You,' he pointed at Jay, 'fuck off.'

I stepped back. Jay continued remonstrating. I felt annoyed now and walked off. I didn't want to go into the club without Jay, but right now I didn't want to spend any more time with him either. He had ruined the evening. I walked on, heading towards town.

The concrete of the sixties office and shop structure gave way to old dilapidated Victorian shuttered shops with occasional gaps covered by large advertising hoardings. Behind the hoardings, there was overgrown wasteland, the dark shapes of buddleia visible though gaps in the fencing. Bomb pecks, my mum called them: the gaps where buildings had been destroyed in the Second World War and still lay undeveloped forty years on.

As I was walking, I saw a figure approaching. There were lots of skinheads around, but even though I had not seen him for a while, I had not forgotten Spooner's purposeful gait. I hoped he hadn't seen me, and I quickly dodged down a side street, but Spooner must have recognised something about my movements and I felt a familiar nausea as I heard his voice behind me.

'Alright, Steve.' Spooner loomed up. He was dressed in his usual skinhead attire: ox blood Doctor Martens, White Sta Press trousers, green flight jacket. He had left school at the end of the fifth form and I had not seen him for a couple of years. His hair was cropped short, as usual, and he had gained a number of scars around his scalp. The crew cut served to accentuate these. The effect was terrifying,

'So, what are you up to, Steve?' Spooner asked. 'Are you still at school?' He grinned and spat. He didn't wait for an answer. 'I'm working at the bakery. I'm getting £50 a week.' He looked down the street and dropped his voice as if he was confiding something personal. 'I'm a bit short tonight. Can you borrow me a fiver?'

I did have a five-pound note and some change in my pocket. Enough for drinks and to cover the fare home on the night bus. I would only need the bus fare now. Still, I didn't want to give money to Spooner.

'I'm sorry,' I replied, 'I've got nothing spare.' I decided I needed to get back on to the main road, it was too quiet where we were. I needed to get away from Spooner. I turned to walk back up to Broad Street when Spooner gently put his arm around my shoulders. It could have been friendly, but his hand was tightening, forcing me towards the doorway of an old factory–

'Leave him alone, Spooner.'

Spooner let go of me and turned to respond to the voice.

It was Jay. He stared hard at Spooner.

Spooner tensed and I felt the skinhead's flight jacket moving across his shoulders, tightening, ready for the fight. But then he relaxed and took his arm away from me. 'Alright, Jayshree. How are you?' He smiled. 'I was just catching up with Stevie here.' He looked up the road towards Broad Street. 'Anyway, I've got to go.' He straightened his jacket and walked away.

Jay and I stood silent, watching him move quickly. Once Spooner got to the main road he turned and shouted, 'Wankers. Paki Raghead.' Then he disappeared around the corner.

Jay looked at me. 'He's nothing to be afraid of. All you have to do is stand up to him and he runs away.'

Nevertheless, that was not the last we would see of Spooner.

MR DAS

Dad's writing confused and exhilarated me. There were more episodes of his life outlined as well as that encounter with Milktooth, I did not know whether it was truth or fiction. There was lots to think about, but the word that stuck out for me was "India".

Dad was definitely olive-skinned and had dark – you might call it black – hair but I had never thought anything of that. Until now. The trouble was that, as usual, I could not get any kind of straight answer from mum. I hesitated to raise what dad had written with her, and it was no use asking Susan. Susan was unavailable. But then more letters from the pickle factory man gave me the push to bring the matter up.

The first dropped through the door a few days after the funeral. I picked it up and looked at it. It was addressed to mum but looked similar to those I had found sent to dad. It was in the same white envelope with the same misaligned typing.

Mum hardly ever had any typed letters, they had all usually been addressed to dad, so her receiving such a letter was remarkable in itself. I gave it to her, and she opened it straightaway. She read it and passed it on to me. 'What does pecuniary mean?' she asked.

I was wondering myself, so I got out the dictionary. 'It's to do with money,' I said, showing her the definition.

The letter was the same short message sent to dad several times previously, but now asking mum to get in touch with this Mr Das.

'So are you going to call him?' I asked, handing her back the letter. I was not sure about him at all.

'I don't know.' Mum folded the letter neatly and sat down. She placed the folded square on the coffee table, staring at it suspiciously as if it were an unexploded bomb. 'I think I'd better ask the solicitor.'

'You should read what dad wrote, Mum.'

'What?' Mum looked nonplussed, as if I had not already tried to show her dad's writing.

'What I found at the factory. I read it all, Mum.' I ran upstairs to get the pieces of paper. When I came down she was still standing in the hallway, holding the letter from the Pickle Man.

When she saw the piece of paper I had brought down, she held up her hand. 'I don't want to read that. I'm not interested.'

'But it's about dad. It seems to be set in the nineteen fifties and says he came from India. Did you know that?'

Mum looked at me as if I was a raving lunatic. 'I don't know what you're going on about. If anything, his family were from Spain.' She laughed hollowly. 'India.'

'Read it, Mum.' I waved the sheaf of paper at her. 'Dad wrote it himself.'

She pushed my hand away. Her voice sounded more gentle now, pleading. 'I don't want to read it, Stephen. Please just put it away. This is more than enough to worry about.' She picked up the letter from Das Pickles and placed it in its envelope, looking a little less terrified now it was somewhat contained. 'Maybe I could ask Susan.'

'What will Susan know?' I was really annoyed now. Susan was just two years older than me but seemed to have taken on the mantle of being head of the family since dad had gone. Mum wanted to consult her and take her advice on all matters. Meanwhile I was still treated like a child.

Susan, though, having got back to Leeds as quickly as she could, was very hard to contact. She hardly ever called and the only way to get in touch with her was by ringing the pay phone in the halls of residence and hoping someone would or could fetch her.

So, mum wasn't able to consult Susan about the letter, and even when a second, exactly the same, came along, she did nothing. The white envelopes just sat there on the hallstand, like big question marks. They weren't the only ones. As well as India, I tried and tried to talk to mum about this Lenny from the funeral. I desperately wanted to get in touch with him. Even more so since reading what dad had written. But mum just dismissed me.

'I don't want to talk about him,' she would say. 'He's not been part of your father's life for many years. We just need to keep away from him. We've got enough on our plates without dragging him into it all.'

And Susan too, before she went off to university again had seem uninterested in pursuing the matter of Lenny any further.

But then, even though mum seemed reluctant to involve me in anything, including the letter business, I did get dragged in. That was the day Jay and I went to the Central Library to revise.

As I left the house that morning, there was a pink Jaguar parked outside. I didn't really take much notice until it slowly started following me down the road. Then I did not look towards it at all. I just speeded up, as if I could outpace a high-performance saloon car by walking fast. In the end, I stopped and looked towards the car. The driver beckoned me over and I reluctantly obeyed.

He lent across the passenger seat and wound down the window. 'Come in and sit down, young sir.' He smiled spectacularly. It was Safari Suit Man.

'I have to catch a bus,' I said, stooping so I could see him better.

'I will give you a lift. It's Stephen, isn't it?' I did not answer and he continued. 'Wherever you are going, I will drive you.' He waggled his head from side to side.

It seems stupid now that I got into his car. Throughout my childhood, I was told not to get into cars with strangers, and the advice still seems worth following even as an adult. But he seemed pleasant enough, and I wanted to know more about him.

Sitting down on the leather passenger seat, I was aware of a very strong smell of aftershave and the voice of Elvis Presley on the car stereo. The Safari Suit Man had dispensed with his suit and was wearing beige slacks and a beige zipped cardigan with a darker brown diamond pattern. He had incredibly hairy left ears. On the lobe of one, I could see there was a large splotch of shaving cream.

'I wanted to speak to you about something,' he said. He had a strong Indian accent, but it was not an accent that I knew from real Indian people, like Jay's mother or grandfather, it was the sort of Indian accent you'd hear when a British person impersonates an Indian, like Peter Sellers in that song Goodness Gracious Me.

'I have written to your mother. I was also trying to contact your father.' Safari Suit Man looked solemnly at me. 'I am so sorry for your loss. He was such a good man. He must have been a very great father to you.'

I nodded, noncommittally, unsure what to say to that. It seemed that that this Safari Suit Man had known my dad at any rate.

'My name is Das,' the man continued, 'Chandra Das. You can call me Mr Das.' He smiled benevolently, as if he were bestowing some great favour upon me. 'Where can I take you?'

I don't know why, it seems obvious now, but I was surprised that Safari Suit Man and Pickle Factory Man were one and the same. I told him I was on my way to the Central Library, and wondered what I was going to discover from him next.

'Oh, very good, very good. It is a wonderful thing for young men to spend time in the library.' He put the car into gear, eased off the handbrake and the car started moving. Immediately he had to brake quickly as a car that had been driving past, sounded a long angry horn. 'Whoops a daisy,' he said, as this time he checked the mirror and started off again.

I pulled at my seatbelt to make sure it was fastened in correctly and held on to the door handle.

'Did you know my dad was from India?' I asked.

'Let's get straight to business,' said Mr Das. 'Let's just say that I knew your father and your Uncle Leonard.' He reached across me and with his short fat fingers attempted to open the glove compartment.

We were just entering a traffic island. As Mr Das struggled with the glove compartment, he cut up a Renault 5 and we were serenaded once more by the sound of a sustained car horn. Eventually he opened the compartment and found a business card, which he handed to me and then, to my relief, went back to holding the steering wheel with both hands. 'This is my business,' he said proudly, as I examined the card. It was similar in design to the letterhead on the correspondence I had already seen.

> Das Pickles
> Makers of the finest pickles and chutneys.
> Get that Das Desi Taste

'My pickles are already found in most Indian and Pakistani grocery stores.' He pointed to the array of shops on the Stratford Road that we were now driving past, shops with white mannequins in the windows wearing

Indian ladies' clothes, saris and salwar kameez, as well as grocery stores with their displays of fruit and veg spilling out on to the pavement. 'Yes, we are well-established in these sorts of shop,' said Mr Das dismissively. 'But my eye is on a greater prize.' He quickly overtook a lorry unloading boxes, by driving into the lane of oncoming traffic, and managing to get back into the correct lane just in time to avoid a collision with an apple green Ford Escort with a curiously low-pitched horn, the volume of which drowned out the sound of Elvis singing Viva Las Vegas. Mr Das seemed oblivious to the drama and continued proudly, 'Very soon, Das Pickles will be on the shelves of all the major British supermarkets, Tesco, Sainsbury, Safeway... they will all be having my name in their stockings.'

We drove on, not speaking, while I tried to take in all this pickle factory and safari suit business. I wondered whether dad and Mr Das were connected from India. I had seen the name Das mentioned in some of dad's writing, but perhaps Das was a common name in India.

Mr Das was loudly and tunelessly accompanying Elvis in Marie's the Name of his Latest Flame and I felt it would be rude to interrupt him. Eventually he stopped singing. I glanced at him, he was looking ahead sadly.

'I have not been lucky in love.' He glanced down at a thick, bright gold band on his left ring finger. 'I was married, but it did not work out. So now, you are all the family I have left in this country.' He turned to me and then had to quickly look ahead as another car horn called him back to the road. Then he continued. 'Do you know anything about an old gold pocket watch?'

He kept glancing over at me as he drove, but I did not know how to respond. I could barely speak. Afterwards, I cursed myself for not asking him all the questions that were racing around my head, but while I was in that car, I was just speechless. He seemed satisfied with that. We drove in silence for a while and then he carried on. 'Speak to your mother and sister...' He stopped speaking for a second as if he were pondering on something '...Your Uncle Leonard too. You have my card, get in touch with me and we can talk...' He looked over at me again and his eyes widened, and his face lit up. 'Talk business!'

I was not quite sure what he meant, so I nodded to humour him.

Now we were near the library and so he concentrated on parking up, not without causing more chaos, mayhem, and the sound of several car horns. I think the serenade was so familiar to Mr Das whenever he drove, that he hardly noticed it.

As I got out of the car, Mr Das gave me a thumbs up, and sticking out his little finger turned it into the universal symbol of a telephone receiver, which he held to his face. As I slammed the door shut, I heard him shout, 'Speak soon, Stephen,' and then drive away to the sound of I'm All Shook Up, accompanied by another car horn.

Jay was sitting on the steps just before the library entrance. I miss that library, the old Birmingham Central

Library, the one I knew growing up. It has gone now. It was a controversial brutalist concrete inverted pyramid, a ziggurat apparently. It had replaced an earlier beautiful terracotta Victorian Library and was symbolic of all that Birmingham gets maligned for. I loved it.

I sat down beside Jay and told him about my suspicion that my dad was from India, and then about Mr Das. Jay showed barely any interest in the India bit, much to my disappointment. The pickle connection seemed to appeal more.

'My mum buys those pickles,' he said. 'Brinjal is our favourite. That's aubergine. "That Das Desi Taste".' He quoted the line on the business card. 'Maybe he wants you to join him in being a big player in the Indian Pickle Market.'

We went into the library, where the long tables were full of mostly Asian teenagers. Eventually we came to a desk lined with the familiar faces of our fellow sixth formers, again mostly Asian. There was not a lot of studying going on. They were all chatting and laughing loudly until a librarian came along: 'Will you lot keep the noise down. This is a library. Not a youth club.'

'It's a youth club,' whispered Jay, as we smiled our hellos to the now silent group. 'It's the only way some of these kids can have a social life. They tell their parents they're going to revise, but really they just come here to meet members of the opposite sex.'

'So, is that why we've come?' I asked. I had been surprised when Jay asked me to come along with him.

'Partly.' He sat down at the table and started getting out his books and a notebook. 'I mean, I can go out to places other than the library, which is more than some of this lot are allowed to do. But I will be expected to marry a Sikh girl. Anyway...' He looked around. 'I was hoping to see Tracey Turnball here, but I think she's stood me up.'

The conversation was ended by a loud, 'Sshh,' from the librarian.

I considered the irony of the situation. Jay found it so easy to talk to girls and could have asked any of them out for a date with no problem at all. My parents – even my dad – would never have minded me dating or bringing a girl back home, yet I had been terrified to ask any out, until I finally got the courage up and Katy Carter rejected me.

The situation was all the more frustrating as I watched other friends pairing up with girls. First, bowling, ice-skating and cinema dates and then going underage to nightclubs in town. Stories of sexual fumblings in dark cinemas and conquests on sofas had emerged and I felt more and more left behind.

We stayed at the library for an hour or so. I revised for a while, but my concentration waned. I looked at Jay, who had been making loud sighs and was now leaning back in his seat, staring up at the atrium. Tracey Turnball had not materialised. I jerked my head towards the broken-down escalators and Jay nodded with enthusiasm. We escaped outside into the bright sunshine and headed off through the crowds of Saturday afternoon shoppers.

As we got to the junction of New Street and Corporation Street, I could hear shouting through a megaphone.

'Show your solidarity with the miners, join the class struggle.' A tall man with peroxide blond hair and wearing a donkey jacket was standing in front of a trestle table covered in newspapers, posters and leaflets bearing the phrase "Victory to the Miners".

Jay started walking towards the table.

'What are you doing?' Panicked, I grabbed his arm.

'This is important.' Jay continued towards the table. 'It's a key battle between the working classes and Thatcher. I want to see what can be done.'

'You sound like my sister.' I did not want to get involved. Still, I followed him over. The tall man carried on speaking through the megaphone. Stood next to him was a tall mixed race girl with long braided hair. She smiled at us and showed a slight gap between her two front teeth. I would have called her half caste at the time, but I know better now. She was so friendly I felt intimidated and did not know what to say. She looked at me and held out a wooden clipboard loaded with lined paper.

'Hi, my name's Jenny,' she said.

I was silent. I couldn't think what to say.

She went on, 'Would you like to support the miners? Sign the petition and have a leaflet. We're holding a rally next Saturday in Chamberlain Square.'

Jay took the clipboard and started talking with her. I wandered away to look in a shop window.

Soon Jay joined me again and we carried on to the bus stop. 'What's the matter? She's nice. Do you want to go to the rally next Saturday?'

'What for?'

Jay held up the leaflet and waved it in my face. 'Like she said, it's in support of the striking miners.'

'I don't think so. What have the miners got to do with me?'

'They've got everything to do with you. The miners are standing up against this government and its policy of destroying the strength of the working classes. Once they've beaten the miners, they'll carry on destroying the other unions.'

The concept did not compute with me at that time. I think I had heard too much of my dad going on about the unions. I needed time to get my head around it all.

Time.

And then of course there would be Mimi.

MISS COSTELLO

The door to Miss Costello's classroom was closed. Jay had a tutorial with her, and I was supposed to meet him outside afterwards. I looked through the glass windows of the classroom door. I couldn't see anyone, but I knew if they were there they'd be out of sight at the back of the room, where there was a carpeted section with easy chairs. I waited.

'Hello, Stephen.'

I turned around. It was Miss Costello.

She went up to the classroom door shaking keys. She knew me, she had taught me English at 'O' level. 'Are you waiting to see me?' She smiled and raised her eyebrows. Her eyes sparked. She was wearing a cheesecloth Indian-style dress, a bright green chunky knit cardigan, an orange bead necklace and these long dangly parrot earrings.

'I... I'm waiting for Jay.' I had a bit of a thing for Miss Costello and back when I had her for English in the fifth form, I'm sure she'd caught me looking at her breasts during a lesson. I hadn't meant to, they had just drawn me in, and I was really embarrassed when she stopped what she was saying to stare at me pointedly. I tried not to look at them again now but the necklace was drawing me in. 'I thought he had a tutorial with you.' I coughed and looked through the classroom window. 'Actually, I thought you were both in there now.'

She struggled to fit a key into the lock, examined the

bunch carefully and selected another one. 'Well, evidently, we're not. I saw him earlier on, in the end.' She opened the door, and as she tried to pull the handle down, she hugged a pile of exercise books closer to her chest. I looked away. Suddenly, the pile collapsed, and the books spilled all over the floor.

I helped Miss Costello pick them up. We were both on our knees and I could see her cleavage. Again, I quickly looked away and continued gathering the books. When we both stood up, I noticed chalk dust on her dress. It made her less forbidding somehow and I relaxed a little.

She smiled. 'Thank you, Stephen.' Her face became serious again. 'I heard about your dad. I'm so sorry.'

I nodded, took a deep breath, and held the books out for her.

Miss Costello walked into the classroom. 'Come in and put them down somewhere. I'll only drop them again.' She spoke without looking as she walked to the desk, and I slowly followed. 'Would you like a coffee, Stephen?'

I placed the books on her desk and looked back at the door.

She pointed me over towards the easy chairs and went into a small storeroom. She emerged with a kettle. 'I'll just go and fill it up.' She went out the door.

The walls were decorated with murals depicting the titles of books. "To Kill a Mocking Bird", "Pride and Prejudice", "Great Expectations", "Cider with Rosie".

There were also pictures of Gandhi, Martin Luther King and Maya Angelou, with quotations below. I remembered all this from my fifth form English classes. I recalled how Miss Costello had taken the dingy classroom and transformed it, spending lunch times painting the murals herself, wearing overalls and standing on a desk holding pots of paint. We all watched her through the windows transfixed, amazed that the headmaster had allowed such a thing. The decoration of her classroom reflected her passion for English literature. It was infectious, and I enjoyed my time under her tutelage.

Miss Costello came back with the kettle and a bottle of milk. 'So, was it coffee or tea?' She plugged the kettle in.

'Coffee, please. Two sugars.' I watched her getting the mugs ready, spooning out sugar from an old Golden Syrup tin.

'Did you finish "Nineteen Eighty-Four?"' She unscrewed a jar of Nescafe.

'Yes, thank you. I really enjoyed it.'

'I don't know whether you're supposed to enjoy it.' Steam rose as she filled the mugs from the kettle. 'It's quite depressing, but I know what you mean. I enjoyed it too.' She placed the coffee on a low table in front of me and sat down. Noticing the chalk on her dress she tried to dust it off. She frowned. 'Well, I enjoyed it once. The trouble is I have to teach it. It can all seem a bit like work after a while.'

I was surprised by this admission. It felt like she was sharing an intimacy with me.

Miss Costello sat back in her chair and looked at me. 'When was the funeral?'

'It was last week, Miss Costello.'

'Call me Claire, Stephen. You're in sixth form now. We can drop the formalities.' She opened a packet of biscuits. 'How did it go?'

'It was OK, Miss... Claire.' I thought about meeting Lenny and then Mr Das. I picked up my coffee and saw her looking at me, waiting for more of an answer. 'Actually, it's all been very weird.'

'Go on.' She blew on her coffee.

'Well, for a start I met an uncle I didn't know I had.'

'Really? From your dad's side?'

'Yes, his brother.' I felt my voice getting tighter.

'Did you know of any other siblings... brothers or sisters?'

'I didn't know of any other family, at all. My grandparents on dad's side died before I was born.' I looked at the biscuits but decided I couldn't eat. 'I didn't know he had a brother.'

Miss Costello frowned. 'So, was there an argument or something?'

I traced some spilt coffee on the table with my finger. 'I guess so. Apparently, my dad caught him in the house, trying to steal something.'

She put her coffee down and let out a big sigh, sitting back in her chair. She looked at me closely. 'Did you get any more details about what happened?'

'Nothing. Nobody will tell me anything.'

I recounted my meeting with Mr Das and that he appeared to know my dad. Then I told her about dad's pieces of writing and how he seemed to have come from India.

'Oh, my goodness, Stephen. You've got so much going on, so many mysteries.' She sipped her coffee. 'I'm not sure about this Mr Das, but maybe you should get in touch with your uncle. He might at least be able to give you some answers. Have you spoken to your mum?'

'I can't get anything out of her.'

Miss Costello frowned. 'It seems strange that nothing was said to you, at least before the funeral.' She looked out of the window. 'Do you have any brothers or sisters?'

'I have a sister, Susan.'

Miss Costello's face lit up. 'Of course, Susan. I remember her. Have you spoken to her? What did she know about this Lenny?'

'She didn't know about him either.'

Miss Costello thought for a moment. 'I think you need to talk to Lenny, Stephen. Be careful, though. It was wrong you didn't know about him before, but you don't really know what he's like and what his motivations are.' She looked away and then spoke again. 'What was your father like?'

I smiled. 'The sort of man who kept his own brother a secret from his son.'

Miss Costello laughed. 'I'm glad you can make a joke out of it.' She looked at her watch. 'So, how is your 'A' level revision going?'

'Not well at all.' I looked to the floor. 'I can't concentrate and I'm not even sure I want to do the 'A' levels I'm doing or even go to university.'

Miss Costello nodded. 'You've been through a lot, Stephen. I'm surprised to see you at school. I don't even think you should be taking these exams now. It's too much for you. Didn't Mr Jones suggest you do them next summer?' She sat forward. 'Better to do them next year. You don't need that stress now.'

'I don't think I can stand another year of physics, maths and chemistry.'

Miss Costello laughed. 'And what will you be doing at university?'

I told her.

'That means you'll still be doing maths and physics in mechanical engineering?'

I nodded. 'Seems like whatever I do I can't get away from it.'

Miss Costello sat forward and looked hard at me. 'Listen, Stephen, you have plenty of time. Think about what you really want to do. Don't waste time on things that don't interest you.' She stood up. 'Like, I suspect, mechanical engineering.' I have to go to a meeting now. 'But please, come and see me again.' She smiled. 'I'm here for you, if you need me.'

I got up and opened the door. 'Thank you, Miss Costello.'

'Claire,' she shouted as I closed the door behind me.

YASMIN: JAKHOO HILL

Yasmin walked across the ridge that crowned the Himalayan town of Shimla, heading towards Christchurch. There were incongruous churches like this all over the sub-continent, left over from the colonisers but still used for worship by Indian Christians.

Yasmin was glad she had come to her hometown while she had the chance, though little was left of the people or the world she had once known. She was still waiting for the results of the lump that had been removed from her breast, but those concerns had been trumped by the desire to visit Shimla. Now here, she felt invigorated by the air and the light she found in the hill station town.

Behind the pretty square-towered church lay the way up to Jakhoo Hill where Lenny, Ronnie and herself had climbed on that day all those years ago.

Yasmin and Lenny were both eight years old. Ronnie had just turned six. He was always the odd one out, wanting to tag along after his older brother and Yasmin, whom he looked upon as a big sister. Lenny would often devise ways to lose Ronnie so he could have Yasmin to himself.

Yasmin liked them both in different ways. Lenny was funny and of course the same age, whereas Ronnie was deep and moody. She wanted to take care of him and she always sensed that Lenny was jealous of this. There was often a tension between the boys as they vied for her attention. Sometimes she enjoyed the importance this gave her, at others the conflict upset her.

Yasmin's father cooked Anglo-Indian dishes for the Merchant family: pepper-water soup, country captain, biryanis, and ball curry with yellow rice. He was a fine cook and would have had no problem finding work amongst any of Ronnie and Lenny's parents' friends in Simla's railway community. Yasmin's mother was ayah in the household and had looked after Ronnie and Lenny since they were babies. So, Yasmin had become a fixture in the household, and had grown up playing with the boys.

She remembered taking them to the chaat shop. Her family lived in the lower bazaar, so she was used to running through the narrow streets, but for the boys, Lenny and Ronnie, the lower bazaar was strictly out of bounds and eating chaat there was even more forbidden. So when the adults discovered this, as well as the subsequent mischief, things were never quite the same for any of them again.

On the day they went up Jakhoo Hill there was no school. The Japanese Army had invaded Burma and there were fears that India would be next; the grownups were too intent on listening to the large Bakelite wireless in the Merchants' flat to follow what the children were up to. Even after forty years Yasmin remembered it vividly.

First, they had gone to the chaat shop, where the owner recounted the legend of Jakhoo Hill. That led them to wander up and play hide and seek amongst the deodar trees on the hillside. But then, when it was

Ronnie's turn to be it, Lenny, tired of the game, led Yasmin up to the top of the hill, leaving Ronnie far behind, his voice getting more and more as he counted out loud to a hundred.

The day was bright and just a little cold. The snows had not yet come, but they would be descending on Shimla soon. Yasmin had felt so free in the sharp bright air, how good it was to get away from the confines of the town and its wartime feel of claustrophobia.

They had gone up to the temple to Hanuman, the Hindu monkey god. The legend was that he had rested there and flattened the top of the hill. Yasmin and Lenny had played there for a while, hearing Ronnie, sounding more and more desperate as he called their names. In the end Yasmin has persuaded Lenny to go back down and find him. But then when they descended to the place where they had left Ronnie, he was gone.

THE PUNJAB PARADISE

'Where is this restaurant?' Mum peered over the steering wheel at some prostitutes standing on the street corner. 'This is a really dodgy area.'

'It's the next right and then down a bit.' I was beginning to wonder whether this had been a good idea.

Mum flicked an indicator and turned right. A row of dusty shops and takeaways came into view. The Punjab Paradise was at the end. Its sign was proudly subtitled with the phrase, Balti Meat.

'Do you think it's safe to park here?' Shaking her head, mum applied the handbrake and got out. I emerged from the other side, quickly avoiding a man staggering drunkenly down the middle of the street. A horn sounded and there were raised voices.

We escaped the tension outside and entered the restaurant. Next to the entrance was a glass counter under which were piles of samosas, onion bhajis and meat-filled flatbreads. A sign scrawled in marker pen indicated the breads were called katlamas. Behind the counter were a microwave, a till and an unshaven man in a grease-stained, once white, coat.

'A table for two please.' Mum smiled tightly at the man.

The man responded by waving at the tables.

'I think we just sit where we want, Mum.' I led her to an empty table. Adjacent was a lady in a very short skirt, low cut top and lots of makeup; she looked like she was taking a break from working the street corner. A few tables further on there was a group of obvious businessmen, wearing grey suits and talking in low voices. The clientele was a mixed bag, but naturally my mum fixated on the woman on the next table and kept glancing over and then looking at me meaningfully.

Finally, mum spoke. 'So how did you find this place?'

'I came here with Jay after the pub.' We had gone to Moseley, and after several pints we had walked down Church Road to this place in Balsall Heath. A curry house, Jay had called it. I was amazed by it: cheap and the food was great. There were aspects, though, I hadn't considered when I decided to bring mum here and I started harbouring regrets when we parked up on the street outside.

I looked hard at the paper menu sandwiched between a tablecloth at the bottom and a piece of glass – that covered the whole table – on top.

Mum looked down at hers and spoke loudly. 'Whatever are you and Jay up to, coming to places like this? You shouldn't even be going to the pub in the first place. You're not eighteen until next month,'

'Mum!' I whispered, looking round the room at the other diners. A tall man wearing combat trousers, a studded leather jacket and with a pink Mohican entered and stood at the counter near the entrance to order a takeaway.

'The prices are good, I'll give you that.' Mum examined the menu. 'Let's hope the food is good too, though you know I've never been a fan of curry.'

'The food here is very good. Jay likes it.'

'Well, I suppose he would be a good judge.' Mum took a paper napkin from a dispenser at the side of the table and started polishing my cutlery. 'I hope this doesn't make us ill. So, what do you recommend? What did you have when you came with Jay?'

I was wondering whether she sat at home working out ways in which she could embarrass me, but I decided the best thing to do was to just humour her. 'Have the chana sag, Mum. It's split peas with spinach. Try it with a naan bread.' I took four cans of lager out of a carrier bag; I had bought them on the way. I opened one. 'Do you want some beer?'

Mum looked around to see where the waiter was. 'Are you sure you can just bring your own drink in.' She tried to put the beers back in the bag. 'Don't make them so obvious.'

I tried unsuccessfully to reassure her, until I was rescued by the waiter who came over with two short heavy glasses. 'Would you like some water, as well?' He wiped the table over with a cloth he unfurled from his pocket.

Mum relaxed a little and allowed me to start sharing out a can of beer, though she eyed the waiter's cloth with mistrust. I gave him our order and took a sip of beer.

'Not too hot for me,' Mum called out as the waiter walked away.

She was getting on my nerves, but I had a motive for getting her to some out with me. I wanted some answers and I had not been able to get anywhere whenever I asked her at home. I thought perhaps if we went out together, the change in environment might make a difference. Mum had seemed pleased and touched when I suggested we go out, but I was feeling maybe I should have suggested somewhere different. Nevertheless, I decided to broach at least one of the issues. I took a deep breath. 'Mum, will you tell me about Lenny?'

She sat up. 'You be careful with Lenny.' She took a long gulp of beer. 'He uses people, he's a waster and he tried to steal from us.'

'So, tell me more about him, Mum. It's hard enough that dad died, without finding out he had a secret brother.' I watched her face.

She looked away. She watched a couple enter the restaurant; the man had long dreadlocks.

I took a deep breath and started examining the menu again. We sat in silence until the food came. I tore off a small piece of naan and half-heartedly dipped it in the bowl, using it to scoop up the chana and spinach, the way Jay had shown me. I was angry, making the food hard to swallow.

'You were brought up better than that.' Mum waved at my hand and then picked up her spoon and tried a tiny bit of her bowl's contents. She tore off a piece of naan then tried a larger spoonful. 'It's actually quite nice.' She smiled.

I picked up my glass and quickly took a drink. 'Please will you tell me about my dad and–' I stopped and quickly wiped a piece of spinach off my chin. Two girls, about my age, had just come into the restaurant. I recognised one as Jenny, the girl with long braided hair who had encouraged Jay and me to attend the miners' rally. The other I had not seen before. She was smaller and had dark curly hair that shot out from her face. She was extremely attractive. They both were. I watched them pointing to samosas and bhajis behind the counter and talking to the man at the till.

Mum noticed me looking. 'Oh, I wondered what had caught your attention.' She looked at them. 'They're both very pretty.' She raised her voice. 'Anyway, how's your studying going?'

I continued looking at the smaller girl at the counter. She was wearing a CND badge, Doctor Marten boots and a combat jacket. She caught me looking at her and I quickly turned away.

Mum tapped my hand. 'And I don't mean that kind of studying.'

The taller, braided hair, girl looked over and smiled. She seemed to recognise me. She said something to her friend who walked over towards us.

My mum noticed. 'Uh oh, she's coming this way.'

The girl gave me a flyer. 'There's a Youth CND meeting in Digbeth on Tuesday. You might want to drop in.' She smiled quickly and walked away. On the back of her combat jacket, inscribed in black marker pen, were the words "Fuck the System".

They were given their food and mum watched them

leave. 'That girl terrified you; you went all red when she came over. She terrifies me too.' Mum pointed at my uneaten food. 'And you've dragged me into this place and now you're not eating.'

In the car on the way home I sat silent. Mum kept glancing over as she drove. We went into the house, and I started to go up to my room.

'Do you want a cup of tea, love?' Mum pointed towards the living room.

I shook my head.

'Or something more to eat? There's ice cream in the freezer.'

'I think I'll go to bed, Mum.' I continued up the stairs.

'Sit down with me for a while... please.' She looked up at me. 'I get lonely on my own now your dad's gone.'

I was annoyed by that. It was as if she was using dad's death against me – and I would have to be careful about that. I could end up sitting in with her every night, never going out, never leaving home. Nevertheless, I slowly walked back down the stairs.

Mum smiled and went into the kitchen.

Then we sat down in the living room, mum in her armchair, me on the sofa. I could have sat in dad's chair, which had the best view of the telly, but none of us would sit there now. I felt detached and seemed to see the surroundings afresh. The room was so nineteen seventies. Dad had built a stone effect fireplace that extended into an alcove with a place to house our giant television. The carpet was brown, and like Jay's, had a swirly orange pattern. This orange was repeated on two of the woodchip-papered walls. Pictures of Susan and me were everywhere. Lucky her. At least she had got away from all of this.

'How are you doing, love?' Mum picked up her mug of tea.

'I'm fine, Mum. How are you?' I picked up the remote control.

'Oh don't turn that on now. Can't we have a chat?'

I threw the remote down on the coffee table. 'We've been chatting, Mum, but you haven't actually told me anything. You haven't answered my questions.'

Mum blew on her tea. 'I'm worried about you, Stephen. It's a big thing for a lad of your age to lose his father.'

'I'm OK.'

'You need to decide what you're going to do after your 'A' levels... if you pass your 'A' levels. I haven't seen you doing any revision.'

'Well, my dad did die, you know.' I sat back heavily into the sofa and turned my face into the brown Dralon.

Mum came and sat next to me. She touched my shoulder. 'I know, love. But you need to pass these exams.' She drank some tea and put her mug back on the coffee table. 'It's what your dad wanted.'

I squeezed my eyes, trying to halt tears. There was a blunt aching in my throat. I took the tissue mum pushed gently into my hand. 'Tell me about dad. Tell me the real story. Why did he keep his past a secret?'

She tapped my knee then sat back. 'You know how your dad and me first met properly?' She twisted her wedding ring. 'We were in a coffee bar on the Stratford Road. He seemed so exotic with his dark skin. He told me his family were Spanish.' She looked at me sharply. 'Not Indian!' Her voice softened again and she continued, 'I didn't have enough money for the jukebox, so he paid. The Everly Brothers: All I Have to do is Dream.'

I had not heard this before. I had never heard anything about dad's family being Spanish. Though of course that was not true at all.

'We went to the pictures for the first date. We saw North by Northwest with Cary Grant and Eva Marie Saint.' She looked at the photograph of dad on the mantelpiece and blinked several times. 'Your dad had a thing about Eva Marie Saint.'

I looked at dad's photo too. I was excited to find out more. 'Did you go to his house? Did you meet his parents?'

'I never met them. They had already died. He was lodging in a house in Sparkhill when we met.'

'Did you meet Lenny then?'

Mum shook her head.

I carried on looking at dad's picture. I could not imagine that man being a teenager We desperately needed a bit more fun and if he had stayed in touch with his brother, we might have had that. I looked back at mum. 'What happened between them?'

She shook her head. 'I don't really know. I think they had a row about some old family heirloom.' She traced a finger across a thin layer of dust on the coffee table and tutted. 'I don't know what it was, and I don't know why they had to make such a fuss about it anyway.' She looked hard at me. 'No thing is worth falling out with your own flesh and blood.'

She looked at a black and white picture of me as a toddler, in which I was holding a giant balloon. 'I think the problems started when their father died.' She straightened her fingers and looked at her wedding and engagement rings. 'But your dad wouldn't tell me what it was all about.'

I thought about what I had found in the factory office. 'Do you think it's what's in that wooden box?'

Mum shrugged. 'I don't know. I don't want to know. If it is, it has created far more trouble than it could possibly be worth. It all came to a head when Lenny came to the house while we were out.' She screwed her nose up in disgust. 'Your dad was angry, and Lenny left the house pretty sharpish, otherwise it could have turned violent.'

'Did he take anything?' I needed to find Lenny. There was so much I needed to ask him.

'Not that I know of.'

'How did he get in?'

'He had found the key. We kept it under the doormat.' She smiled and shook her head.

'Oh, so he didn't break in?'

Mum widened her eyes. 'That doesn't make it any

better. He came into our house without permission. I don't care about any heirloom, whatever it was. I wish your dad had given it to Lenny in the first place. I just didn't like him sneaking about our house. We had to change the locks. Your dad never spoke to Lenny again.'

'Did Lenny try and get in touch?'

'He called on the phone and sent letters, cards for birthdays, cards at Christmas, but your dad stuck to his guns. You know how stubborn he is.' She took a deep breath. 'Was.' She was silent for a while. 'To tell you the truth, once Lenny had come into our house like he did, well that was that for me.' She finished her tea and put the mug down on the coffee table.

'What was Lenny's job, Mum, what did he do?'

Mum stood up. 'That's enough now. I'm tired and I need to go to bed.'

I was being stonewalled again. I tried a different tack. 'Where did dad grow up?'

Mum thought. 'I think it was in Winson Green. He was always a bit vague about that sort of thing.'

At least that fitted in with what dad had written. 'We know next to nothing about his childhood. Don't you think that's a bit strange? Didn't you want to find out more?'

Mum looked down at the floor and rubbed her hand across her chin. 'He wasn't the sort of man to be interrogated and I suppose I found the mystery about him interesting. Part of what attracted me to him.' She smiled. 'He was so handsome.' She picked up her empty mug and mine and moved towards the door. 'But he didn't seem to want to talk about the past and I respected that.' She looked at the clock. 'It's getting late, and I have work in the morning. Goodnight, love. I enjoyed our little chat.'

I picked up the remote control to turn on the television. I was not going to get anything more out of my mum. She seemed to know as little about my dad as I did. I was going to have to find Lenny. The trouble was that I knew barely anything about him either.

THE LEGENDARY FIGHTING COCKS

The bus stopped by Digbeth Civic Hall, opposite the coach station and just down the hill from the Bull Ring.

As we were getting off, I took the folded flyer out of my pocket and looked up at the pub, saying to Jay, 'The Old Bulls Head. This is the one.' Between two extravagantly etched Victorian pub windows, there was a doorway with a lighted Ansell's sign above. Pubs were likely to be either Ansells or Mitchells and Butler; in those days, pubs in Birmingham would usually be tied to one brewery or the other.

I'd been past The Old Bulls Head many times on bus journeys into town, but I couldn't imagine where in the pub the meeting would be. But to the side of the pub was another entrance with a piece of paper bearing "Youth CND" inscribed neatly in black marker pen. Jay had seen it too and was already moving towards it. I'd shown him the girls' flyer a few days earlier. He had readily agreed to attend, especially when he heard about Mimi and Jenny.

We went up dark stairs and turned left at the top. The room was full of young people, on chairs arranged in rows that faced a makeshift stage bearing a central table. Behind the table was sat the tall peroxide blond-haired man we had seen shouting through a megaphone in town on the day we visited the Central Library. We found a couple of seats and sat down. The pub had been refurbished at some point. There was a bar in the corner that would have been elegant at one time but unfortunate attempts to modernise it meant the wooden countertop was covered in red Formica. A fluorescent strip light was in the ceiling and the plugged-off pipes in the walls showed there would have once been gas lights. There was a musty smell in the room; I wasn't sure whether it was coming from the pub or the charity shop coats that seemed de rigueur for many of those assembled. These old tweed coats were from a different age, but the various CND, Anti-Nazi League and Rock Against Racism badges on the lapels reflected the current times. There were also plenty of combat jackets, and studded ones on the backs of a few punks. In front of me, a pink Mohican held rigid by hair gel, meant I struggled to get uninterrupted views of the stage area. One of the girl punks was Asian. She wore heavy eye makeup and had a pierced nose with a chain linking to an earring, another Mohican crowning the whole ensemble. I had never seen an Asian girl looking like that before. Behind her, I noticed Jenny and the girl who had given me the flyer. Jenny smiled a hello and waved. Her friend looked over but did not seem to recognise me.

Jay noticed and I leant over and whispered, 'She's the one that gave me the leaflet.'

Jay nodded approval.

The meeting started. A lot of the talk was about a march and free concert to be held in London. There was also going to be a benefit gig at a large pub called The Mermaid on the Stratford Road. That was to raise money to help pay for the coaches down to The Capital. Jenny, who had gone to the front of the room, told us all the arrangements. She was looking for volunteers to help print posters. Jay put his hand up.

'Great,' said Jenny. 'Can anyone else help?'

Jay grabbed my arm and pushed my hand up too. I instinctively pulled it down again, but Jenny had noticed already.

'Seems like that's two.'

The meeting continued. Resolutions were proposed, seconded and passed. I was impressed at the way the other people in the room felt able to speak up and express their views. I did not speak and voted with the majority to pass all the proposals. To be honest I barely understood a lot of what they were going on about, but even if I had I would not have wanted to vote against the majority view; I was afraid any dissent would provoke hostility and abuse from the rest of those assembled.

After the meeting we went outside. The girl from the Punjab Paradise was standing chatting to Jenny. Jay grabbed my arm. 'Come on, we're going over.'

'No.' I pulled my arm back. Of course, I wanted to go over, but I just didn't know what I would say.

'Well, I'm going.' Jay made his way over to the girls and I followed slowly, terrified but yet glad he was taking the initiative.

'Hi.' Jenny smiled at us. 'Thanks for volunteering to help print the posters.'

'No problem at all,' said Jay. 'When do you need us? You're Jenny, right?'

She smiled. 'That's great. Yes, I'm Jenny.' She pointed her friend. 'And this is Mimi. Mimi's going to help with the posters too.'

Jay introduced us. Mimi glanced at us unsmiling, nodded briefly, and looked away.

I coughed to try to regain her attention. 'Er, we met before. At the Punjab Paradise. You gave me a leaflet for today's meeting.'

Mimi looked back at me, still unsmiling. 'I gave out lots of leaflets to lots of people last week.' She turned to Jenny. 'Shall we make a move? The Daves are on at The Fighting Cocks.'

Jenny frowned. 'Hold on a sec, Mimi. We just need to sort timings. Tomorrow at 1 o'clock at Birmingham Poly? I'm an art student so we can print the posters there.'

Jay smiled. 'That's OK with me. Stephen?' He turned to me.

I had a physics practical session the next day. I couldn't miss it. I looked at Jenny and Mimi. Jenny was waiting for my answer, Mimi was watching the peroxide blond man talking intently to the Asian punk girl. Her chin was down, and she was biting hard on her thumbnail. She pushed her dark curly hair back and I saw the soft down behind her ear. We would get to spend time together printing posters... I nodded to Jay. 'Yes, tomorrow should be fine.'

Jenny clapped her hands. 'Great. Listen, guys, we're going to The Fighting Cocks in Moseley to see this really good band. Do you want to come?' She reached for

Mimi's arm. 'Mimi, could we give them a lift?'

Mimi turned back to Jenny. 'What?'

'Can we give Stephen and Jay a lift to The Fighting Cocks?'

Mimi shook her head. 'There's no room. It's full of papers and stuff.' Her eyes went back to the peroxide blond man. 'And I was going to give Rick a lift.'

Jenny persisted. 'I don't think it's that bad. I'm sure they could squeeze in with Rick in the back.'

Mimi walked quickly over to Rick, who was still speaking to the Asian girl, and spoke briefly. He shook his head and Mimi walked quickly away, calling to Jenny, 'Come on, let's go.' She reached a dark green Mini van, opened the door at the back and then got in the driver's door.

Jenny got in the passenger door while Jay and I clambered into the back. I was on the hard metal floor. There was a pile of Socialist Movement newspapers which Jay sat on.

He attempted some humour. 'So, this is Mimi's Mini.'

Jenny and I laughed but were stopped by a retort from Mimi.

'Ha bloody ha, I've not heard that one before.' She turned. 'And get off those. I have to sell them.'

Jay sat on the floor next to me, pulling a face at Mimi's back.

Jenny and Jay chatted easily as we made our way into Moseley. Mimi was silent and I took the opportunity to look at her from my position on the floor of the van. All I could see was the back of her head and her hands moving the steering wheel and changing gears. But that was enough for me, bewitched as I was. Eventually we turned off the High Street and parked on the drive of a large and elegant Victorian house just a little down Chantry Road. Apparently, this was Mimi's house, just round the corner from The Fighting Cocks. As we emerged from the van, Jay was mumbling under his breath, 'Would you look at that house. It's even got a tower.'

I walked backwards, looking up at it.

Mimi dug into a canvas army surplus shoulder bag that was studded with badges, some of them bands. There was a CND symbol and a large badge bearing the line: "If the Tories get up your nose, picket". She pulled out some keys and turned to Jenny. 'Come inside a second, Jen.' She ignored Jay and me completely, walking up to the front door of the house.

Jenny looked at us apologetically. 'We'll catch you up.' Then as she followed Mimi, I heard her say, 'What's the matter with you?'

Jay and I walked round the corner to the pub. I had never been there before, but I had seen it from the outside, and I remembered hearing the name on illicit late-night listening to the John Peel show on Radio One, using the little pink earphone on my radio. Peel would detail venues where various bands would be playing. He always called this pub. "The Legendary Fighting Cocks".

We climbed the stairs to the first floor. Outside the room was a poster: Entrance £2.00. NUS Cards/UB40

£1. Nowadays we think of UB40 as the Birmingham band but back in those days, it was just as well-known as the card they gave you when you were unemployed. Just inside was a man sitting at a table taking money.

Jay bent down, speaking to him. 'We're in sixth form. We're not unemployed and we can't get in the National Union of Students, so we don't have those cards.'

The man shrugged. 'Well, you'll have to pay the full price, then.'

Jay frowned. 'That's hardly fair.'

'Listen,' the man said, 'if you're still at school then you're too young to be here in the first place. So if I were you, I would pay the full price or fuck off home because its way past your bedtime.'

Jay took a deep breath and looked like he was going to say something more, but on looking at the man's face appeared to think better of it. He turned to me. 'It's two pound.'

We paid the man and went in.

The room was packed. There was a thick pungent smell and the air was heavy with smoke. It took me a while to realise the smell must be cannabis. Once we had drinks, I looked over to the stage where the band was getting ready to start. There was the sound of guitars tuning and a voice speaking 'one, two, one two' over the mics. I blinked then, because over in the corner of the stage with a guitar slung around himself was someone who looked just like Lenny, a cigarette hanging from his lip, his arm stretched tuning the guitar.

I turned to Jay. 'That's Lenny, over there. My uncle, the one I told you about.'

Jay looked impressed and I felt really proud. My uncle was in this band! And best of all I could speak to him once again.

The music was tight and exhilarating. After a few bars a tall man in a long trench coat walked on stage, took off the coat and launched into the vocals of the first song. It had a reggae feel and the lead singer was charismatic in his movements and the way he engaged with the audience. Soon the whole floor was bouncing as the crowd danced away. I watched Lenny. He had a battered electric guitar, its white paint worn down to the bare wood in places. He played confidently and owned his place on the stage, moving with the lead singer and every now and again joining in with backing vocals.

After a few songs Mimi and Jenny came in. Jenny moved towards us and danced next to me. I felt awkward and self-conscious. I was trying to move to the music but was worried I might look stupid. Mimi seemed to be standing back, keeping apart from us.

After a while, the frontman announced the band was taking a break and the musicians started moving off the stage. Lenny leant his guitar against an amp and stepped carefully between the monitors and microphone stands. I stared at him, willing him to catch my eye and recognise me. He snaked through the crowd towards where I stood. I thought he must have seen me, but then he was about to carry on past. I quickly built up the courage.

'Uncle Lenny,' I felt stupid calling him uncle, but it seemed disrespectful not to,

He looked confused for a second and then his face filled with a large smile and he put his hand on my shoulder, pulling me into a hug. 'Hello, son. It's great to see you. Come on let's get a drink.'

I followed him over to the bar. This evening was just getting better and better.

There was a quite a crowd at the bar but Lenny went to the side where a section had been raised to allow staff in and out. Lenny held his hand up and winked at the barman, who finished pulling a pint, put money in the till and – ignoring the sea of hands waving pound notes – came right over. 'What you having, Lenny?'

Lenny asked me what I wanted and I asked for my usual lager.

'You don't want to drink that, son. You want a proper beer.' He looked up at the barman. 'My usual and the same for my nephew here.'

The barman grinned. 'Two pints of bitter. Right you are, Lenny.'

While he was pouring the drinks, Lenny turned to me. 'I'm so glad to see you, son. I've been wanting to talk with you, but it's so hard.' His voice lowered and he looked sad. 'You know, what with your mum and everything.'

'I've been wanting to speak to you too, but I didn't know how to find you. I've got so many questions.'

Lenny grinned and ruffled my hair. 'Well, you've found me now, son and you'll find it hard to get rid of me. Here.' He pulled a short betting-shop pen out of his pocket, took a beer mat off the counter and peeled off the top layer, revealing a white section underneath. Then he wrote a telephone number down and gave me the beer mat. 'Call that number and ask for me and we'll arrange to get together properly.' He looked around the crowded room. 'We can't talk in here.'

I put the beer mat in my back pocket.

Lenny gave me my pint, his face all serious again. 'And don't lose that number.' Then he grinned. 'Don't worry. If you do, just ask in here.' He nodded towards the bar staff. 'They'll know how to get hold of me.'

We walked back to where Jay was talking to Jenny and Mimi was still standing apart. She was looking at her nails and biting her lip. But when she saw me coming over with Lenny she pushed her hair away from her forehead and moved forwards. I introduced Lenny to them all. Jenny grabbed Lenny's hand and shook it. Lenny pulled her hand closer to him and kissed the back of it. He then kissed Mimi's hand too. Finally he shook Jay's hand.

'I love the band.' Mimi was smiling now. Her cheeks had reddened and she looked even more beautiful. 'So, this is your new venture? Aren't you with Needless Alley anymore?'

Lenny laughed. 'We split up a few years ago now, love.'

I looked at Lenny, amazed. I had heard of Needless Alley, they had a few hits back in the early seventies when I was very young. The biggest had been One Night Band.

Even I had heard of it. They had used it in an advert on the telly.

Jay leant in. 'Why didn't you tell me your uncle was in Needless Alley?'

I spoke in his ear. 'I only just found out.'

'That's weird.' Jay drank the rest of his beer down and shook his head. 'Your family is so weird.'

Lenny was engrossed in talking to the girls. They were both looking up at him, their faces all lit up. I was thinking about how this new revelation would put me in the good books with Mimi. After a while Lenny looked up at the stage where the band were coming on again. He placed his hand on my shoulder and squeezed gently. 'Back to work. See you later, son.' He then carried on back up to the stage.

Mimi came up to me. 'How do you know Lenny M?'

'He's my uncle.' I tried to be as nonchalant as I could and took a sip of my pint.

'That's amazing. He's a legend. I love that song, One Night Band. I play the album all the time.'

I smiled, nodding in what I thought was a knowing fashion. 'Oh yes, it's a great album.' I knew of the song but I wasn't aware there had been an album, too.'

'Yes, Blind Alliance. It's a classic. You must have heard it loads of times, being in the family and all.'

Once again, I nodded knowingly, wondering if I had enough money to pay a visit to the HMV shop.

The band started up, a song with a driving and infectious calypso beat. Mimi took my pint off me, placed it on a side table, grabbed my hands and led me into a dance. I could feel the soft warm skin of her fingers wrapped around mine. I looked up at my rockstar Uncle Lenny as he set off into a blistering guitar lick, and all seemed well with the world.

    Ha!

YASMIN: THE GOLD WATCH

Yasmin walked down to the flats where the Merchants had lived. The block was still there, a little worse for wear, perhaps, but as she looked up, she could see the front door to the flat and she remembered Lenny bringing her back to it after they had been to Jakhoo Hill.

By the time they reached home that day it was dark and both Lenny and Yasmin's mothers were standing near the entrance to the flats, looking out for them.

'Where have you been?' Lenny's mother was peering at them through the dusk. 'Where is Ronnie?' Her voice initially angry sounded panic-stricken now.

Yasmin's mother was staring hard at her daughter. She didn't say anything. She didn't need to. Yasmin knew her mother was angry but she was too scared to worry about that, she was also too busy worrying about Ronnie. He must still be up that hill. In the dark.

'We went up Jakhoo Hill.' Lenny looked down at the floor, his voice was tight and he sounded afraid.

Yasmin looked at him, wondering whether he would tell the truth.

'Ronnie went off,' Lenny said. 'We couldn't find him.'

Yasmin stared; the lie seemed treacherous.

Just then Lenny and Yasmin's fathers appeared through the gloom.

'We've been looking all over for you.' Lenny's father looked hard at his son. 'Where's Ronnie?'

'They've been up to Jakhoo Hill.' Lenny's mother was

crying now. 'They've lost Ronnie. I think he's still up there.'

His father looked at Lenny. 'I'll speak to you later.' He turned to Yasmin's father, who seemed scared rather than angry at her and Yasmin was thankful for that. 'Get the flashlights, we'll go and search for him.'

It was a long desperate wait for the men to come back that night. Lenny and Yasmin were fed in silence, their mothers pacing around the flat, starting at any noise coming from outside. Eventually they heard the sound of the fathers and they saw them all come through the door to the flat. Yasmin was so relieved to see Ronnie was with them. He was pale and refused to look at Lenny or her. Ronnie's mother ran up to him and embraced him tightly, then led him through to the bedroom.

They had found Ronnie in the woods on the hillside. He had heard his father calling and ran towards his voice, cold and shivering. He said that after he gave up looking for Lenny and Yasmin he tried to find his way down but then as darkness fell he had curled up for shelter under a fallen tree, scared of the monkeys.

The boys' father took his belt to Lenny that evening. He said he did not blame Yasmin for what happened. Despite that, her mother would not speak to her. But Yasmin did not need any punishment for what happened. She and Lenny had betrayed Ronnie, putting themselves apart from him. For her it created a loss in the relationship between the three of them – and it was a loss she still felt keenly, forty years later.

That was why, back then, she showed Ronnie the watch.

The watch was a gold hunter's pocket watch. It had been originally given to Yasmin's great grandfather by the Maharaja of Puranpur, when he was in charge of the Maharaja's polo ponies. The watch had an enamelled section on the case, with a polo player painted on, the horse caught in mid gallop as its rider, head wrapped in an extravagant turban, swung a polo mallet.

Yasmin showed it to Ronnie a few days after the incident on Jakhoo Hill; she took him to her house in the lower bazaar because Lenny was still in disgrace and not allowed out to play. Ronnie should not have gone so far as the bazaar again, and both children would have joined Lenny in disgrace had they been caught, but no-one ever knew. Ronnie did not tell Lenny about the watch, even though he was amazed and intrigued by it: the beauty of the gold and painted enamelled case, as well as the mechanism within.

Yasmin sighed. Now the watch was gone and so were the Merchants. She went up to the flat to knock and ask after the family, but the people there had never heard of the Merchant family and, alone, Yasmin wandered back up to The Ridge.

BIRMINGHAM POLYTECHNIC.

Corporation Street is a broad road leading off New Street in the city centre, or "town" as us Brummies call it. The street was built in Victorian times, inspired by the great boulevards of Paris. Now, many might feel comparing Corporation Street in Birmingham to Rue de Rivoli is stretching a point, but back in 1984 I had never been to Paris or pretty much anywhere else. So, I was impressed by the long city centre street, stretching off into the distance. I still am.

It was along this street and towards the tall terracotta tower of Central Hall, that Jay and I walked on our way to the Art Faculty at Birmingham Polytechnic. The polytechnic was spread across the city, but this section was located right on the edge of town, next to Aston University and at the end of Corporation Street.

'She said to meet her by the entrance, at two.' Jay reported his telephone conversation earlier that day with Jenny. 'She sounded really pleased I was going to help.'

'Did she say Mimi would be there?' I tried not to sound too desperate. I had spent a long time deciding what to wear before leaving the house, even though my wardrobe was fairly limited. In the end I was wearing my jeans, a black t-shirt and a denim jacket my mum got me from her catalogue. I had attached a CND badge to the lapel.

'Yes, yes, she said it would be her and Mimi. But do you think Mimi is interested in you?'

'She danced with me at the gig. She seemed interested.'

'Yeah, but that was only after she found out Lenny M is your uncle.'

'So what! If Lenny has provided a way in, then that's no problem as far as I'm concerned.'

There was a man shaking a yellow bucket, collecting for the miners. Jay stopped and dug in his pocket for change. 'We're right with you, comrade.' He tossed coins into the bucket.

I watched for a moment and then, realising I was expected to contribute too, followed suit and we were both given yellow "Coal not Dole' stickers. I stuck mine next to my CND badge, imagining Mimi seeing it when we met.

But then Jay spoilt my moment by continuing to warn me about her. 'I just don't want you to get hurt. She seems a bit of a femme fatale to me.'

'What's a femme fatale?'

'We did it in English. It means lethal woman; a woman who lures men into trouble. Costello spent hours going on about how it's an example of sexism in art and literature and stuff, then she had us write a whole essay about it.'

The idea of a lethal Mimi luring me in sounded very appealing. I was more than ready to be lured.

We walked on up towards the top end of Corporation Street until we reached a patch of grass with some benches.

'We're still early. Let's have a seat for a while.' Jay took a Golden Virginia tin from his pocket. Inside, amongst the tobacco and rolling paraphernalia, were two neat hand-rolled cigarettes. He held one up triumphantly. 'Do you fancy a doobie?'

'What's that?'

'Cannabis, marijuana, pot, hashish.' Jay lit the joint. 'My brother calls it dope. I nicked a bit from his supply.'

'Doesn't it get you addicted?' I felt excited, yet worried. Where was this going to take me? Would I end up wandering around like some crazed maniac, craving for another fix of drugs?'

Jay inhaled deeply and blew out sweet-smelling smoke. 'Naaahh, you're thinking of heroin. This stuff is good for you. There's no reason why it should be illegal.' He offered me the joint.

I looked around instinctively, checking for police. But I just saw people going about their daily routines. There was a group of students nearby, gathered around a bench, chatting and laughing, but no one else near, and no one seemed interested. Back then, people didn't really know the smell of cannabis like they do now, unless they already smoked. You just had to watch out for the police.

Jay touched the joint to my fingers 'It's OK, mate, no-one's interested. Just have a toke. It's nice, man.'

I inhaled from the joint and then coughed. The smoke went up my nose and into my eyes. I bent over, continuing to cough, wiping tears with the sleeve of my jacket.

Laughing, Jay took the joint off me and then took another deep inhale, expertly blowing a series of smoke rings into the air. 'Suck on it and then breathe in gently through your nose.' He passed the joint back.

This time, I managed to breathe in the smoke successfully and felt a strange sensation percolate through my brain. I looked at Jay with a stupid grin.

He grinned back. 'It's good, yeah.'

We finished the joint and carried on heading towards Birmingham Poly, through the Aston University buildings. As we walked through the campus, I felt a strange sensation, a hyper-awareness of my surroundings. Colours looked different, sounds came at me with a disorientating resonance. I felt unable to speak. As we reached the Polytechnic entrance, I was nervous. I had already felt on edge about meeting Mimi, wondering what I would say to her and now, I was regretting having that smoke, as I felt disorientated and unable to engage in any conversation at all, let alone speaking to a woman I was trying to impress.

Jenny was standing in the entrance hall. Mimi wasn't with her. 'Hi guys.' She smiled brightly. 'Thank you so much for coming to help.'

I looked around, expecting Mimi to appear. She didn't.

Jay started talking to Jenny and I followed the pair down stairs and along corridors. Jenny turned every now and again to check I was keeping up. As we entered the print room, I looked around the room, still expecting

Mimi. She wasn't there. She must be running late, I thought.

Everywhere in the print room seemed to be splattered in ink. Jenny showed us a template she had made of the poster. She had cut out spaces for lettering and a simple design. She attached the template into a wooden frame and explained how we would help her, passing sheets of paper and drawing ink over the template and then drying the posters in drying racks. I noted that Mimi was not mentioned.

We worked hard until there were many posters drying in the racks and more besides pegged on a clothesline. The poster was simple but communicated the event perfectly and I was impressed with Jenny's obvious talent and expertise. I noticed that Lenny's band, The Daves, was playing, as well as a band called Pandora's Socks.

I was planning on seeing Uncle Lenny before then. I was going round to his after school on Friday. I had managed to get through to him earlier in the day. It had taken a couple of calls, The first was answered after many rings by an elderly lady with a strong accent that I thought might be German. She sounded angry as she told me he wasn't in, but still I made the second call an hour later. I was desperate to get hold of him. She answered again and I heard a loud sigh after I asked for Lenny, then there was silence for several minutes while I wondered how long I should wait before putting the receiver down. Eventually I heard the friendly voice of Lenny and we had made our arrangements to meet up. I was excited at the thought of, at last, meeting him properly. I was looking forward to discovering the truth about my dad and where he had come from, as well as asking Lenny about Mr Das.

We stopped the print operations for a coffee. There were mugs and a kettle in an adjacent smaller room. Jenny asked me to help her.

Jay followed. He was going on about The Mermaid, the pub where the gig was to be held. I had seen it from the bus many times. It was a massive Victorian pub on the Stratford Road in Sparkbrook.

'All the Irish guys, the navvies, the builders, stand outside there early in the morning. They're waiting to get picked for work. The trucks stop by, and they point out who they want. At the end of the day, they all get dropped off and they pile into The Mermaid.'

'So will they be going to the gig?' I asked.

Jay laughed. 'They're not interested in the gig. They just want a drink.'

'It's a great venue,' explained Jenny. 'It's on several bus routes, there's a massive room upstairs, and they can get a late bar.'

'Actually, the guys downstairs might like that,' said Jay

'It's going to be great,' said Jenny. 'Your uncle's band is playing, Stephen. They're so good.' She concentrated on spooning out instant coffee. 'Will you be there?'

'We'll be there,' said Jay. We walked back into the main print room with our coffees and Jay took another look at the poster. 'This is very good, Jenny. So, are you doing a degree here?'

'I'm on a foundation course,' She turned to me. 'What are you doing Stephen?'

I told her without enthusiasm about my 'A' levels and the offer I had for a place at Leeds to do Mechanical Engineering. 'I don't know whether I really want to go,' I added.

'I'm doing English and History 'A' levels,' cut in Jay.

Jenny ignored him. 'You should take a year out, Stephen. Why do something you're not sure about?'

'I'm planning on a gap year,' said Jay.

I looked at Jay. I had never heard him mention a gap year before.

'I'm going back to India. To my roots. I want to find myself.'

'Oh wow, that would be amazing,' said Jenny. 'Have you been before?'

'I went with my parents when I was about five. I can hardly remember anything about it. My mum wants to go again with me, but I don't want to go with her. She'll want to go to the home village in the Punjab and meet all the relatives. They'll probably be trying to find me a wife.' Jay grimaced. 'No, I definitely don't want to go with her. I want to travel round, see places, like the Taj Mahal.'

'I'd love to go to India,' said Jenny. 'It's my dream, to travel round there, taste the food, experience the mysticism. It seems like a very spiritual country.'

'Yeah, man.' Jay grinned, looked directly at Jenny, and pointed at himself. 'And you've got your own bit of India, right here.'

Jenny turned to me. 'Are you interested in going to India?'

'Oh, yeah,' I said. In fact, the idea had never even occurred to me before. The thought of travelling anywhere had not occurred to me. I had never even been abroad, so setting off on a tour of India had been completely off the spectrum. But now I was starting to discover some family connection to the sub-continent, the idea of travelling there held an appeal.

'We could all go together,' said Jay.

I wondered whether Mimi would go too.

'We just need to get some cash,' he continued. 'Maybe we could stand outside the Mermaid and get work on the building sites.'

Jenny looked us both up and down and laughed. 'You never know.' She moved over to the drying posters. 'Anyway, come on. We need to get tidied up.'

Later, as Jay and I caught the bus home after smoking the second joint in Jay's tin, I wondered why Mimi had not come. When I had asked Jenny where she was, Jenny shrugged and looked sad for a moment. 'That's Mimi.'

While I sat on the bus mooning after Mimi, Jay was in a better frame of mind. 'I think that went well. I think she likes me.'

'Why didn't you ask her out for a date or something?'

'I'm going to see what happens at the gig. Make my move then.'

I looked out of the window, wondering when I would be able to make my move on Mimi, and then, even if I did get the opportunity, whether I would be able to work up the courage to make any real kind of move at all.

The gig was going to be a week Saturday, in ten days' time. Jenny had asked us to go out fly- posting on Thursday night, to advertise the gig. I had seen gigs advertised by poster on old buildings and boarded up shop windows, but I'd never considered how they got there. I wondered what it would involve. Most of all I wondered whether Mimi would be there for the fly-posting. That got me thinking about India and imagining Jay, Jenny, Mimi and Me all going off together.

'You've never mentioned going to India before,' I asked Jay.

'I've thought about it a lot, but never seriously,' He gripped tight on to the bus seat's hand rail as the bus turned a tight corner. 'Don't you think it's a good idea?'

'How would we afford it?' I looked out the window at the Stratford Road, busy with its usual bustle. We passed The Antelope, a typical Irish pub. 'What about what you said, standing outside The Mermaid? Get some work on the building sites.'

'I wasn't really serious,' said Jay. 'They're not going to want a couple of nine stone lads like us. No, I can get work in my uncle's shop. He's been trying to get me to work for him for ages. Why don't you get a job too?'

'Where?'

'Sainsburys. Do some Saturday work. Once the 'A' levels are out of the way we can work during weekdays. We just need airfare money and bit extra. It's not going to cost us much once we're in India.'

I had seen other friends from sixth form working in the supermarkets, stacking shelves, working the tills. I hadn't considered it, but it seemed a good idea even if we didn't go to India. As for my 'A' levels, they seemed more and more pointless. I was awed and terrified about travelling to India, but I needed something different to do, something to focus me in a new way. Hopefully Mimi would go too.

KOFTAS AND YELLOW RICE

The address was a street of massive Victorian mansions in Moseley. I checked the house number against the one I had scribbled on piece of paper from the pad by the phone. Forty-five was a particularly dilapidated looking example, the garden overgrown, and dark green paint peeling from the window frames, behind which hung filthy net curtains. I walked up the driveway past a yellow GPO Morris Minor van. There was a padlock keeping the van's back doors secure. Someone had written "Preen Me" in the coat of grime that covered it.

I turned my attention to an array of ten black plastic doorbells lined up in symmetry next to the double front door. I saw Lenny's name and pushed the bell, hearing a distant steady ring. After some time I heard footsteps and eventually the door opened. Lenny was unshaven and wearing tracksuit bottoms and a white vest bearing the phrase "No Problem". He managed to pull off the whole ensemble with his inimitable style. He smiled, ruffled my hair, and ushered me in. The floor had once been beautiful with terracotta tiles in a geometric pattern, but now the tiles were cracked and stained. There was a musty smell undercut with a hint of cat piss.

Lenny was holding some envelopes that had been put through the door by the postman. 'Hold on, son, I'll just check these.' He sorted through them, kept a couple that were evidently his, then put the rest under a door on the left. 'These are Stella's, the lady in the front downstairs flat.' He looked towards the back of the hallway, past the stairs, where there was another door. He lowered his voice. 'There's an old Austrian lady, Gerda, lives there. She's a bit senile. You spoke to her when you called the other day. If we don't get to the door in time, she takes our mail. We have to wait for when her niece visits to get it back. Come on let's go up.'

I followed Lenny up the old staircase to a second floor. The bright daylight outside struggled to enter the hallway and so Lenny had to push timed light switches to illuminate our way up the stairs.

'The light will go out before we get to the top.' Lenny led the way, up stairs covered in dirty, threadbare carpet, to reach the first-floor landing. 'There it goes.' We were plunged into darkness and there was a loud crash. 'Bastard bike.' Lenny's voice cut through the gloom. The lights came on again as Lenny found the next switch. 'This place is a dump. I don't know why she had to put that there.' Lenny wrestled the bike back against the wall, knocking off a large piece of plaster in the process.

I followed him into his flat. It had once been one large bedroom, now split into two parts, with a kitchen to the smaller side and a bed cum living room to the other. The bathroom was along the hallway, shared with other residents. Lenny waved me on to a large cat-scratched leather sofa and went into the kitchen to make tea. There was large amplifier in the corner with his battered white electric guitar on a stand beside it, a wire snaking from the instrument to the amplifier. On the floor, close by, was a record player. Two large speakers serving this turntable sat on either side of a large ornate Victorian fireplace, above which was a poster advertising Duke Ellington at Newport Jazz Festival,1958. There was a wonderful aroma of Indian food cooking.

Lenny came in with a tray containing an old brown teapot, cracked mugs, sugar and milk. He set the tray on an old wooden clothes chest that served as a coffee table. I had to move a large ashtray full of spent cigarette ends out of the way, to make room for the tray.

'I hope you're hungry, son. I've cooked you up something to eat. I'm really pleased you felt able to come and see me.' Lenny settled himself down and took his tobacco tin off the table. 'Thank you, son.'

'It's OK.' I was at a loss what else to say. Lenny seemed so grateful, but it was me that should be thankful. I had so many questions. The trouble was, now I was there, I didn't know what to say. I looked for something to hold on to. I found a tortoiseshell guitar plectrum on the chest coffee table. I toyed with it, feeling the edge against my fingers.

Lenny noticed. 'Do you play?'

'I want to.' I looked over at the guitar. 'I need to get something to play on, though.' I had been wanting to learn to play for ages and had spent much time looking at an electric guitar in mum's catalogue.

'I've got an old guitar you could use to get you started. I could show you a few chords and stuff.'

I nodded enthusiastically, imagining myself playing in a

band at The Fighting Cocks, like Lenny, Mimi dancing in the audience. 'Your band is great. We really enjoyed the gig.'

'Oh, The Daves? I play in a few different bands. Anyone who'll put up with me. I like to play jazz, nowadays. I'm usually out every Friday night with Steve Oberon at The Red Lion on Ladypool Road.

I wondered about his band's name, The Daves. 'How did you get that name, The Daves? Is there more than one Dave in the band.

Lenny had pulled his tobacco tin. He looked up at me, puzzled. 'No, there's no-one called Dave in the band.' Then he looked down and continued pulling out Rizla papers.

'I didn't know you were in that band, Needless Alley.'

Lenny looked up. 'You didn't know? Nobody told you?' Then he thought for a while. 'I suppose they didn't. You haven't been told anything about me.'

I didn't know what to say. I looked around the room, wondering how someone who had been on Top of the Pops, ended up living like this. 'Do you have a job?' I asked wondering whether it was an impertinent question. I was wondering if Lenny just lived off the money he had made being a pop star.

'I'm on the dole,' said Lenny. 'There's no work for me, only music. And that doesn't pay. I got next to nothing from being in Needless Alley. That song was used in an ad, and I got nothing. We were screwed by the record company.'

He took three cigarette papers, stuck them together, spread tobacco out and then burned a brown lump for a few seconds. I recognised the strong sweet smell of cannabis and wondered whether he would pass any on to me. Lenny quickly and expertly rolled the joint and then placed it, unlit, into his mouth and poured the tea. He held the milk bottle up to me questioningly, and I nodded. He added a splash to both mugs and then held up a battered bag of Tate and Lyle, a spoon sticking out of the top.

'Two, please,' I said.

He spooned out two for me, and then one for himself and then stuck the wet spoon back in the sugar. My mum would have gone mad if anyone did that at our house, but then there was a lot about this whole situation she would not approve of. I didn't tell her I was going to see Lenny, I said I was going around to Jay's.

Lenny lit his joint and then looked out of the window 'We should have met sooner. It has all been stupid and unnecessary.'

I assumed he was talking about his estrangement from my dad and so I decided to dive straight in to the question at the centre of the whole situation. 'I need to ask you something. They said you burgled mum and dad's house?' I picked up my mug of tea and stared at a crack in the side.

Lenny quickly looked at me. 'It wasn't like that, son,' he said. 'There was a misunderstanding. I didn't ever get the chance to explain myself.' He took a drag from the joint and then a sip of tea.

I thought about the wooden box. I wondered if Lenny had been looking for that. It seemed very old, and when I thought about it, the box had an Indian feel about it. I considered mentioning the box to Lenny, but even though I had a good feeling about him, something made me decide to keep the box to myself for a while, until I found out more.

Lenny interrupted my thoughts. 'Did you know that your father and I grew up in India?'

I put my tea down and sat back, staring at him. So, it was true.

Lenny was still speaking. 'We were both born in Delhi but spent most of our childhood in Simla, a town in the Himalayan foothills. They call it Shimla nowadays.'

I tried to imagine my dad of all people, growing up in the Himalayas.

'So, your dad never told you about India,' he went on after a while. 'He didn't tell you about your heritage?'

When I did not reply, Lenny said, 'He didn't, did he? Of course he wouldn't have told you, knowing him.

Finally, I took a deep breath. 'Why would dad keep it a secret from me? Does my mum know?'

'Probably not.' Lenny pulled on the joint. 'He was ashamed.' The heady sweet smell of cannabis grew stronger in the room. 'Plenty of our people are ashamed of where we come from. Who we are. It's tragic, it really is.' He moved his head back and blew smoke up at the cracked, stained ceiling.

I looked at Lenny closely. He had dark skin. His hair was greying but the original colour was black, like dad's had been. 'Are we Indian?'

'We're Anglo-Indian, a mix of Caucasian and Indian,' replied Lenny.

'Apparently, dad said he was part Spanish.'

'Yes, plenty of Anglo-Indians will say that.' Lenny flicked the ash off the joint.

'But why be ashamed of who you are? Why keep it a secret?'

'You have to know India, know history, to understand that,' replied Lenny. 'When the British first went to India, they formed the East India Company which had its own Army; soldiers were recruited from Britain for it.' He took another long drag on the joint and another cloud of the sweet smoke expanded in the room, catching the sunlight coming through the dirty bay window. 'Well, these men got together with Indian women and had children. Mixed race children. After a while, that practice stopped. Marriage between Indians and the British was discouraged. The mixed-race children grew up and weren't considered marriageable by the fully-white British, while the mixed-race offspring would not marry full Indians. So, they married amongst each other, and a new race was formed: the Anglo-Indians.'

'So why be ashamed of it?' I felt annoyed, though whether it was due to my father hiding his past, or that Lenny wasn't going to offer me any of the joint, I wasn't quite sure.

'Because they had Indian blood, they were considered lower class by the British. Often, they would pretend that their dark skin and hair was due to Spanish or Portuguese blood. That only made the British despise us more. They called us chichis and other names.'

'I wish dad had told me,' I said. 'There's so much more I want to know.'

'You're right.' Lenny laid the smoking joint in the ashtray. 'It is interesting and I'm glad that you want to find out more. It shouldn't have been kept a secret from you.'

That made me ask another question. 'So, do you know Mr Das, Chandra Das?'

'Who?' Lenny looked startled.

I told him the story, about the man in the cemetery. The letters. The lift into town.

Lenny grew more and uncomfortable. 'It's best to keep away from him, son. He's been trying to get in touch with me. I didn't realise he was trying to contact your dad and then you, too. I saw him at the funeral. Buggering about in the mud. The man is an idiot. He's a disaster.'

'Well, his pickle business seems to have gone well.'

'Yes, that's typical of him. He comes out of everything OK, but he causes chaos for everyone else around him.'

'So, how did you and dad know him.'

'Well, that's a long story.' Lenny stubbed out the joint. 'Are you ready to eat?'

So he wasn't going to tell me about that either. I thought again about the wooden box. Well, if he wasn't going to talk about his attempted burglary, I definitely wouldn't mention the box yet.

Lenny disappeared into the kitchen and came out with a tray bearing cutlery, a jar of Das mango chutney and a steaming plate. 'Here, son. Have some proper Anglo-Indian cooking.'

I looked at the plate of food. There was a huge steaming mound of yellow rice with green peas in. On top of this were a number of meatballs in a thick sauce. Scattered on top were some finely chopped green leaves.

'That's ball curry and yellow rice, son. The proper Indian name for the meatballs is koftas.' Lenny came back in with his own plateful. 'I've put some fresh coriander on top, it makes it really tasty.' He spooned out some of the chutney, passed the jar to me, sat down and started to eat. 'This is a staple food in the Anglo-Indian household.' Your grandma used to cook it for us when we moved to England. Before that, in India, we used to have a cook make it for us.'

I was enjoying the food, but found it very spicy-hot. I put the tray to my side.

Lenny looked up. 'What's the matter, son?'

I told him I needed to get some water.

'Stay where you are. I'll get you a beer. That will be better.' Lenny got up and went to the kitchen. I heard the click and hiss of cans being opened and Lenny re-emerged with two cans of beer bearing red diagonal stripes.

'Jamaican Red Strip lager,' said Lenny placing a can in front of me on the coffee table and touching it with his own can. 'Cheers, son.'

'Did you make this curry yourself?' My annoyance at his failure to explain Mr Das was dissipating with the serving up of the curry and beer. I had never known my dad make anything more complicated for me than beans on toast.

'Of course,' Lenny said. 'I love cooking.'

'How did you learn to make this?'

'Friends. Cookbooks. Watching your grandmother. All I can do is an approximation, but it's my own version.'

I pointed to the jar of mango chutney. 'That's Mr Das's business.'

Lenny looked over at me. 'Listen, you keep away from him for now. I will tell you how he's connected with our family, I promise. Just not yet. Let me deal with him. I'll see what he wants, even if it's just to stop him bothering you.

TOMMY DEATHRIDGE

It was a perfect night. The sky was clear, and the stars dusted the sky like diamonds.

I had Mimi on my arm, walking her back home. The gears were clicking into place perfectly. I was all loved up. I breathed in the sheer beauty of the situation, inhaling the sweet subtle scent of Mimi herself.

Going out fly-posting had gone well. Mimi had shown up and, along with Jenny and Jay, we had gone around pasting the posters up on disused boarded-up shop fronts and any other surface we could find. We were nearly caught by the police at one point. After that, we had gone to the pub, and it had felt like I was making good progress with Mimi.

Then, a few days later, we went to the gig at The Mermaid, and now I was walking beside her. Just her and me. The gig was great. Lenny had played and, once again, the band was amazing. I hadn't much chance to speak with him, though. He was busy doing the gig and knew lots of people there, who all wanted to talk to him. I didn't mind. I was more interested in Mimi for now.

Jay and I both arrived later than we wanted to. He was working at his uncle's shop and I had been messing about with vegetables at Sainsburys. But as soon as we got there, Jay and I made straight over to where we could see Mimi and Jenny sitting. Jenny made room for us, and Mimi smiled spectacularly at me. I loved that smile.

I ended up being with Mimi all night. We chatted. We

danced to the bands. Mimi introduced me to all her friends. Jay started by speaking with Jenny, but she moved away and was soon with some other people, leaving Jay spending a lot of the evening by himself. I felt a bit bad about that – not too bad, though. It would have been the same if things were the other way round, and I would have understood, like I'm sure he did that night.

At the end of the evening, Mimi looked up at me and asked, 'Are you going to walk me home?'

Now, it's a long enough walk from The Mermaid to Moseley, remembering there was then the walk back to my house, but I didn't mind. It meant more time on my own with Mimi. She might even invite me into her house.

She had taken my arm and everything was all perfect. She was going on about Jenny and politics but could have talked about anything, and I would have listened. I was just enjoying the sound of her voice.

'Jenny's doing that foundation course at the poly, and she cuts hair in her mum's salon at the weekend, but what's the point?' She looked up at me. 'The priority is dealing with the politics. If the bomb drops, then an art degree will be useless.'

'Protest and survive.' I repeated the current slogan of CND, thinking it might impress her.

'Yes, but ultimately we need a revolution.' Mimi let go of my arm for a moment to pull her bag strap more securely onto her shoulder and I felt a sense of panic until her arm engaged with mine once more.

I considered my own suburban home. Revolutions

happened in other countries, not Hall Green, Birmingham. 'How do we get to the point of revolution?'

Mimi let go completely now and I wished I had said nothing. 'We engage with the workers, the disaffected, the youth and build a movement. That's what we're doing with Youth CND.' She was becoming more animated now. 'We take an issue that the youth are concerned about. e.g. the threat of nuclear war and we use it to educate around politics in general.' Mimi took my arm once more and I relaxed again. 'So, do you want to come and sell papers with me on Saturday?'

I thought about the pile of Socialist Movement newspapers in Mimi's car. I didn't understand the stuff they all went on about, and I couldn't imagine myself talking to people about socialism in the way I heard Mimi, Rick and the others debating. Jay seemed to fall into that effortlessly but I struggled. I had no idea how I would manage it. But I would do anything to spend time with Mimi. 'That would be great.' I replied.

Mimi held my arm more tightly and I breathed in the scent of the night once more.

We were approaching her house in Chantry Road now. I could see her van parked on the drive. I was aware of a figure sitting on the wall on the opposite side of the road, but Mimi appeared not to notice. As we reached the driveway of her house Mimi stopped and looked up at me, smiling. Her face was illuminated by the streetlamp and her eyes sparkled. Afterwards I felt like I was supposed to kiss her; to kiss her properly, tongues intertwining and all that business, but I couldn't even give her a peck on the cheek, I was nervous and my awareness of the figure sitting on the wall over the road didn't help. When she let go of my arm and moved her head to look into her bag for the keys, the moment was gone. I really didn't mind. I was happy with our walk home and with her hand on my arm. Things could carry on progressing slowly but surely.

Anyway, it turned out best that we didn't launch into a long kiss at that particular time.

'Can we meet again?' I asked.

'You're going to help me next Saturday with the papers. Get to the ramp in town by ten o'clock.' She grabbed my arm and pulled at the sleeve of my cardigan. It was an old Arran one of my dad's, too big for me, which I thought gave me a Bohemian air, fitting in with my new Moseley set of friends.

She stroked the arm and looked at me sheepishly. 'Can you wear something other than that cardigan.'

With that, Mimi turned and walked up the drive. I stood there, wondering what was wrong with my cardigan, but loving the fact of her starting to direct what she wanted me to wear. I watched Mimi let herself into the house and close the door with a brief wave and a smile. I then turned to start the long walk home.

'Oi, you.' The shout came from over the road. 'Come here.'

I carried on quickly up the road.

'Fuckin, come here.' The voice was louder and thick

with the scrape of late nights smoking, drinking, and fighting. 'Don't make me come and get you.'

I stopped and looked over. A tall middle-aged man was standing, swaying.

'Come and sit down, mate.' The voice was softer and the man beckoned. 'I ain't going to hurt you. I just want to talk.' His accent came from the very bowels of Birmingham.

I slowly crossed over the road. I did not want to antagonise this man. I would see what he had to say.

'Here, come and sit down,' The man moved up the wall a little to make way for me and I reluctantly sat. 'I don't mean you no harm, mate.' I just want to talk.' His voice was slurred. I suppressed a retching sensation as I was assailed by the warm sweet odour of beer.

'What are you doing with my daughter?'

I looked over at the house and then glanced carefully over at the man beside me. He looked slightly dishevelled, but his clothes were smart: a blue three-piece suit and loosened bright yellow tie. Gold cuff links flashed, and a gold chain looped into the waistcoat pocket.

The man belched loudly. 'Are you courting?' He looked around as if checking for any eavesdroppers and lowered his voice. 'Her tells me nothing.' He put his hand on my shoulder, whether this was to steady himself, threaten me or was an act of affection, I couldn't tell. 'Are your intentions horrible.' He stopped to think. 'No, I don't mean that.' He thought again. 'Are your intentions honor...' He stopped again. 'Honourable. That's it.' He laughed and then stopped and looked fiercely at me. 'Because I don't want anyone messing with my daughter.' He looked over at his house and his voice lowered. 'That girl means the world to me.'

I slid a little down the wall away from the man. I wanted to run and keep running. I was terrified.

He noticed. 'It's OK. If you're a good lad you don't need to be worried. I just know what young lads are like. I was young myself once.' He smiled as if reliving a happy memory and then his face darkened again. 'So don't fuck with my daughter.' He shook his head and put his hands to his face. 'I'm sorry, mate. I've had a few too many.' The man reached in his jacket pocket and pulled out a packet of Benson & Hedges. 'I'm just having a few smokes before I go in the house. The missus don't like me smoking at home.'

He offered me a cigarette, but I declined, and he then spent a while trying to light his, but his hand was shaking, and the flame wouldn't stay long enough against the unlit tip. 'Give me a hand, mate.' He held the lighter out towards me.

I took the lighter and lit the cigarette while the man cupped his hands around it.

He took a deep drag. 'So, how long have you been courting?'

'We're just friends.'

'Friends.' The man laughed and then looked morose. 'That girl won't speak to me no more. She just looks right through me.' He looked at his cigarette. 'And I gave her everything. Private education at Edgbaston Ladies' College.' He waved his cigarette near my face. 'Do you know how much that costs?'

I remembered seeing the girls coming out of that school. It was on the way to the Botanical Gardens, nestled amongst all the sugar white Edgbaston mansions. The girls wore straw hats and burgundy pinafore dresses, looking like they were from another world. I glanced again at Mimi's house. It was another world.

'She's been on good holidays. I bought her that car. She wanted a Mini because it rhymed with her name.' He had smiled briefly but became morose once more. 'I grew up with fuck all.' His voice slurred heavily, emphasising the expletive. 'We lived in a back-to-back house in Hockey. I had to work hard to get what I've got now. And then she goes around preaching socialism – fuckin' socialism – and yet she looks down her nose at her own fuckin' father.' He stopped and sat quietly for a moment. I started to stand up. 'Wait a minute. What's your name?'

'Stephen.'

'Stephen what?'

I hesitated but I felt there was little choice 'Merchant.'

The man thought a while. 'I know a Lenny Merchant, what plays guitar, was on Top of the Pops back in the day.'

'He's my uncle.'

'Are you Ronnie's son?'

'Yes.' I was amazed this bloke knew my dad and

quickly wondered whether it was good for my chances with Mimi or not.

'How is he?'

'He died.' I said it like it was a matter of fact, but still it was hard to break the news of my own father's death to someone who evidently had not known.

He put his hand to his heart. 'Oh no. I'm sorry to hear that, Stephen. It's a hard thing to lose your father when you're a young man.' He stopped. 'Well, it's hard whatever your age. You still need a father.' He took a deep breath. 'I remember your dad and Lenny, back in the day. I see Lenny round Moseley, drinking and playing in the pubs, but I hadn't seen your old man for years.' He smiled and looked into the distance. 'The Merchant boys. Fresh off the boat from India.'

It seemed everyone but his own wife and children knew my dad was from India.

'Your poor father.' The man put his head in his hands and his voice became muffled. 'I've done bad things in my life; I've not done right.' He looked up. His eyes were red, but he smiled and seemed suddenly full of hope 'But now, I've found the Lord Jesus Christ. I'm going to make things right. Do you have religion, Stephen?'

I didn't know what to say. I had not been brought up with religion in my life, I barely ever thought about it. I had only been to Church for weddings and a funeral.

'You need to find God, my son. Don't waste your life like I have. Find salvation now, while you're still young.' He smiled. 'I seen the fucking light.' He looked at his watch. Then he got up. 'And now it's time for me to go to bed.' He put out his hand. 'The name is Tommy. Tommy Deathridge.'

I stood up, thankful I could finally escape. Tommy's grip was tight, and I felt my hand being crushed for a moment. He smiled and I saw a flash of gold.

'Come round one day, Stephen. I like you. You're a good lad. Tell Lenny, Tommy says hello.'

He swerved his way across the road and up the drive and I started my long walk back home. Mimi was as good as my girlfriend, and I had met her father. He was a bit scary, but he liked me. Things were looking up.

YASMIN: FIRE

Yasmin walked through the lower bazaar, taking in the multitude of noise, smells of food, the bright flashes of colour from the Desi Sari Store, the solid blue of Ubhi Jeans. She stopped by a kitchenware shop, buying some shiny metal food tins, before wandering down to where she knew her childhood home had been. She was still remembering that night. The night of Partition.

There weren't so many Muslims in Simla, but they had, until then, always got on well with their Hindu and Sikh neighbours. On the Partition night, she had woken to shouting, the sound of breaking glass and then the crackle of flames. She heard her father moving quickly. 'Get up,' he said, his voice hard and insistent. She was aware of her mother sobbing, yanking at her insistently. Breathing quickly and noisily the family moved to get out of the burning building. Thick smoke was coming up the stairs and into the single room that all the family shared. Yasmin was coughing. They were all coughing. Tears were streaming down their faces. Yasmin's father had opened a window, then he grabbed her, pushing a wooden box into her hands and hurriedly hanging a key on a chain around her neck, before lowering her down on to the lower roof next door. Below she could see the crowd cheering and jeering at them. A man climbed up on the roof to join her. It was the sahib. He moved to reassure her then looked up at the window to help, but the smoke was already too thick. He took her to the roof edge and carried her down to the street. Yasmin looked back up at the window where she had last seen her father but all she could see was the smoke, and then – flames.

Now, as she thought back to that night, Yasmin looked up at the balconies of the building that had replaced the one in which her family had lived. A little girl was leaning over the metal rails and, catching Yasmin's eye, she smiled. Yasmin waved in return, before quickly making her way back to the hotel. She needed to lie down.

BROCKWELL PARK

I decided that Jasper smelt of beans. Baked beans. Ordinarily, I did not mind the smell of baked beans. But from Jasper the odour was nauseating. The problem was compounded as the coach went past the HP sauce factory and the normally pleasant odour of brown sauce wafted through the coach. Stifling a retch, I looked out to the left at the chimneys of Aston Hall, incongruent amongst the industrial landscape and the floodlights of Villa Park.

We were going to the Youth CND demo, a convoy of coaches from Colmore Row, taking us to central London. From there we would march to Brockwell Park in Brixton, where a free concert was being held: Madness; The Style Council; The Damned; Hazel O'Connor; Clint Eastwood and General Saint. I was really looking forward to the music. Even more, I'd anticipated spending the day with Mimi but somehow I was stuck sitting next to Jasper and his stale beany odour. Worse still, Shane Spooner was at the back of the coach.

I had first seen Spooner and his skinhead mates standing amongst the gothic gravestones of St Philip's cathedral as we all waited for the coaches.

'Spooner. What's he doing here? I didn't know he was interested in nuclear disarmament,' I said, instinctively stepping to the side, putting Jay between me and Spooner's line of sight.

'He's not interested in CND.' Jay turned to look at Spooner and his friends. 'They're going to see the bands.

Which I suppose is the whole point. Attract them with the bands and then convert them with the speeches in-between.'

'I don't want the likes of Spooner being converted.' I was horrified, picturing Spooner and his mates sitting in on a Youth CND meeting. Noticing Jay was glaring malevolently at Spooner, I said quickly, 'Stop staring, he might see us.'

'I don't care if he does.' Jay shrugged. 'I'm not scared of him.' He looked at me. 'You shouldn't be either. He's just a coward.'

All the same, I tried to keep my head down and avoid getting anywhere near Spooner and his mates. This was difficult as I was also trying to keep an eye out for Mimi. I had not seen her since the night I walked her back from The Mermaid and then met her dad. We were supposed to have been selling papers together, but she had not shown up.

Eventually I saw her and Jenny lining up to get on a coach further down Colmore Row. I tapped Jay and pointed them out, walking quickly so we could get join them.

'Can't we get on a different coach?' said Jay, catching up with me. 'You don't have to go running after her all the time.'

I ignored him and carried on along the line of vehicles. I almost slipped over as I clambered up the coach steps. As we walked along the aisle, I tried to affect surprise at the sight of the two girls sitting side by side,

'Hello, Stephen.' Mimi said my name heavily, emphasising the last syllable and then looked out of the window.

Jenny smiled at me.

I stopped. There was a single empty seat behind Mimi and Jenny, next to Jasper.

'There's room for both of us to sit together further back,' said Jay.

I stood looking at the empty seat, unsure whether to take it or go to the back of the coach as he was suggesting.

'Come on, sit down for fuck's sake.' A tall man in John Lennon spectacles stood impatiently behind Jay. After him was a line of people, all waiting to get to a seat.

I took the place next to Jasper.

Jay sat down heavily in the empty aisle seat opposite, next to Liz, a bespectacled petite dark-haired girl wearing a leather biker jacket and reading an ancient-looking paperback. I recognised her vaguely from Youth CND meetings. She looked up from her book, shyly acknowledged Jay and then carried on reading.

As the coach filled up, Spooner and his skinhead friends got on. I quickly busied myself searching in my rucksack, but nevertheless felt a sharp rap on my shoulder. I looked up.

'Alright Steve.' Spooner ruffled my hair, grinned, and carried on to the back of the coach.

Jay looked over at me. 'Don't let him bother you, mate.'

Jasper nudged me. 'Is that skinhead a friend of yours?'

'No, he's not,' I said. 'I just know him from school.'

We talked for a while after that. Jasper appeared to be about fourteen. He was wearing a grubby green snorkel coat, zipped up tight to a chin dotted with acne and occasional long straggling hairs. At some point the snorkel's shoulder had torn and there was an inexpert repair, a jagged line of uneven black stitches. Jasper's hair was greasy, mousy and had formed itself into a bob, more through a deficiency in cutting, than any stylistic intention. As I spoke with him, I realised that he was in fact nineteen. He had completed his 'A' levels and taken a year off. I discovered that Jasper was a member of the Revolutionary Communist Party. Impressively, he had a place at Cambridge.

'I'm going to read law,' explained Jasper. 'I'm going to attack the system from within.'

As the coach worked its way along the M6 and then the M1, Jasper entered into an argument about the Labour Party with Rick, who was sitting behind us. Jasper leant over the back of the seat, drawing diagrams in the condensation on the window to illustrate his points. Meanwhile Jay seemed to be getting on very well with Liz; they had spoken continuously and carried on throughout the journey down. I tried to engage Mimi in conversation a few times, without success. Jenny was friendlier but it was harder to speak with her, as she was by the window. I got my novel, War and Peace, out of my rucksack and tried to read, hoping that Mimi might turn around and notice the title.

I had never been to the capital before and so, as we came off the motorway and into the city, I looked eagerly through the window, taking in the sight of London red buses and tube stations. I was enthralled by everything, even the unfamiliar colour of the terraced houses' brick. The very fabric of the city looked and felt so different to Birmingham. As the coach parked up, we got out and were met with a fine drizzle. We walked round through the slick damp streets to the Embankment, where the demo was due to start. The road was closed off and I looked up the river. I was awestruck by the busyness of it, the different boats moving around, the majestic bridge by the Houses of Parliament and the clock tower I had always known as Big Ben. Thousands of youths were assembled along the road, and I felt overwhelmed with a great sense of solidarity: part of this movement, part of history. The Birmingham Youth CND group had gathered close together. Mimi was standing by Rick who was engrossed in a conversation with a very tall skinny man, made even taller by a high-spiked Mohican haircut. I heard him referred to as Spider.

Jay and Liz were still engrossed in conversation. I stood with them for a while but was hungry now I was out in the fresh air and not so close to Jasper. Nearby, a caravan had been set up and was selling burgers. The smell of frying onions was irresistible, and I wandered over to the food stall. I decided to get one for Jay too.

'No, thanks,' said Jay loudly, when I handed it to him. 'I'm vegetarian.'

'Ewwww,' said Mimi who, had moved over into the group. 'You're eating the corpse of a dead animal.'

'You're vegetarian?' I asked looking at Mimi. Both her and Jenny nodded slowly, stepping back in disgust from me and my two burgers. I turned to Jay. 'You're not vegetarian.'

'I am vegetarian.' He looked towards Liz, who was also looking at me like I was some kind of psychopath, and added, 'It's part of my religion.'

'But I've seen you eat meat. And you're not even religious.'

'Well, I've stopped eating meat now. And anyway,' he looked down at the burgers distastefully, 'I've never eaten beef.'

I stared at the food, ashamed and annoyed. I knew Jay ate meat but now I came to think of it, I was unsure whether I had ever seen him eat beef.

'Vegetarianism is a petty bourgeois deviation from the class struggle,' said Jasper. 'I'll have his burger.'

'Why does everything have to be in the context of the class struggle?' said Jenny, 'I just don't want to eat meat.'

I gladly gave a burger to Jasper and then walked away. I took a small bite, but suddenly sickened by the smell of the meat and onions, I threw it all in a litter bin, trying to wipe the thick congealing grease from my fingers.

Marshalls wearing CND vests mustered us all into place and very gradually we started to move. The rain became heavier and, as we approached Westminster Bridge to cross the Thames, I donned my bright orange cagoule. The bridge was temporarily closed to traffic to allow the march to cross, and horns sounded from the cars waiting for us all to pass and the road to reopen. I wondered whether they were sounding in support or opposition.

The traffic horns were drowned out as the march turned the corner by Parliament. The proximity of the seat of government worked to inspire and embolden us, and Rick, the cone of a loud hailer to his mouth, led us in a call and response, articulating a distorted Maggie and the rest joyously responding with Out:

> Maggie, Maggie, Maggie,
> Out, out, and out,
> Maggie, Maggie, Maggie
> Out, out, out
> Maggie,
> Out,
> Maggie,
> Out,
> Maggie, Maggie, Maggie,
> Out, out, out.

This went on for a while as we crossed the bridge and into the streets of South London. Later, Mimi had the loud hailer and started singing to the tune of Camptown Races:

> Nuclear Bombs kill policemen too

> Join us, join us
> Nuclear bombs kill policemen too
> Join us on our march.

As she sang, she was directing the loud hailer at the two policemen accompanying this section of the march. The officers smirked in response, and I suddenly lost my sense of solidarity. Even from the lips of Mimi, the song seemed pathetic and the whole endeavour futile. I wondered why I was on the march, what was the purpose of it? If I was just coming along to be close to Mimi and see the bands, then I was no better than Spooner and his friends.

In hindsight, I think that was the moment which led me to start taking the movement and politics more seriously; by questioning my motives I put myself into a frame of mind that made me more open-minded to what was really going on during that day in London.

As if on cue, though, Spooner et al literally loomed into view. The skinheads had disappeared as soon as they got off the coach and I had not seen them on the march. But now, as Mimi carried on singing her song, I saw them leaning on street railings near Brixton tube station. They were drinking cans of Kestrel lager. They started laughing and pointing at us all, shouting, 'Wankers,' thumbs pressed to index fingers, hands shaking in the perennial schoolboy hand insult.

Suddenly there was a sharp movement, and a hooded snorkel-clad figure ran to the railing, vaulted over and punched the much taller Spooner in the face. Spooner's features screwed up in astonishment and pain and he staggered backwards from the force of the punch. I stood shocked, in disbelief, as I realised the attacker was Jasper. Before Spooner could retaliate, the two policemen waded into the fight, taking Jasper to one side, radio static buzzing as they called for help. A large group of Youth CND marchers had moved on to the pavement and were surrounding the skinheads. I stayed on the road, away from the confrontation.

'Look, everyone, get on with the march,' shouted Jenny, addressing those assembled on the pavement.

Rick was squaring up against one of Spooner's friends.

'Just leave it to the police, you'll only cause Jasper more trouble than he has already. Ignore them.' Jenny pointed at Spooner and his friends.

More police arrived and Jasper was taken into the back of a transit van, while Spooner's lot were shepherded down a side street.

'Move along, now.' A large policeman addressed us all. 'We're going to keep your little friend in the wagon for now. We'll decide what to do with him later.'

'Fucking pigs,' said Mimi.

I nodded in agreement, looking over to Jenny and Liz who were talking with the police, Jenny's arms moving as she appeared to remonstrate with them. The two girls came back.

'There's nothing more we can do at the moment.' Jenny shook her head. 'Basically, he's assaulted someone in full view of two policemen. He doesn't have a leg to stand on.'

'Fucking pigs,' repeated Mimi.

I nodded emphatically in agreement once more, though silently thankful the police officers had been there to handle the situation.

We decided there was nothing more we could do for Jasper now, so we carried on with the march.

As we approached Brockwell Park, we heard the boom of music over a PA system, amplified unintelligible speech occasionally cutting in, and my earlier disillusionment was replaced by feelings of excitement and anticipation. Joining the assembled crowd, I could see the stage. A white-haired man was orating on nuclear disarmament. I listened intently as the man explained the power of nuclear weapons and articulated the arguments for unilateral disarmament. I was enthralled. What the man said really frightened me. How close the world had come to annihilation; the delicate, precarious balance of second-strike capability, where peace was held in place by the fact that if one side bombed the other, the other side could strike back, was terrifying. Unilateral disarmament meant that one side disposed of its nuclear weapons; the other side would then have no need for its own atomic bombs and so would get rid of them too. The USSR was not intent on invading Europe or the United States, according to the speaker. Both sides had built up nuclear arsenals in a fit of paranoia that had lasted since the end of the Second World War. It all made sense to me. My previous disillusionment, my questioning of my motivation was dispelled, and I felt a new sense of solidarity with what was going on in this London Park; I was no longer just on this march to be close to Mimi.

'We've missed The Damned,' said Mimi. 'Apparently, there was a stage invasion too.'

I had never heard of The Damned, but I attempted to look suitably disappointed as I tried to catch the end of the white-haired man's speech. Afterwards, The Style Council came on. I had never heard of The Style Council either.

'It's Paul Weller's new band,' said Jay. 'He was in The Jam.' Jay looked at me questioningly, waiting for some recognition.

'Yes, I know The Jam,' I said, irritated. 'A Town Called Alice.'

Mimi laughed. 'It's A Town Called Malice.' She put a heavy emphasis on the M.

I felt myself reddening.

'You're getting mixed up with the novel, which is where the song's name comes from,' said Jenny. 'I thought the same at first.'

I was grateful for Jenny's intervention.

'How can there be a town called Alice?' Mimi carried on laughing and then concentrated on the band again.

I tried listening to the band but found it difficult, the atmosphere near the stage had become edgy and I could see missiles being thrown as The Style Council played. In the melee at the front of the crowd, I could see Spooner and his mates, hurling bottles and mud.

As the concert went on the acts became increasingly irritated by the behaviour of the crowd. It was not enjoyable and Jenny suggested we go and see what was happening with Jasper. We looked around the various stalls until we found a large tent labelled Welfare. At the entrance, there was a harassed-looking woman wearing a yellow CND tabard and holding a walkie talkie. Jenny went in and spoke with her. The woman talked on the radio, nodding.

Jenny came back out. 'They've been in touch with the police.' She pulled the hood of her cagoule closer over her head as the rain grew stronger. 'Apparently there's a holding area towards the back of the festival. If we wait until later tonight, they might let us take him back with us. I think we might miss the coach though. She said they're only releasing people once the crowds have dispersed.'

It turned out Liz had some friends in a squat near Camden, so she arranged for us all to sleep there. We could hitch lifts back up the motorway to Birmingham the next day.

Later on, we finally located Jasper. He was in a dark blue transit van, parked outside a block of Victorian apartments near Herne Hill Station. There was a whole line of the vans and Jasper was right at the end.

'Oh you've come for Citizen Smith,' said the policemen, standing on the street next to the van. We could see Jasper inside, still enclosed in his green snorkel. 'You can have him, with pleasure. We're sick of him, going on about El Salvador and Trotsky and The Fourth International.' The police officer screwed up his face. 'He pen and inks a bit too. We were thinking of having a whip round to get him a bar of soap.'

Jasper climbed out of the van and raised his fist in the air.

'Oi, watch it, Trotsky,' said the policeman. 'We can still do you for assault. It's just I hate those fascists more than I do you lefties.'

I was glad we couldn't get home; it was more chance to spend time with Mimi. But in truth, I barely got any chance to be with her. I ended up sharing a bed with Jenny, at her suggestion, and it wasn't how it sounds. We were respectably head to toe in a single bed, me worrying whether my feet smelt, while Jay and Liz shared a double bed with Mimi. Also quite respectably, according to what Jay told me later, as we both hitch hiked back to Birmingham.

GUITAR

Lenny laid the guitar case on the floor and knelt in front of it. The latches let out satisfying clunks as he unflicked them; it seemed to me that Lenny was paying homage to the instrument inside. As if to confirm this, he paused in the opening and appeared to be examining the case itself, running his palm across its surface. There was nothing remarkable about it, except perhaps its evident age. It had once been black but was now faded by grime and time. Scratches wove across its surface like lines on a map. There was a sticker stating "Musicians Union Says Keep Music Live". I wondered what sort of instrument was inside; what its journey had been and where it might take me.

I had been at home, bored, thinking about Mimi when the phone rang. It had been a boring time overall. My eighteenth birthday had been and gone, with nothing much happening except I went to a Berni Inn for a Steak and a legal pint of beer with my mum. Susan sent me a card. Jay had forgotten, but then I hadn't bothered with his birthday either.

When the phone went, I rushed into the hall, picking up the receiver, hoping, as I did every time I heard a ring, it would be Mimi's voice on the other end of the line. As usual I was disappointed. Instead, it was a man's smoky voice crackling though the receiver.

'Hello, son. How are you doing?'

I was too busy bemoaning the fact that this was not

Mimi, to register who was calling. Whoever it was seemed to know me.

'Hello, hello. Is that Stephen?'

'Hello,' I said neutrally, trying to place the voice.

There was a pause. 'It's Lenny. Don't you recognise me? Don't you remember your old Uncle Lenny?' A dry laugh crackled.

'Yes, yes. I know it's you Len... Uncle...' I attempted to recover.

There was another laugh. 'Listen, son, just call me Lenny. I'm not used to being called uncle. It makes me sound like an old man.'

I tried to think of a reply.

'Anyway,' Lenny continued. 'How about meeting up again sometime? You wanted some guitar lessons.'

'Yes, I do. That would be so good, but I don't have a guitar...' Lenny had said something about a guitar for me.

'Don't worry about that. I've got something you can use for now, until you can get sorted. At least you can see how you get on before you spend any money.'

Arrangements were made and once more I turned up at Lenny's, excited to see my new guitar. The beginning of the visit followed a similar pattern to before. I followed Lenny up the stairs, the light went out and a tirade of expletives sounded as he collided once more with the bike resting on the top landing.

'She always puts it in a different place.' Lenny's voice resonated through the darkness, and I waited halfway up the stairs until he found the light switch.

Inside his room, leaning against the sofa was the guitar case. When Lenny finally opened it I was disappointed. I had expected an electric guitar. I knew it wouldn't be a Fender, like the one he had resting in the corner, but I had hoped for something cooler than this old battered acoustic guitar. Something that would impress Mimi.

'She's a beauty,' said Lenny, taking the guitar out of its case. He played a few notes and strummed a chord, shook his head, and then alternated between turning pegs and playing strings until he could finally play a chord that satisfied him.

'Listen to the sustain on that.' Lenny struck a note and looked at me, waiting for the note to die. It took some time and I looked away from his expectant stare; I wasn't quite sure what sustain was.

Lenny sensed my disappointment. 'This guitar may not look like much but it's a great instrument, solid sides and top, made in the 1950's I think, in Spain. The action is great.' He played a burst of fantastic, what I now know to be, flamenco guitar. 'You'll learn better on this. Then, when you've learnt the basics and you're ready to join a band,' he looked over at his own Fender Stratocaster, 'you can get yourself an electric guitar.' He fingerpicked a twelve-bar blues and then handed the instrument to me. 'This, my son, is a proper guitar.'

I held the instrument by its neck, looking at it, still unimpressed. I looked inside it. there was some writing in pencil on one of the wooden struts. I could make out the name Olga and the rest looked like Spanish. I swung it round onto my knee and nervously strummed the open strings.

'Here, come on, son. We'll start your first lesson.' Lenny showed me how to hold the guitar and to play notes correctly, then he taught me a few basic chords. After I had been going for a while, trying to bend my fingers into impossible shapes and making an awful racket, Lenny stood up.

'Time to put the kettle on. So now you've got to take this home and practise until your fingers bleed.' He laughed. 'I'm joking, but you do need to practise every single day. If you can only do half an hour that is better than nothing. What's half an hour to a young lad like yourself? You've got nothing else to do.'

'Well, there is the revision for my 'A' levels and my job at Sainsburys.' I felt a mixture of irritation at Lenny, who actually did seem to do little more than play guitar and idle about, and panic at the thought of the pile of neglected books in my bedroom. Since starting work at the supermarket, I was struggling to find any time for revision.

Lenny shrugged. 'Maybe. It depends what you really want. If it's important to you, you'll do it, whether it's these 'A' levels or playing an instrument.' He pointed at the guitar. 'Put it away now and I'll make us a cup of tea. There's something I want to talk to you about.'

I practised the chords a little more as he went into the kitchen, then carefully placed the guitar in the case, wondering what Lenny was going to say. It sounded ominous.

He returned with two mugs, placed them on the coffee table, sat down, and let out a long sigh before reaching for his cigarette papers and tobacco. 'I saw you at the gig, hanging around after that girl. I've been worried about you; she seems like trouble. I've seen her about before at parties and gigs in Moseley. Are you seeing her?'

I cringed. I was aware of my uncle's gaze and looked around the room avoiding eye contact, wishing this conversation could end. I finally answered, 'Sort of.'

'What does that mean? Sort of?' Lenny asked. 'Seems like she's leading you on. Seems like she's got you exactly where she wants you. People like that enjoy the attention they are getting, and they don't care how much they hurt your feelings.' Lenny turned so he was facing me now and the movement caused me to reluctantly look at him. He carried on. 'You're hanging around her like a little dog and it looks as if she's using you. I hate to see it, son.' He put a hand on my shoulder and his voice, which had started to increase in volume, softened. 'Just keep away from her, I know it's hard when you're in...' He stopped, looking up at the large dusty paper lampshade hanging from the ornate plaster moulded ceiling. 'When you have feelings for someone. Just leave well alone.'

I stared hard at the filthy carpet. I felt obliged to reply in some way but could not think of an adequate response. Lenny had Mimi wrong. I wanted him to like her. I thought of her father and recalled him mentioning Lenny and my dad.

'Her dad seemed to know you,' I said. I thought this connection may help change Lenny's mind about Mimi.

Lenny looked confused. 'Her dad? Who is her dad?'

'Tommy,' I said. 'Tommy Deathridge.' It had not been difficult to remember the name. It was Mimi's surname after all. I looked at Lenny expecting a smile of recognition at the name of an old friend. Instead, I saw a look of deep concern.

'Say that name again,' he said quietly.

'Tommy Deathridge.'

Lenny had been rolling a cigarette, but he quickly put it half-rolled on to the coffee table. It fell on the floor, scattering tobacco onto the already debris-littered carpet. Lenny did not seem to notice. 'Tommy Deathridge?' he repeated.

'Yes.' I remembered then how intimidating I had found the man. Perhaps Lenny had had a similar experience.

'Do you know who he is?' said Lenny.

'I just know he's Mimi's father.' I was scared now by this reaction.

Lenny laughed mirthlessly, looked down on the floor towards the scattered tobacco and Rizla paper, which he kicked under the coffee table. He started assembling a fresh roll up. 'Tommy Deathridge is a bad man. You might call him a gangster. You know that nightclub in town, "Tommy's"?'

I nodded, recalling Jay and me unsuccessfully attempting to get in. 'You mean...'

Lenny nodded. 'Yes, he owns it, and he runs a lot more beside. And now you're running after his daughter. Be careful, Stephen. Be very careful.' Lenny gathered the mugs and picked up the overflowing ashtrays. He stood up and took the things out to the kitchen. 'How did you get to meet him?' asked Lenny as he re-entered.

I described my meeting with Tommy.

Lenny stood still. 'And what exactly did Tommy say to you?'

'He asked me not to fuck with his daughter,' I said, trying to inject some humour into the situation, frightened and exhilarated by my use of the f-word with my uncle. I could not recall using the f-word with an adult before.

'I bet he did,' said Lenny. 'And you say he said to remember him to me?'

'Yes. How do you know him?'

'I've seen him around. Working on the music scene, you get to come into contact with people like him. He's always been alright with me, though my policy has been to steer clear of him as much as I can.' Lenny remained standing, looking down at me, his voice getting louder. 'Which is why I'm definitely warning you off from his daughter.'

'He seemed to know my dad too.' I decided to steer the conversation away from Mimi.

'He did?' Lenny seemed surprised by that and then shrugged. 'Tommy Deathridge knows a lot of people.' He sat down again. 'Anyway, even before I knew who her father was, I wanted to warn you off from that girl. Your old man isn't here anymore, so, when I can, I'd like to try and take his place in offering fatherly advice.'

He coughed and I looked away from him, unsure what to say. I could never have imagined my dad talking to me like this, looking out for me in this way. Still, I thought Lenny had it wrong about Mimi.

'Treat them mean and keep them keen,' said Lenny.

I couldn't imagine Mimi allowing me to treat her mean. That just sounded ridiculous. I decided to try and change the subject. 'Can you tell me more about Chandra Das? How do you know him?'

Lenny let out a long sigh. 'Your dad and me had no choice.' He rolled another cigarette and was silent for a while, blowing smoke rings that were caught in the spring sunshine streaming through the grimy window.

I wondered whether he was going to say anything more. He seemed as if he might carry on; might tell me more about himself and my dad and Mr Das. I didn't want to break the spell so I stayed silent and waited.

Lenny just sat there smoking. He didn't tell me anything. Which was a shame, as I might have told him what I knew from reading through dad's papers. But I still did not trust Lenny completely, so I did not tell him about what my dad had written.

YASMIN: PARTITION

Yasmin looked up at the grand building. It was now called the Institute of Advanced Studies, but when she was a child, it was the Viceregal Lodge, the summer palace of the Viceroys, where the British rulers had escaped the crippling heat of the plains to rule the whole of the sub-continent during the summer months.

Yasmin remembered how Ronnie, Lenny and she had come up here, to the top of Observatory Hill to catch sight of Nehru, Jinnah, Ghandi and Mountbatten, as they held the Independence talks. These had culminated in the partition of the Indian sub-continent, the formations of the Muslim state of Pakistan and a separate India. The non-violent independence campaigner Gandhi had never wanted the partition. He had wanted the whole of British India to become one independent state undefined by religion. Partition had been a tearing apart and, as new borders were created across the Punjab and Bengal, vast numbers of people moved: Muslims to the new Pakistan, Hindus and Sikhs to the new India.

On Yasmin's partition, as the sahib had carried her down from the roof that night, some of the mob had come over to them, but they were stopped by an elderly lady.

'Bas,' she had screamed, and the men had moved away sheepishly. By now flames were licking out of the building windows and there was no option of either further attack from the mob, or for Yasmin's family to be rescued.

'Hai Rabba,' the old lady said, coming over and stroking Yasmin's hair, trying to soothe her. The old lady took off her scarf, wrapped it around Yasmin and walked away without looking back, muttering, 'Hai Rabba' continuously.

They cut up a flight of stairs. There were lots of these running up diagonally between the streets that ran across Simla's steep slope. Yasmin was small for her nine years but still it must have been hard work carrying her. The smell of burning and sounds of shouting and breaking glass cut threateningly through the night. Yasmin caught site of the body of a young man splayed out, face down, arms spread, and a pool of blood emerging from the head. The sahib gently pushed Yasmin's face against his shoulder, pulling the scarf over her head, and moved quickly past the corpse.

They came back up on to the Mall, the main street running up Simla's hillside, and reached the Gaiety Theatre, where Yasmin knew they held pantomimes and shows. Outside the old gothic style building there was a different type of drama. A gang of men was gathered. The sahib stopped at the sight of them, and Yasmin hoped he would turn back, but then, to her horror, he carried on. As they got closer, the men moved towards them.

'Bas.'

The sahib stopped at the command and turned to face them.

The men came over and, seeing the sahib more

closely, the one who had come out with the command spoke in English. 'Where are you going?'

Yasmin stared at the man. He was wearing a Nehru cap, and traditional dress. Yasmin recognised him. It was Prakash Das, the owner of the Das Emporium, a large store that sold linen and household items. Even as a child, she knew he was a prominent figure in the town. Das came over and pulled the scarf from Yasmin's face. She looked up, terrified.

'Where are you taking her?'

'I'm taking her to my home. Her family are all...' The sahib looked down at Yasmin and lowered his voice. 'There was a fire.'

Das nodded. 'She's Muslim. She needs to go to Pakistan. There is a refugee camp at Amritsar. She can be repatriated from there.'

Yasmin held on tightly to the sahib; she did not want to be taken away. This family was all she had left now.

'You work on the railway?' Das asked. The sahib nodded. It was an easy guess. Many Anglo-Indians worked on the railway and his clothes were typical of what an engine driver would wear.

'Your name?'

'My name is Merchant,' Yasmin heard him reply. 'William Merchant.' She could feel him stand taller as he replied.

'You should look after her. For now,' answered Das. 'But she needs to be taken to the refugee camp in Amritsar.'

He stopped, pointing to the wooden box Yasmin held tightly in her hand. 'What is that?'

Das tried to take it, but Yasmin had it held tight.

Das slowly unravelled her fingers. Yasmin struggled, but the sahib held her tightly.

Das freed the wooden box and tried to look inside. At first, he couldn't open it and turned around the box until he found a bit that he could slide out, showing a keyhole. He looked at Yasmin, frustrated, and then he smiled as he noticed the key on the chain around her neck. He took it roughly, yanking the chain over her face and opened the box. Inside was the gold pocket watch.

Yasmin struggled wildly through this, crying out as the sahib continued to hold her tight.

Das examined the watch intently, holding it up see it better. He called over to his son. Yasmin recognised him. Chandra. He worked in the shop.

Suddenly they all stopped, listening. There was the sound of marching feet and then a troop of soldiers approached.

Yasmin felt the sahib relax a little. She did too. She recognised it was the Simla Rifles who had been trying to keep things under some control.

'Is everything OK?' An Indian officer pushed through the crowd of men. 'Are you OK there, Bill?'

He seemed to know the sahib, and Yasmin's sense of relief increased.

The officer looked at the box held open in Das's hand. Das looked up at the officer, grinning, and slowly shut and locked the wooden box. Then he gave it, along with the key, back to Yasmin.

Das nodded slowly, looking intensely at Merchant. Then he moved away, the men following.

'Yes, clear off, the lot of you,' said the officer. 'I don't know what mischief you've got planned, but if I were you, I'd get off to your homes. There has been enough trouble tonight.'

Das and the men moved away, but as he left, Das spoke once more to the sahib. 'That girl needs to go to Pakistan. We will check.'

'Be on your way,' said the officer. He lowered his voice and looked at the sahib. 'I'll walk back with you. He spoke a few words in Hindi to the men. Two stayed with the officer and the rest marched off down the Mall. The officer nodded at Yasmin, who was still being carried by Merchant. 'Poor girl.'

The sahib shook his head slowly.

'The lower bazaar?' asked the officer.

The sahib nodded.

'Say no more,' said the officer, shaking his head. 'That we have come to this.'

There was no further trouble as they went up the Mall, past Christchurch and over The Ridge. As they moved towards the block of flats where she knew the sahib lived, Yasmin could see the memsahib looking out for her husband from the walkway of the third floor.

'Looks like she's been worried about you,' said the officer. 'He looked around him and lowered his voice. 'If

I were you, I'd be very careful of that Das. He has some very unpleasant friends. You need to get this girl out of Simla as soon as you can.'

The sahib took leave of the officer and slowly climbed the stairs up to his home. Yasmin recalled how she had struggled again at that moment and the sahib had relaxed and put her down, allowing her to climb the stairs herself.

As she ruminated on all that had happened back then, Yasmin walked round the garden of the old Viceregal lodge, idly watching a mali cutting grass. She had still ended up losing the watch that night, and so far she had found no success in tracing it.

TURBAN

Jay and I arranged to meet on Bog Island.

Bog Island was the very centre of Moseley Village, a small triangle of land stranded between traffic lanes at the junction of Saint Mary's Row and Alcester Road. It had once been part of a larger village green, now mostly swallowed up by the road system. There was no green there now, except perhaps the flaking paint on the subterranean toilets' cast-iron railings.

It had been a busy time. I'd finished my exams but found it hard to apply myself properly and felt I had not done very well. I was also putting in plenty of extra shifts at Sainsburys. There was a lot on my mind, what with all I was finding out from Lenny, as well as what my dad had written. I still hadn't told Lenny about the wooden box, or about dad's papers. I needed to find out more from him before I shared it all. We had planned for me to go and see him every Wednesday evening for a guitar lesson and, I hoped, for Lenny to fill me in.

On the last day of the exams, there was a Youth CND meeting, then we – Jay and Liz, who were rapidly becoming an item, Jenny, Mimi, and myself –had gone for a drink in Moseley. I told them about my discoveries of an Indian past, but no-one seemed to care that much.

'You might have Indian blood but you're not Indian,' said Jay.

'Why not?' I asked.

'Well, for a start, you didn't even know about any

Indian connection until now. You were just brought up like any other white boy, with all the same advantages.'

'What advantages?'

'No-one looks at you and thinks you're brown,' said Jay. 'You don't have to put up with racists like Spooner, do you?'

I was thinking that I put up with plenty from Spooner.

'It's funny, isn't it,' added Jenny, 'my dad was black, from Nigeria apparently, but I never met him. I grew up with my white middle class mother from Cheltenham and because of the colour of my skin and my afro hair, everyone assumes I'm of Jamaican heritage, and they assign a whole set of cultural values to me that I don't possess. Going on to me about chicken, rice and peas and trying to speak to me in Patois. I don't have a clue about any of that stuff.'

That got me thinking, so what are we? Are we what other people think we are, or do we assign our own identity? I would have liked to discuss more, but the conversation moved on to Indian food.

'I'd love to be able to cook a good curry,' said Liz.

'I'll teach you,' Jay offered.

'Can you cook?' I was surprised.

'Yes, of course.'

'I've never had any of your cooking.' When I ate at Jay's, it was either Jay's mum or his sister Narinder that cooked.

'Why don't you cook at mine this weekend?' Mimi suggested. 'My parents are going away to the villa in Spain for a week on Saturday, so I have the place to myself. You can cook for us and show Liz what to do.'

'I can do Saturday,' said Jenny. 'Everyone else?'

All of us nodded, except Jay who was not looking so enthusiastic.

'Jay?' Jenny looked at him expectantly.

'Er yeah,' said Jay. 'That should be OK. But it might be difficult; I'll need all the spices and equipment.'

'Well, we do actually have a kitchen with a cooker and things,' said Mimi. 'And you can bring all the ingredients with you.'

'I suppose so,' said Jay.

'That's great,' replied Jenny. 'I'm so excited.'

I looked at Jay. He seemed worried and I wondered whether he could really cook at all. Still, it would be wonderful to spend an evening round at Mimi's house.

So here I was, waiting on Bog Island, excited about the evening ahead. I looked expectantly for a number one bus coming down St Mary's Row with Jay aboard. Instead, a rusted red Ford Cortina drew up. Jay was in the passenger street and his brother Bal was driving. Jay got out, passing carrier bags and a flat metal pan to me.

We crossed through traffic and turned into Mimi's road.

As we walked, I examined the metal pan. It was almost flat, slightly concave, with a wooden handle. 'What's this?'

'It's a tawa.'

'Yes, but what's it for?'

'It's for making roti.'

'Chapattis?'

'Yes.' Jay seemed distracted and not in the mood for conversation.

We rang the bell at Mimi's, but there was no reply.

'Where are they?' Jay put bags on the floor. 'What shall we do?'

'I don't know.' I swung the tawa like a tennis racket.

'Will you stop using it like that, you'll break it.'

I brought the tawa down to my side and looked at Jay. 'What's the matter with you?'

'I'm fine. I just want to get on with this cooking. I wish I'd never offered now.'

'Let's go round to The Prince.'

Jay swung his two carrier bags at me. 'What about this lot? I don't want to have to lug it all over the place.'

'Well, we can't just wait here.'

So, we carried everything round the corner to The Prince.

The Prince of Wales pub occupied a proud and simple 19th century building. It had a bar at the front and two small rooms at the back. We found a seat in the corner of one of the back rooms and Jay went out to the serving counter to get the drinks. The room looked more like the living room of a house. There was a chimney breast boasting an original Victorian fireplace, painted white and framing a Canon Miser gas fire. Round, wooden-topped and cast-iron tables and brown PVC-covered seats filled the perimeter of the room. Above this seating there was wood panelling with push buttons, presumably to call for table service. But the buttons had not rung bells for many years. In the corner of the room was a juke box playing Sweet Home Alabama.

A mixed bunch of people populated the room. In one corner was a smartly dressed elderly couple. A green tartan pull-along shopping trolley stood next to their table, indicating they had stopped off following a late afternoon shopping trip. He had a pint of bitter; she nursed a half pint glass of mild. Further along was a group of punks I recognised from the Youth CND march the week before. Their Mohicans and black leather were in sharp contrast to the appearance of the elderly couple who, nevertheless, seemed to pay no attention to the punks as they slowly and silently worked at their drinks. Further along sat a bearded middle-aged man with long straight hair and a Fair Isle sweater. Grubby jeans and cowboy boots were visible below the table. He was immersed in The Guardian, a tin of rolling tobacco before him.

'So will you go round in a minute and see if they're back?' Jay took a long sup of his pint.

'Why don't you?' I was irritated by Jay's behaviour.

'I need to look after the bags and things.'

'Well, I could do that.'

Jay shook his head, put his pint down, and without looking at me, walked out.

I felt bad. I wished I'd just agreed to go in the first place. Now I felt petty and didn't know what to do with myself without Jay.

After a while he came back. 'They're here. They've

been in the other room all the time. Didn't you think to look?'

'Well, you could have...' I stopped and smiled sympathetically at him, wanting to break the tension building up. 'Did you end up walking round to Mimi's?'

Jay stared blankly at me. 'Yes, I ended up walking round to Mimi's, even though they were here all the time. Let's get another drink.'

We gathered everything up, I got more drinks, and we moved into the other room. Mimi and Jenny were sitting at a table with Rick. Mimi nodded at us but continued her conversation with Rick. Jenny made room beside her on the long bench. 'I'm so glad you came to find us here. I was worried we'd miss you. We were just coming back off the bus from town and then we saw Rick and he invited us in.' She lowered her voice. 'I did try and tell Mimi we should get back to hers, but...' She looked at Mimi who was still engrossed in a conversation with Rick.

I went to the toilet. When I came back, Mimi was still talking to Rick. They were leaning close to each other, Rick saying something, and Mimi listening intently, smiling. I sat down heavily next to Jay on the bench and tried to join that conversation, avoiding the sight of Mimi and Rick. Apparently, Jay had argued with his mum before coming out, which explained his foul mood. He seemed to be brighter now he was talking to Jenny.

'She wanted to know where I was going,' Jay was telling Jenny. 'She saw me taking all the cooking stuff. She's worried I'm seeing a girl.'

'Wouldn't she want you to see a girl?' Jenny asked.

'Not unless she was Sikh and mum had been involved in finding her, checking out her family and which village they were from in the Punjab.' He rotated his beer glass on its edge, the froth coating the sides. 'I'm sick of it all.' He pointed at his turban. 'I'm sick of wearing this.'

'It looks good,' said Jenny. 'It's part of who you are. You'd just look like everyone else if you got rid of it.'

'I want to look like everyone else,' said Jay. He looked at his bags scattered around on the floor. 'I really need to get on with the cooking.' He nodded at Mimi, still talking to Rick. 'Do you think we'll be able to get a move on soon?'

Jenny leaned in to interrupt Mimi and Rick's conversation. Mimi looked irritated. Nevertheless, we finished our drinks and made our way over to Mimi's house, leaving Rick behind.

Mimi had forgotten her key, though, and for a moment I was anxious if the evening would go ahead. Luckily there was a spare key hidden under a flowerpot next to the front door.

Mimi's house had a proud Edwardian exterior. As I walked into the hallway, I noticed it had been tastefully decorated with Laura Ashley wallpaper and fabrics. I also could not fail to notice, looking through into the lounge, a large shotgun mounted on the wall.

Liz arrived soon after. She joined Jay and Jenny in the kitchen, where Mimi was showing them where everything was. I sat in the sitting room on an enormous Chesterfield facing a large inglenook fireplace. On either side of the fireplace were enormous HiFi speakers.

Walking over from the pub, I had tried to engage Mimi in conversation, but she was distant and distracted. Now she had disappeared into the kitchen with the others. I didn't know what to do with myself, so I started trying to roll a joint. I picked up a large book on urban photography from the shelf of the large coffee table and laid the joint paraphernalia out. My first attempts were bad, but I was slowly improving and after a few stops and starts I managed to get something together. I was impressed with the results and was holding the joint up to admire when Mimi came in with a bottle of wine and some glasses.

'Ah, you've created an aperitif.' She smiled and went over to the record collection.

I looked uncertainly at the unlit joint. 'Er, is it OK, if...'

Mimi smiled and waved dismissively. 'It's fine. I could do with a spliff.'

She went over to shelves containing records and started flipping through, eventually pulling out a shiny gold LP. She took the inner sleeve out and handed the gold cover to me. I tried to make out the writing: Exodus. It was a record by Bob Marley and the Wailers.

'Do you know it?' Mimi asked.

I recognised some of the track names but hadn't heard of the LP. First there was the click and hiss of the needle catching the record, then a rhythmic bass seemed to come out of the ground. Quiet at first, it became louder and louder until the record came fully to life with a drum roll and Marley's voice cut in singing Natural Mystic. I knew of Bob Marley, but I had never heard music sound like this before. The bass coming out of those massive speakers rolled though into my chest and I was captivated.

Mimi came over. She grabbed the unlit joint out of my hand and lit it up. She held it between her lips and inhaled, screwing up her eyes against the smoke. As she did this, she poured a glass of wine for both of us, gave one to me and started dancing round the room, blowing great clouds of smoke into the air. The evening sunlight caught the clouds, and it seemed that Mimi was dancing through mist.

She passed the joint to me, and I inhaled deeply, the music and the cannabis working in synergy as I lay back on the sofa and watched Mimi dancing. She came over and, with both hands, pulled me up and led me into the dance. I felt awkward at first, but I think I relaxed into it. Afterwards I thought I should have kissed her, but I was too nervous, and the moment passed.

We ate in the kitchen, sitting around this enormous farmhouse-style oak table.

'There's aloo palak, that's potato and spinach; dahl, which is lentils; rice, and roti – they're flatbreads,' Jay explained.

'It looks and smells wonderful,' said Jenny, sitting

down.

'Well done, Jay,' said Liz, giving him a kiss.

The food, in my opinion, was not very good. For a start, the potatoes were not cooked and there didn't seem to be any salt in the dahl. It was not like the food Jay's mum or sister cooked. Still, no-one else seemed to mind and Jay received plenty of compliments.

Mimi got out a bottle of Thunderbird wine. 'It's mentioned in the Ian Dury record, Sweet Gene Vincent,' she said, unscrewing the bottle top.

I had never heard of the record, though I recognised the name Ian Dury. Regardless, the connection gave the wine an air of the exotic. I took a sip; it had a strong chemical taste. 'It's very nice,' I said.

'It's disgusting.' Jenny made a face.

Nevertheless, we all drank the bottle of Thunderbird as we ate and then Mimi opened another. After the food, Mimi rolled a joint.

'Your cooking is really good, Jay,' said Jenny, refusing the joint that Mimi passed on to her.

She never partook in smoking. 'How did you learn to cook?' she went on.

'I watched my mum,' said Jay. 'She has shown me a few things.'

'So, your food is Punjabi? Where is the Punjab?' Mimi asked.

Jay explained how the Punjab was in the north of India.

'Punjab means land of five rivers,' explained Jay. 'Pun

is five. You see, it has–'

'Five rivers?'

Jay looked annoyed and I felt guilty for interrupting. Mimi asked about Jay's religion.

'My family are Sikh, but I don't really follow it myself.'

'Is the turban part of the religion?' asked Liz.

'It's part of the five K's,' explained Jay. 'Khanga, a wooden comb; Kara,' he waved his wrist to show a steel bangle, 'Kirpan, a special knife; Kachera,' he looked embarrassed, 'special underpants and...' he pointed to his head, 'Kesh, uncut hair.

'So do you have all those things?' Mimi asked. 'Including the underpants?'

'I left the knife at home and my pants are classified information,' said Jay, grinning. He turned to Jenny. 'Anyway, you can cut hair. Will you cut mine?'

Jenny shook her head. 'Why? Your turban looks great.'

'Please don't cut your hair, Jay,' said Liz.

Jay ignored her, looking towards Jenny. 'Please, will you cut it for me?' He took his turban off, revealing a topknot. He placed the black turban on the tabletop.

Mimi picked it up. 'It's all stiff. How does it get like this?'

'I soak it in starch and then I wrap it. When it dries it becomes stiff like that.' Jay turned to Jenny. 'Please will you cut my hair.' He reached up, undid the topknot, and let his hair fall. It was long and luxuriant and reached down to his back. Jay looked different and his long hair gave him a feminine appearance.

'Your hair is beautiful,' said Jenny. 'Some women would kill to have hair like that. How could I cut it?'

'Jay, just leave it like that. Your hair is amazing,' said Liz.

Mimi stood behind Jay, ruining her fingers through his hair. 'It's so soft.'

I couldn't stand seeing Mimi paying attention to Jay like that. 'If you want to get it cut, go to the barbers on Monday,' I said.

Jay looked at Jenny. 'Please will you cut it.'

Jenny shook her head. 'No, not tonight. Not now. You've been drinking. If you still want it cut tomorrow, I'll do it for you then.' She looked at his long hair and shook her head. 'What would your mum say.'

'It's not my mum's hair, it's mine. I'm sick of it.'

Mimi crossed the kitchen, opened a drawer and walked back over, snipping a large pair of scissors in the air.

'I'm not cutting his hair.' Jenny shook her head. 'Not now, at any rate. I need proper hairdresser's scissors.'

Mimi combed through Jay's hair with her fingers. 'Shall I do it?'

'Go on, then,' said Jay,'

'No!' Jenny and Liz said in unison.

Mimi stood, uncertain, running her fingers through Jay's hair. His eyes were screwed shut, as if he was expecting a blow to the head. We watched, mesmerised. I felt horror pounding in my chest, but whether this was about Jay losing his hair or seeing Mimi so intimate with my friend, I couldn't tell. Suddenly, Mimi pulled the hair into a ponytail and cut it off. It took several goes to get through. Lengths of black hair fanned out across the floor. Mimi continued, cutting the hair short across the back, and then trying to cut around the ears. It looked awful.

Liz's hands were over her face.

'Oh my God, stop it,' said Jenny. 'Let me finish it off.' Jenny took the scissors from Mimi and spent some time trying to tidy up Jay's hair.

To see Jay with short hair was quite disorientating. But it was a disorientation that had been going on all evening. The dance earlier, and the amazing bass of the Bob Marley record, had seemed to mark something new, a different phase in my life. Now I wanted to be alone with Mimi again, to have that kiss and perhaps more. But she seemed more interested in Jay's hair. I couldn't make her out. At the start of the evening, she had been more interested in Rick, then the dance, and now she had gone again.

For Liz it was all too much. The heavy mascara she wore was running down her face as she packed up her things and silently left the room. The slam of the front door prompted Jay to leave the room too, his hand running through his now short hair, another slam confirming that he had followed Liz out into the night.

Jenny, Mimi and I moved back to the sitting room. Mimi put on a Dr Alimantado record, The Best Dressed

Chicken in Town. A haze of smoke filled the room and we sat quietly, dub reggae moving hypnotically around us.

After a while, Mimi got up. 'I'm ready for bed. You can stay here, if you like. Jen, there's your usual bed upstairs.' She looked at me. 'There's the sofa or...' She shrugged 'Whatever, just sort yourself out.'

Jenny, who had already been falling asleep, went off with Mimi and I was left alone. There were other bedrooms – why had Mimi not offered me a bedroom? Was she inviting me to her room? She had said, 'There's the sofa or...'

I tried not to look at the shotgun mounted ominously on the wall and then crept up the stairs. Mimi's room had her name on the door on a china plaque, a relic of her childhood. I crept in and could see her looking up at me from her bed. I took off my trousers and got in with her. I tried to kiss her, and she rolled over, her back to me. She did not say a single word but lay there resolute and unmoving like a brick wall. I stayed for a while, wondering what to do, then, ashamed, I got up, gathered up my jeans and crept back downstairs. Once dressed, I escaped out through the front door and into the night air.

MIMI

It was three weeks after the night Jay had his hair cut before I got to see Mimi again.

It was three weeks during which nothing much happened. I just worked at Sainsbury's mindlessly sorting greengrocery until I started to feel I was turning into a vegetable myself.

I saw Jay a few times. We were well on our way with arranging the trip to India, but he was busy a lot with Liz, so less interested in spending time with me.

It was Mimi who got in touch with me in the end. I was surprised and elated to hear her voice on the phone. I had already tried several times to call her. Usually Mimi's mum would answer – a smoke-cracked voice drawling in middle class vowels, asking me who I was and telling me Mimi wasn't there. On one occasion she sounded drunk, and it appeared that the phone was taken from her by Mimi's father.

'She's not here,' had been the curt reply, the telephone struggling to contain his thick register, the resultant crackle adding an additional element of menace to the man.

There had been no Youth CND meeting where I might have been able to rely on seeing Mimi. When I had met up with Jay at the pub, I hoped I'd see her then, but I had no luck there either.

So when she called me, I felt I could hardly breathe.

'Hello... Stephen?' She sounded uncertain, nervous.

This tone of her voice was unfamiliar to me.

'Mimi?'

'Ah. Hi Stephen, how are you?'

'I'm fine, Mimi. How are you? I've been trying to get in touch. Did your mum tell you?'

'Are you free tonight?'

I paused. I had offered to take mum out that evening She had been feeling down and I thought it would do her good.

'Er, yes. Yes, I'm free... Where? When?' I could go out with mum another night.

We arranged to meet outside The Fighting Cocks in Moseley.

My preparation for the evening started with a very long bath. I loved baths. I still do. I run the water to a really hot temperature and then luxuriate in it, reading. I was still steadily working my way through War and Peace, but on that day I found it hard to concentrate, the thought of an evening alone with Mimi uppermost on my mind. I was hoping Mimi's mum and dad would be away again and she would invite me back and things would go more successfully than last time. I gave up on trying to concentrate on War and Peace and lay back giving in to the anticipation of the night ahead.

I planned to wear my new donkey jacket. It was a fine sunny day and I wondered whether I may be a little too hot in the coat, however when I considered the other choices in my limited wardrobe, as well as Mimi's previous comment about my clothes, I decided the donkey jacket was my best option. I spent a long time in front of the hallway mirror, carefully siting my CND and a new Coal Not Dole badge on the black PVC shoulder-covering.

That was when mum came home from work. She was an assistant in a shoe shop in Kings Heath. 'Where are you going?' She stood by the open front door, keys dangling in her hand, looking me up and down.

'I'm going out.'

'Oh.' She looked puzzled. 'You'll be back in time for our night out?'

'Can we go tomorrow instead?'

She threw the keys on the gas meter cupboard next to the front door. 'But I thought we agreed to go out tonight.' She put her handbag down and pushed past me, taking off her jacket. 'I've been looking forward to going out. I haven't even got anything for tea.' She moved into the kitchen. 'I can see you've had something to eat.'

'I'm sorry, Mum, something's come up. We can do it tomorrow night.'

Pans clattered in the kitchen; cupboard doors banged. 'Forget it, Stephen.' She came out and faced me. 'I don't know what has come up that's so urgent, but I'm sure it's not more important than keeping a promise you made to me. You're getting selfish and thoughtless.' She stopped and stared at me.

I moved closer to the door, desperate to get out, to get away from the situation, worried too that this might make me late for Mimi.

But mum hadn't finished. 'What has got into you? You've changed.' She turned to go back into the kitchen, and I thought that was her last salvo. I was wrong. She turned around. 'And you've left the kitchen in a right state. You've been home all day while I've been at work, and you've even left your breakfast things for me to sort out.'

'I've been busy, Mum.'

Mum just stared at me for a while before replying, a little sarcastically I thought, 'Well, you could have found some time in your busy day to wash up.' She turned and went back to the kitchen. 'Just selfish and thoughtless,' she repeated before slamming the kitchen door shut.

I had meant to wash up the kitchen detritus that built up through the day; the cereal bowl, the toast crumbs, the open, empty bean can and the saucepan I used to make myself something to eat before heading out. But I'd run out of time, and now if I stayed any longer, I would be late for Mimi. I took a final look in the mirror and set out.

I arrived at The Fighting Cocks ten minutes early, then waited half an hour outside the pub, frequently looking down at my watch and up at the Alcester Road for Mimi. The sun was still shining, and I was hot in the donkey jacket. Consequently, I had sweated a lot on the walk up and I could feel my t-shirt sticking to my back. At least the jacket would hide that, but I was beginning to think I was not in the best state to meet Mimi, after all. At one point, I started walking towards her house to meet her.

Then I worried she might be coming from somewhere else. I quickly went back to my place outside the pub and continued waiting.

After a long while I thought to check inside. Immediately, I heard her voice as I pushed through the heavy wooden doors. She was sitting on the long bench seat facing the bar. The pleasure I had at the sight of her was dampened considerably by the fact that she was not alone. She was with Rick and a number of other people I had seen at Youth CND events.

I tentatively went over to join them.

Mimi saw me. 'Stephen.' She patted the seat next to her. 'Sit next to me.' She looked at her glass which was nearly empty. 'Actually, would you get me a drink while you're up? I'll have a pint of lager dash, please.'

'Would you get me a pint too?' Rick held up an empty glass. 'Bitter. You're a top bloke.'

I took the glass from Rick and felt obliged to ask the rest of the group if they wanted drinks. Taking their orders, I wondered if I had enough cash for the rest of the evening.

I took the seat next to Mimi, considering how and when we were going to be alone. There didn't seem to be much prospect of it. Mimi and the rest were engrossed in a conversation about the miners' strike. Then Jenny arrived, got a drink and sat next to me. I wondered if she had been invited out by Mimi too.

'Aren't you hot in that coat?' Jenny asked me.

'No, I'm fine,' I lied, hoping the amount I was

sweating wasn't making me smell.

Jenny shook her head and took a sip from her drink. 'Where's Jay?' she asked.

'I'm not sure,' I replied. 'I didn't know we were all meeting up like this.'

Jenny looked at me strangely. 'Did Mimi ask you to come out?'

I hesitated. Being asked to meet up seemed an intimate thing between Mimi and me. I felt uncomfortable discussing it.

Jenny said, 'Only, you see, Mimi called me to meet her as she was upset about something. But now, I've come here expecting to see Mimi alone and I find a whole crowd of people. So, I just wondered, did Mimi invite you out?'

I nodded slowly, looking down at the table, wondering what Mimi was up to.

Jenny was silent for a moment. 'How were Jay's family about his hair?'

I recalled how Jenny had tried to tidy up Jay's hair after Mimi had cut it. 'I think his mum was really upset,' I said. 'She's still not speaking to him.'

'It was such a shame to see all that beautiful hair cut off.'

'I think he feels a lot better about it now. He had been wanting to stop wearing a turban for a long time. He just hadn't worked up the courage to do it.' I was still getting used to the sight of a turbanless Jay with short hair. In truth though, I was envious of Jay's determination to take such a bold step against his mother. If I had been in that position, I don't think I would have done the same.

After a while, Rick and the others left, saying they were going over the road to a caucus meeting of the Socialist Movement group. Later, they were coming back to see the band playing upstairs. Mimi told us she was going with them, which was strange because I still thought she was having a date with me. Mimi stayed with Jenny and me for a while longer though, while she finished her drink.

That was when things got difficult.

Mimi was still talking about the miners' strike.

'We're going up next week. Rick's organising a minibus.' Mimi smiled. 'We're going to throw eggs at those scabs still going down the pit.'

I didn't like the idea of Mimi spending a day travelling around in a minibus with Rick. 'I'm not sure that's right.' I took a sip of beer. 'I mean... well... I support the miners and all that, but...' I looked up, trying to find the words. 'The miners who are on strike have a right to picket, but do...' I wanted to say 'people like you' but changed it to, 'people like us have a right–'

'Of course we fuckin' do.' Mimi's voice rose. 'This is a key moment in the workers' struggle. Those miners going to work are fuckin' scabs. Betraying the cause. We have to make it difficult for them. We have to support our brothers on the front line.'

'Well...' I started. This was going all wrong.

Jenny intervened. 'Stephen's right, Mimi. Those miners going to work have families to feed. How can we judge them?'

Mimi picked up her pint, took a long drink and slammed it down on the table. A splash of beer hit me in the face.

'You know nothing, Jenny Wainwright.' Mimi's voice was loud now, and people were looking over. 'They are fuckin' scabs. Fuckin scabs letting the side down. And you're a scab for supporting them.'

Jenny stood up. 'I know you live in a great big house in Moseley and that daddy provides everything you need. It's easy for you. This miners' strike is just a bit of fun for you, but for those miners it's a real crisis and a dilemma. You have no right to judge them for carrying on working.' She snatched up her bag.

I watched Jenny leave. I turned to Mimi. 'I'm sorry–'

'Shut up, Stephen,' She looked at the door where Jenny had just left. 'You're such an idiot. You know nothing. Absolutely nothing.' She stood up too and went out the door.

I supposed she was going to the meeting over the road.

I sat alone, looking down at my pint, wondering what to do. Wondering what was wrong with Mimi. I shouldn't have provoked her with my stupid statement about the miners' strike. Should I just go home, or stay at the pub? I knew Mimi would come back with the rest to see the band upstairs.

In the end, like the stupid, lovesick fool I was, I just waited until I saw her come back through the doors along with Rick and the rest of them. I'm sure she saw me, but she just carried on up the stairs.

Then I spent a while wondering whether I should go upstairs and see if Mimi was OK. Maybe she was waiting for me to apologise, and she would be even more annoyed with me if I didn't try and resolve matters. I could not stand that Mimi was upset with me. That's one of my many weaknesses – even now. I can't stand the disapproval of others. Over the years I've found there are people who will take advantage of that to manipulate. But of course, I didn't know that back then.

When I did go upstairs, Mimi was talking to Rick. I tried to join them, but she turned away from me. Then I stepped back and stood alone, watching the band, though I was unable to concentrate on anything else but Mimi. I kept glancing over towards her. Seeing her close to Rick was almost unbearable. When he moved away I went over again. I bent down a little and moved my head close to hers, meaning to make some comment about the band, but she moved her head quickly, her dark hair swishing against my face. She strode quickly away, leaving me alone with her lingering fragrance and the memory of the feel of her hair against my face.

That was when I decided to give up and start the long walk home. The night sky was clear and cloudless, a bright full moon lighting the deserted streets. But any beauty of that night was not apparent to me as I strode home, kicked stones, and cursed the miners.

When I did get home, I discovered I'd forgotten my key and had to ring the bell a few times. Finally, the hall light came on and, through the dimpled glass of the front door, I saw the shape of my mum descending the stairs. She went away from the front door and I saw her look blankly through the front room window at me, I supposed she was checking who was knocking the door so late. She opened the door without facing me and wordlessly went back up to bed.

RONNIE: PARTITION

'You need a burra peg my friend,' Dr Basu said to father. 'You can get me one too,' he added, sitting down in the cracked brown leather armchair and resting his head back on the antimacassar.

Father gathered glasses and poured two whiskies. His hands were still shaking and mother, who had just entered, would notice he spilt some of the Johnny Walker on the sideboard top. He wiped it away quickly with his sleeve, looking round to see she was near.

Unusually for her, she didn't bother about the spilt whisky. Mother had been busy looking after Yasmin. She'd drawn the poor girl a bath to get rid of the smell of smoke and to try and calm her down.

Lenny was in bed, but I hadn't been able to sleep, what with all that was going on, and so I had waited up with mother for father to come back from work.

Father settled back in his chair and took large gulp of the whisky. He held the glass up, trying to control his shaking hands and looked at the liquid, as if trying to focus his thoughts and calm his mind. He started the story afresh.

He had brought in the up train from Kalka. In Kalka things had been bad, with looting and burning; the station master told him there were dead bodies on the streets. Father was glad when the engine had begun the climb out of the town into the deodar-lined hills. He looked back along the train, seeing thick, menacing smoke over the town below. It was a tense six hours up to Simla. Normally when he did the up train with Joe De Souza as his fireman, there was laughing and jokes. This time they stood in terrified silence every time they entered one of the stations on the way. They were glad as they drew into Simla and came to a halt.

But that didn't last long.

As father handed over to the next driver he heard things had been bad there too.

'They've been attacking the Muslims. It's in retaliation for what has been going on in Lahore and other places. Tit for tat,' said Jimmy Smith, a tall Anglo-Indian who father played tennis with at the club. 'Be careful walking up the hill, there's a lot of trouble about. Avoid the lower bazaar. It's really bad around there. They're not bothering with us, but still you still need to be careful.'

The lower bazaar was where Mohammed Pir, our cook, his wife and Yasmin lived. In Simla, Muslims were in the minority, so they were vulnerable to attack. Father headed up The Mall and stopped. He looked down towards the lower bazaar. As at Kalka, there was the smell of burning in the air. He moved to carry on up The Mall, thinking of mother, Lenny and me. He stopped again and took the way heading down – towards the bazaar.

He was right to be concerned. Yasmin's house was burning and there was a mob outside. Father watched Yasmin being lowered from a window by Mohammed on to the roof of the place next door, and he quickly climbed up to help. Mohammed nodded with grim relief as he saw father and went back inside to help his wife. Yasmin recognised father and went to him, and he gathered her in his arms and waited for Mohammed to come to the window again.

But Mohammed did not come back and the smoke became too dense so that, even outside, father could hardly breathe. It was a hard climb down with Yasmin held tight with one arm.

Father told how they had climbed up through the streets, how he had been rescued from a difficult situation by Subedar Singh from the Simla Rifles. It had been fortunate that father knew Singh from the Railway Club where the soldier would often pop by for a drink.

There was no further trouble as they went up the Mall, past Christchurch and over The Ridge, escorted by Singh. Mother and I were standing on the balcony outside the flat's front door and I could sense her relief as father and the Subedar came into view. I could see father was carrying a child.

'What has he been up to?' said mother, looking down as father said goodbye to the Subedar and approached the stairwell.

Father came in and followed mother into the kitchen, still holding Yasmin. I tagged along behind, unnoticed it seemed, in all the drama.

'I've been worried, Bill.' She grabbed a cloth and opened the oven door, taking out the covered plate of food that Yasmin's father had prepared earlier. It was the usual routine when father was on the late run. We would eat earlier, and his meal would be kept warm in the oven for him.

Mother took the cover off the plate. 'It's all dried out.' She stared at the plated meal. Father looked too. There were lamb cutlets and vegetables. The gravy had baked at the edges. In any case, he did not feel hungry.

'We need to take care of Yasmin,' he said.

Mother looked up. 'Yes, the girl.'

Father placed Yasmin on the ground. She stood carefully, her legs could hardly support her.

Mother dropped down and stroked the girls hair, looking her over. 'And you. Are you hurt?' She was talking to father but she wouldn't look at him.

'I'm fine, Mary.'

Mother knew he was staring at her. He could not stand it when she was annoyed with him, but she could not help herself. 'You could have been killed.' Mother took Yasmin in her arms and finally looked at father. She lowered her voice. 'The rest?'

Father shook his head.

She closed her eyes, said once more, 'You could have been killed,' then stood up. 'This girl needs a bath and I will make up a bed, though God knows where. She can't sleep in the boys' room.' Mother looked at the plate of food. 'You need to eat.' She walked Yasmin through towards the bathroom and turned. 'And we need to talk.'

Mother got Yasmin sorted and reluctantly settled her on a camp bed in mine and Lenny's room. Lenny slept through the whole lot. Then Dr Basu knocked on the door to see whether father had got home. Mother had spoken to him earlier when father didn't return on time.

The whiskies and father's telling of the night's events followed.

'So, what will you do with Yasmin?' Basu asked.

'We can't give her in to Das,' said father. 'He will send her to that refugee camp. Who knows what it's like there. The girl has lost all her family. She needs looking after.'

'And who will look after her?' Mother asked. 'She can't stay here. It was foolish enough that you risked your life to save her. It's best that we keep out of all of this as much as we can.'

'I wasn't thinking she could stay here,' replied father, though mother knew he thought that might be the best option.

'Leave it with me,' said Dr Basu. 'I will see what I can arrange,'

'Do you know about this?' Mother held up a small wooden box. She had the key, she must have taken it from Yasmin. She easily found the sliding section, inserted the key and opened up the box. Mother held a golden pocket watch up, swinging on its golden chain.

I recognised it as the one Yasmin had shown me before.

'Why on earth would the girl have this?' Mother opened the watch to look at the face, showing it to father and Dr Basu. 'This must be worth a fortune.'

'Her father passed it to her from the window. I don't know how he would have got it,' said father.

'I think we need to take care of this for the girl.' Mother scooped up the chain, popped it in the wooden box and locked it.

Dr Basu got up from the chair. 'I think it is time for me to go. I will make some enquiries and then get back to you regarding the girl. There must be something we can do rather than sending her to Pakistan.'

A few days later, Yasmin was dressed in Lenny's school uniform, cap in place and her hair gripped over her ears and hidden under the shirt collar. Then Dr Basu walked her down the hill and took her on the train to Kalka.

That was the last we ever saw of her.

She was adopted by a friend of Dr Basu. He was a doctor too.

But Yasmin did not get to take the watch. That was kept by mother. She did not think it was safe to leave Yasmin in charge of it. But keeping the watch led to a further trouble, this time with Chandra, the son of Prakash Das.

THE SOCIAL

Back in the 1980s the licensing laws were strict. By 11pm or earlier it would be chucking out time at the pub and you had to find somewhere else to carry on socialising. A legal late bar might be found on Saturday night if there was a charitable, fundraising event – like they had at The Mermaid to raise money for CND. Then there was the odd illegal pub lock-in. These were often near police stations, as the presence of police officers would provide protection for the licensee. There were also the nightclubs in towns: Edwards, Snobs, Faces or Tommy's, but they weren't our scene. Jay and I had given up on those after not being allowed into Tommy's.

That's how I discovered the Moseley late night life. There would be house parties. There was the Jamaican style blues party; heavy reggae pounding out from a cellar down Trafalgar Road. And there were "socials".

A social was a party held by one of the left-wing groups. Usually in one of the large Victorian house shares in one of the streets off Church Road. You would pay to get in, then you could get some food, usually a veggie curry, and some beer or wine, often home-brewed.

On the night I ended up at my first social, Jay and I had gone to drink at the Prince of Wales. I was excited on the way there, hoping I would see Mimi, but at the same time nervous. I didn't know how she would react to me. I would not be able to stand it if she ignored me the way she had at the Fighting Cocks. And I hadn't seen her since then.

As it was, she was fine.

'Stephen!' She greeted me warmly as I walked into the back room. She was standing up, talking with a group that included Rick, Jenny and Liz. Mimi put down her drink, rushed over and gave me a tight hug and kissed me on the cheek.

'Where's mine?' Jay asked.

Mimi gave him a hug too, but it wasn't like the one she gave me. I was ecstatic.

We went and joined the group. Jay kissed Liz and she straightened his shirt collar for him. They seemed to be getting like an old married couple more and more every day. That was what I wanted, someone to care for me the way Liz obviously cared about Jay. I looked to Mimi, but she was talking to Rick.

Jenny interrupted my thoughts. 'We're going to a social after the pub, are you coming?'

So, once the pub closed, I ended up walking down to the social with Mimi, Jenny and Rick. Jay and Liz went back to Liz's house.

There, I saw Lenny.

'I've just popped by quickly after the gig. How are you doing, son?' He was rolling a cigarette and had his guitar case leaning against his side. We talked a while. I asked him if he had seen Das yet.

Lenny shook his head. 'The man is an idiot. He's a disaster. I'm still not sure we should have anything to do with him.' Then he changed the subject and asked me how I had been getting on with my guitar.

In truth I had not been getting on very well. I had learnt the chords to Mr Tambourine Man by Bob Dylan, but it sounded awful, and I was having trouble getting my fingers to stay in the right places on the guitar frets. I didn't have much hope.

'Just keep at it, son. Keep at it.' Lenny smiled. 'You'll be sounding like Hendrix in no time.'

He went soon after that and left me alone at the party. I could not see Mimi or Jenny anymore and I was wondering whether to just go home when into the room came Miss Costello – Claire as I was trying, with difficulty, to call her.

'Stephen,' she greeted me warmly.

She was a little drunk and, putting her arms out, she gathered me into an embrace. I could smell her perfume mixed with the smell of stale cigarette smoke.

'This is my friend, Sue.' She turned to her friend. 'This is Stephen, one of my sixth formers.' She stopped. 'Well actually, he's not one of my sixth formers.' She shook her head. 'Well, anyway, I know Stephen from school.'

Her friend was tall and slim with reddish hair cut into a neat bob. She had bright red lipstick and was wearing a red skinny-ribbed top and jeans with a black and white dogtooth scarf. She had small eyes that she had worked to emphasise with make-up. I found the effect very attractive. She smiled thinly at me in a way that made me feel I had disappointed her in some way.

Claire and I talked for a while, her friend standing

there smoking and looking bored, then they went off to get some food and drinks. I wandered round and saw Jasper. I chatted with him for a bit and then, not being able to find Mimi or Jenny, I decided it was definitely time to go home.

As I was making my way to the front door. I came across Sue. She was sitting on the stairs, idly smoking a cigarette.

She called me. 'Hey, you, whatever your name is. Have you seen Claire?'

I told her I hadn't and moved to carry on up to the front door.

'Don't go, come and talk to me for a while.' She patted the stair next to her and shuffled close to the wall to make room for me.

I hesitated.

'Oh, come on. Sit down and talk to me,' she slurred. She seemed very drunk.

I sat down next to her. She smoked in silence, flicking ash on to the floor and rubbing it into the carpet with her foot. I didn't know what to say and was about to get up and go when she started speaking.

'She's gone off to see him, you know,'

I didn't know what she was talking about.

Sue looked at me. 'Her fancy man. He came here and now they've disappeared. He just clicks his fingers and she follows him wherever he wants her to go.'

'Do you mean...' I struggled to think how to address Miss Costello

'Claire. Yes, Claire. Who else would I be talking about,' said Sue, stubbing her cigarette out against the wall. 'We share a house. We're old friends, Claire and me. Went to teaching college together.'

After that we chatted and Sue told me she was a teacher at a local girls' school. Then Mimi and Jenny came in from outside; the stairs Sue and I were sitting on were opposite the front door. They both looked at me.

'Ooh you look very cosy there,' said Mimi.

Jenny did not say anything.

'We was just... just chatting,' I said unnecessarily.

Mimi said, 'You mean "we were"–'

'Who the fuck are you, correcting his grammar,' cut in Sue. 'Only his teacher or his mother should do that.'

Mimi looked at her for a few seconds. 'Well, which one are you?' Then she walked off down the hall without looking at me. Jenny gave me a sad, disapproving look. She must have thought I was messing her friend about.

'Come on let's go.' Sue stood up.

I wondered what she meant.

She looked down at me. 'I want you to walk me home. You're not going to leave a lady to walk home on her own, are you?'

I stood up, not sure what to do, but I knew I had to leave this social.

We walked through the streets of Moseley to where she told me that she lived. It wasn't much further for me to go home anyway. She took my arm like Mimi had done and whether it was to steady herself or a sign of affection, I wasn't entirely sure, though every now and again she became unsteady and swerved into me, laughing, and sending us both across the pavement into either a garden wall, a parked car or off the kerb and onto the road. Eventually we turned onto a street of small, terraced houses. I stood on the pavement and watched her enter the gate of the front garden. She dug in her handbag for keys and then looked up at me.

'Aren't you coming in for a coffee?' She turned her back and opened the door.

I thought, why not? I followed her in, through the front room and into the back. The house was a right mess. You could tell that there were great intentions: the walls painted in bright colours; some cool, framed black and white photos on the walls; a lot of expensive funky ceramics. I had seen similar stuff in this shop in Moseley called Pottery and Pieces. The trouble was everything was covered in a thick layer of dust. There was a stuffed ashtray on the stained coffee table and plates with left-over food stacked beside it. The kitchen was also filthy. Washing-up for several days covered the surfaces. The cooker was caked in grease and covered in dried up remnants of food.

Sue was in no fit state to make any coffee, so I made it. As soon as I had put the drinks down on the coffee table and sat down, she was on me, kissing me, pushing her tongue into my mouth. I could feel her breasts against me. I was aroused but nervous. I was not sexually experienced. I was worried how I would perform with this older woman.

My worries were replaced with new concerns though when we heard a key in the door.

'Oh no, that's Claire.' Sue quickly moved off me. 'Go up to my room. I don't want her to see you here. It's the front bedroom, the one on the left. I'll come up in a minute.'

I sat there a little confused.

Sue pushed me. 'Quick.'

I went through the door she was pointing at. It led directly on to a staircase.

I could hear Claire coming through now. She was not alone. There was a man's voice and I recognised it. I crept quietly up the stairs and went into the front bedroom. I did not turn on the light but, if anything, it was in even a worse state than downstairs. There were clothes strewn on the floor and on the bed where I sat. There was a pair of scrunched-up knickers on the floor beside the bedside table. I sat there for ages, hearing the indistinct voices talking downstairs. Finally, I heard Claire and the man coming up the stairs and into her room.

I waited ages for Sue to come up. I had been all excited with her kiss and was anticipating what would happen when she appeared. Instead, I had to listen to the sounds of Claire and the man loudly making love in the other bedroom. Eventually, when it got quiet and I guessed they must have fallen asleep, I crept back down the stairs. Sue was lying fast asleep on the sofa, her head flung back, loudly snoring. There was a sliver of saliva running down her chin. I quietly went up to the front door and let myself out.

It had been a strange night. But perhaps the strangest thing of all had been the man who had come back with Claire.

It was Mimi's father. Tommy Deathridge.

RONNIE: SMOKE

The thing I remember about seeing Birmingham for the first time was the smoke. It was everywhere. It literally smeared the sky, venting from these great, tall factory chimneys rising out of the murk like blasted trees. It emerged from the endless terraces of houses. It got into everything, leaving behind only dust and blackness. Every now and then the stalagmitical array of chimneys was breached by a black church steeple or tower. For ages, I thought the buildings in this city were constructed out of some kind of black stone. Then I realised they were just coated in soot.

That was what faced us when we arrived in Birmingham on the train. The vibrancy and colour of India replaced by smoke, drabness and black. Inside the train, the atmosphere was as black as that outside. Father, Lenny and I were in disgrace, for some reason. Mother could be like that. Moody. She would not speak to any of us except her sister, my Auntie Betty, who had met us off the ship. When mother wasn't looking, Auntie Betty slipped us the occasional wink and a grin.

Father wasn't speaking to anyone anyway. I think that was because of what happened at Euston.

Excited by being in a British station and seeing a British loco, father had gone up to speak to the driver and fireman and ask them how he could become an engine driver in Britain. He had taken Lenny and me with him.

'Hello, there,' said Father.

The driver was standing on the footplate, holding a mug of tea and a cigarette. The fireman, who was shovelling coal, stopped and stood looking at us, resting on his shovel. The driver took a drag on his fag.

'I'm a driver, myself,' continued father. 'I worked on the Indian Railway. I'm hoping to be a driver here too.'

The driver shrugged, threw his cigarette down and stubbed it out with his foot.

The fireman resumed shovelling.

'How do I apply for a job?' asked father.

The driver took a sip from his tea and then threw the dregs on the platform, splashing father's shoes and trouser legs.

Father turned away. He looked down at his shoes. I knew he had polished those shoes to glass before we got off; excited for his first steps in the motherland. He kept his head down and walked back towards our carriage. 'Come on lads,' he said to Lenny and me.

As we walked away, I heard one of the men mutter, 'Bleedin' darkies.'

After independence many of the Anglo-Indians had looked to ways of moving away from India. Even though we were part-Indian ourselves, we did not feel welcome in the country anymore. We were too associated with the British. We had made it that way ourselves, I suppose. In spite of the struggle for Independence, the British Raj seemed like it would last forever and the Anglo-Indians had found their own unique place in it, serving and identifying with the British, while looking down on the full-blooded Indians. The British had used the Anglo-Indians to work on the railways, in the post office, in the military and as clerks. Once the British had left, we Anglos found it more difficult to get jobs or promotions. I had got used to being told to 'Quit India,' having to walk past protestors holding banners outside the railway cantonment. A way out was provided in 1948. The British Nationality Act gave commonwealth inhabitants like us the right to live in Britain. Additionally, following the war, countries such as Australia and Canada had been welcoming immigrants. The Merchant family had a number of options for leaving the country we had been in for generations and my parents decided we had to take one of them.

First, my father wrote to an aunt, Leila Merchant, who had moved back to Britain just after the war. I remember finding Aunt Leila's reply in my parents' bedroom, when I was going to take a look at that old watch of Yasmin's, like I often used to. Though mother and father had always referred to Britain as home, the thought of leaving India, where all my friends were, seemed unthinkable.

Dear William

Your letter to hand, strange you should say you have not met me because when you were transferred to Lahore you came and saw us and spent the day with us. I expect it was so long ago you may have forgotten. You were tall and thin. Well, in 1947, my married daughter Eva and her husband and two daughters, as well as my daughter Marjorie, who is a nurse, arrived here and they bought a bungalow. After they had settled in, Uncle Harry and I arrived here early in 1948. Uncle Harry had been having heart trouble and fell asleep in February 1949. He was 76 years old.

Well, I am glad that you are thinking of coming here. This is the best place for the education of the boys. Boarding schools are very expensive, but in the day schools children are educated free. The government gives eight shillings to every child under sixteen except the eldest.

The problem would be housing, as boarding houses, or people who may have a rooms to spare, will not take in children. That is the most difficult part over here. If you can afford to buy a house, they range in price from £1600 upwards. The building societies would lend up to half if you could put down the remainder in cash. Furniture is also very expensive, It would cost the best part of £200 to furnish a house, or half that amount if you bought second-hand.

Your wife should certainly come with the children as no one else could take that responsibility. Perhaps you may have some friends who could help them till you get your own house. I am very sorry we could not help you in that way as we have not a corner to spare. Houses are small, not like India, and there are no servants. We have to do everything ourselves. Sweeping, cleaning, cooking all meals, buying ingredients, meat and vegetables.

Everyone has to do it. Shops are near – you soon get used to it.

I have heard that you can get assistance for your passage if you can show your British ancestry. You should first of all write to

The Commonwealth Relations Office
King Charles Street
Whitehall
London

Enclose copies of your claim and ask for assistance for your children's education and passages. I have heard that some people have had such help.

Secondly, you should try to interview the British High Commissioner in Delhi and find out if you can get any assistance from him.

Below, I have copied a letter I received from The Commonwealth Office showing your father's father and grandfather. It will help you if you come to this side of the world.

I do hope I have made everything clear.

With love and kind thoughts to you and your wife and family

Yours affectionately
Aunty Leila Merchant

*Commonwealth Relations Office
King Charles Street
Whitehall
SW1*

23 June 1949

Dear Madam,

In reply to your letter of 25 May I show below the result of searches made among the records preserved in this office.

*Samuel Henry Merchant
Son of William Merchant, Gunner 1st Battalion and Elizabeth his wife, born 13th January 1834 and baptised 4th March 1834 Secunderabad (Madras: 15/564). Enlisted at St Thomas's Mount 4th June 1852 as Gunner 3rd battalion, Madras Artillery. Volunteered to Royal Artillery as Gunner in 1861. Pensioned as Sergeant 11th April 1872.*

His father

*William Merchant
Born Colchester Essex (no date given).
Enlisted London 25th April 1826 for Madras Artillery (aged 22) Embarked for Madras on "Lady Raffles" 22nd May 1826. Removed to 1st Battalion -Ooty 26th June*

1832.
Schoolmaster Sgt 1st Battalion Ooty 26th June 1834.
Pensioned 4th March 1851.
Died 11th January 1852.

In the end, father managed to make all the arrangements to get back home to England. There being no room at the inn so far as Aunt Leila was concerned, Auntie Betty was willing to take us. She had met and married an English serviceman during the war and then moved to his home in Birmingham.

I wondered what it would be like living in England and, in spite of my worry about what occurred on the journey, I awoke with excitement on the last day of our twelve day trip from Bombay to London.

It was the ship's hooter that woke me. That was followed by a similar blast from further off and I was aware of a change in the ship's movement, an indication we were not on the open sea anymore. I climbed out of my bunk, feeling the cold of the metal rails on my bare feet, and looked out of the port hole. Thin daylight and fog obscured my view. I decided to go up on deck for a better look. I tried to wake Lenny to get him to come too, but he was still fast asleep, so I quickly got dressed and went by myself.

There were a few others about up on deck – migrants taking in their first sights of England. The thick fog allowed only a hazy view of the Thames shoreline. It was utterly uninspiring, and I thought of all we had left behind in India. Yet, this grey, cold foreign place before me was the land I had been taught to call home all my life. Unfortunately, the mother country was not living up to expectations on that morning.

As I looked along the rail I saw father, also taking in his first sight of the homeland. He looked down in surprise as I joined him. 'Ah, so you've woken early too.' He ruffled my hair like he did. 'So what do you make of it?' He looked out toward the blurred Essex shoreline and then back to me, smiling. 'It will be fine once you get used to it. We will be better off here.' He flicked a piece of flaking white paint from the deck rail. 'I can get work on the railway; I heard they're crying out for drivers.' He put his head back, inhaling deeply, looking out at the thin strip of flat shoreline. 'Your mother can get a teaching job and we can live in a nice English house.' He looked back at me. 'You and Lenny will have better prospects than in India.'

I looked down the deck rail and saw Peter, the stowaway. I tried to look the other way but it was too late. He was already coming towards us. I did not want father to know anything about what had gone on involving all that.

I excused myself and quickly went over to speak with Peter. Whatever he wanted to say, I did not want him to say it in front of father. Especially if it was to do with anything that had happened after we left Port Said.

'What is it?' I spoke quietly and led Peter away from where father stood, smoking and looking out at the shoreline.

'I'm worried,' said Peter. 'What is going to happen when we leave the ship? Is the plan going to work?'

At first, Lenny and I had not realised Peter was a stowaway. He was older than us, about seventeen or eighteen, but he had a vulnerability that made him quite childlike. He had asked me to get him some rolls when we went to breakfast. Then he wanted a blanket. And soon we learnt how he had managed to sneak on board the ship at Bombay. He was Anglo-Indian like us, but had not been able to get proof for an assisted passage to England. He didn't even have a passport!

In the end, we let him sleep on Lenny's and my cabin floor. Every evening, during the first part of the journey, we let him in, making sure he was out early in the morning, in case mother or father popped by.

We didn't know how he was going to get off at Tilbury but it came about that Chandra Das would help with that one.

Das was a bit older than Peter. We recognised him from Simla, where he had worked in his father's shop. We had spoken with him a bit at the beginning of the journey when we got on at Bombay and he told us he was going to work in his uncle's spice business in London. With all the people going over from India, there was more demand in Britain for Indian ingredients. The Das's were aiming to profit from that.

One night when we were in the ship's billiard room playing snooker, Das suddenly asked us, 'Do you know anything about a watch? A pocket watch?' He looked sneakily at us both for a moment and then made to concentrate on examining the arrangement of the snooker balls.

I think he could tell I knew something about it.

He went on, 'That girl had a watch on the night of Independence. Your father took her home. But I heard that when she left to go down to Kalka on the following day, she didn't have that watch anymore. That was a beautiful watch. I wonder what happened to it?'

I looked at Lenny. I think he knew there was a watch but I don't think he knew it had come from Yasmin. He didn't say anything and neither did I.

Das just smiled, nodded and chalked the tip of his cue before taking a shot. He missed and the white rolled into a pocket. He did not mention the watch again that night. It was as if he was just mentioning it in passing, but there was something about the way he brought it up that worried me.

Das didn't know about Peter at first, but he must have noticed us always sneaking food out of the dining room. One day, not long after we had left the Suez Canal and got into the Mediterranean, Das followed me back after breakfast and walked into our room without knocking. Peter's bed was still made up on the floor in the narrow space beside our bunks. He stared at the makeshift bed and then at all our faces.

'You don't have a ticket, do you?' Das looked at Peter.

'Please don't tell anyone...' I began, before being

nudged by Lenny.

'I won't tell,' said Das. 'But I will want something in return.'

That's why I went and got the pocket watch from my parents' cabin. It was what Das wanted for his silence; he wouldn't believe us when we told him there was no watch and would not take no for an answer. We felt we had no choice because we couldn't let Peter be caught. And if Das informed about Peter, Lenny and I would be in huge trouble too.

It was late in the evening when Das came to collect the watch. We were already in our room, with Peter in the top bunk, though I planned to turf him out soon enough and make him sleep on the floor. Das came through into the cabin and watched greedily as I reached into my suitcase and slowly drew out the wooden box containing the watch.

INDIA

People talk about going to India and having some kind of amazing spiritual experience. I'm not sure about that, but I think my trip out there, back in 1984, was the time that I really began to grow up. There were high points and low points. And, as often turns out in life, it's when we hit a low point that we really have an opportunity to improve ourselves.

Certainly, the train from Old Delhi to Kalka was a low point. I pulled the sheet over myself and felt under the pillow to check my passport and wallet again. My suitcase was under the seat cum bed below, secured with a chain I'd been advised to purchase by a friendly man I spoke to at Old Delhi Station. The train was creaking and screeching like some kind of wounded beast and this cacophony intruded into my already semi sleeping state and woke me.

I wondered where Jay was. The two of us had been travelling together, due to go to Shimla and then travel on to Amritsar to see the Golden Temple. Unfortunately, we had become separated in Agra, after we had visited the Taj Mahal. I didn't know what to do at first, but in the end, I decided to keep to the itinerary we decided on prior to the trip. But being on my own, I was lost and concerned. Up until we had become separated, I had relied on Jay to sort out the complicated arrangements and baksheesh involved in negotiating our way around the sub-continent. Now I was having to do it by myself. I was managing but I was way out of my comfort zone.

This train was a sleeper going to Kalka. From there I would change and get on the toy train to Shimla. It was romantically called The Himalayan Queen, though there was nothing else romantic or royal about it. I was supposed to be travelling first class; mum had asked me to do that where I could, and stay in decent hotels rather than the hostels she had heard other backpackers used. She had even given me extra money to better make sure I complied.

The compartment I was in slept four. During the day the beds folded so that there were two rows of seats facing each other. A door led out to a corridor that ran the length of the carriage. When I had gone to bed, I was alone in the compartment, but during the night a man had come in and got into the other bed. He had kept clearing his throat noisily and occasionally going out into the corridor to spit on the floor. I made a mental note to be careful where I trod when I went out the compartment.

My mouth felt dry and there was an awful taste. My head was aching; I had run out of water. A vendor had come down the train shouting 'Paani, paani,' which I had learnt, too late, meant water. I looked out the window for distraction and saw we were coming into a station. There were hundreds of people sleeping, illuminated by the platform's meagre light bulbs, and a cow standing amongst those waiting to join the train. I wondered whether it was supposed to be alighting, too. I looked at the station name. It was Chandigarh.

A new man came into the room and set about settling himself down in the bed below. I felt under the pillow again, touching the embossed surface of my passport like it was a talisman; the coat of arms and the inscription inside promising, apparently, that I was to be protected by Her Majesty's Government. I needed to urinate now, but the thought of once more visiting the shit-splattered hole in the floor behind the door marked "Toilet", did not inspire me to move out from my bed.

So, I lay there, unable to sleep and thought about what had led to Jay and me becoming separated in Agra.

We had been to the Taj Mahal and were on the way back to the hotel in an auto-rickshaw, when he started going on about Mimi.

'I don't know why you bother with her,' he said. Then he just let it out with no warning at all. 'Did you know she's sleeping with Rick?'

I felt sick.

'She's just stringing you along because Rick is running hot and cold with her. He's not into conventional relationships, apparently.' Jay lit a beedi, one of those Indian cigarettes. I had tried one. They were disgusting, but Jay was still persisting.

I sat silent digesting what he was saying.

'I think she enjoys all the attention you give her. But you just look stupid, mate.'

I did not speak and stayed silent all the way back to the hotel. He tried to engage me in conversation but I couldn't speak to him. I knew he was looking out for me, but I was too upset.

I think that led to us becoming separated. The next day we were due to go to Delhi. I was still sulking. He went to find a toilet and then I got fed up with waiting for him and got on to our train. It left and he wasn't on it. When I got off at Delhi, I expected to see him alighting from a different part of the train, but he didn't. What else could I do than carry on to Shimla alone?

I traced my finger up the compartment wall, feeling the cold, Formica-like surface. Jay's words had been hard to take but he was right, and I was starting to see that my obsession with Mimi was formless. I had created a version of her that did not exist. She was actually quite uninteresting; she went on about politics and seemed to have no interest in life other than to be the centre of attention. I guess that was why she had invested a small (actually very small) focus of her attention on me, because she enjoyed my devotion. It's funny, but once I realised that, on my way into the Himalayas, it was like a turning point. I saw Mimi for what she was, and I was set free.

I untangled my feet from the sheet wrapped around them and swung myself out of my bunk and went to use the first-class hole in the floor.

The train journey from Kalka to Shimla was magnificent enough. My guidebook told me the aerial distance was thirty-five kilometres. The narrow-gauge train had taken five hours to get there, climbing nearly five thousand feet, through the tree-covered foothills, as it wound its way ever slowly upwards through tunnels and across bridges.

As it happens, Jay and I were to meet up again in Shimla. I was composing a shot with the snow-studded Himalayan peaks and Shimla's half-timbered buildings and square-towered church, when I saw Jay through the viewfinder. He was strolling across The Ridge. We had an immediate argument about how we had come to be separated – and then we calmed down and started to enjoy being in this amazing part of the world.

Jay managed to get in with me at Clarke's Hotel. Lenny had suggested the name as one he recalled from his childhood, and it felt good to stay somewhere with a link back through the years. At the hotel I spoke to the manageress and told her about my family's history in the town, including that my dad and his brother had attended Bishop Cotton School.

'I know a teacher from that school.' She picked up the reception desk's telephone receiver. 'I'll give him a call. His father taught there too; he might remember your family.' I was anxious. I did not want to inconvenience this nice lady or the teacher and his retired father. 'It really is no trouble.' Waving away my protests she made the call. Arrangements were made and I went to afternoon tea at the teachers' house. I invited Jay, but he was not interested and spent the afternoon watching television in the hotel room.

I walked down one of Shimla's steep narrow streets looking for the address. A porter carrying a whole wardrobe tied to his back and secured with a tight band across his forehead, walked slowly up towards me; there were no cars allowed and I was getting used to seeing such sights, though I never failed to be amazed at how the porters managed to carry such heavy loads. I found the apartment building and climbed a dark narrow staircase. A door bearing a nameplate matched the name the manageress had written down: Ajay Sood MA. I pressed the bell. I was so pleased to be visiting the house of an Indian for tea. So far, I had been eating and staying at hotels, but to visit someone's house felt like I was really experiencing the real India. I was looking forward to Indian home-cooking. I imagined samosas, bhajis and Indian sweets. Maybe masala chai. Just like a visit to Jay's house.

A slim man, who looked to be in his early thirties, wearing an open-necked shirt and a cardigan, opened the door.

'Mr Sood?' I looked at the man, who smiling shyly, offering his hand.

'Call me Ajay. 'The man shook my hand lightly. 'You must be Stephen. Please come in.'

I followed Ajay through a small hallway and into a large, dark sitting room. The floor was tiled and swept clean. There were several bookcases lining the room. I sat on a small sofa next to a coffee table on which lay The Times of India.

'Would you like to take some tea?' Ajay picked up the newspaper and folded it carefully.

'Yes, please.' I grasped the chair's wooden armrest, feeling the coldness of the varnish.

Ajay disappeared for a moment. The heads of two small boys peeped round the doorway.

I smiled. 'Hello.'

The heads disappeared and Ajay came back in and sat down. 'Tea is on its way. My father is just finishing his afternoon nap and will be with us shortly. How are you finding India?' Ajay leant forward looking at me.

'It's amazing to come here and discover where my father and uncle grew up,' I replied. 'Thank you for taking the time to see me. Shimla is my favourite part of India so far.'

'You know it was the summer capital of the British Raj?' Ajay leant back on the sofa, adjusting a cushion. 'The summers in Delhi were too hot for the British, so they decamped up here where it was cooler and then went back to rule from Delhi during the winter.'

I had read about this in the guidebook but nodded politely. The door opened and an elderly gentleman came in, slowly moving with the help of a stick. Ajay got up quickly and went over to his father. 'This is the young man we were talking about.'

The elderly gentleman, sat down, taking a long look at me. I had stood up to shake his hand, but he had been too preoccupied with the business of sitting down to take the proffered hand, and I was left stranded. So I slowly, awkwardly, sat down again.

He examined me curiously. 'No, I don't remember

teaching you at all, young man.'

'You won't have taught him,' said Ajay, 'He's from Britain. His father went to Bishop Cotton.'

'What was his name?'

'Ronald Merchant,' I replied. 'His brother is Leonard Merchant.'

The old man scratched his head and looked out the window where a monkey scampered past. Ajay went over to a bureau in the corner and started looking over some papers.

'Merchant, Merchant.' The old man screwed up one eye and looked to the ceiling. 'Did he play in the cricket team?'

I had no idea. I wished Lenny were here to help. A lady entered, bearing a tray of tea, which she placed on the table. She smiled at me. I assumed she was Ajay's wife and I introduced myself. She tilted her head from side to side with another smile and left the room, re-entering with two plates. One was filled with small sandwiches, the other with small fancy cakes that reminded me of Mr Kipling cakes back home. I dismissed any hopes of authentic Indian foods.

'Merchant.' Ajay was holding a piece of paper. 'This is interesting. A lady came to visit from the UK earlier in the year. Like you, she was looking for history of her family. Rita, at the hotel, sends people to us quite frequently.'

I worried again that I was just another stranger troubling Ajay and his family and must have shown it.

Ajay tried to reassure me.

'No, no it isn't any trouble at all. We enjoy it.' He smiled at me and then looked at the paper in his hand. 'The lady asked about a Merchant family. She said her parents worked for them in the 1940s. Fortunately, she left her address and a telephone number.'

I sat up quickly.

'I remember a Masters.' The old man raised his head hopefully.

Ajay shook his head at the old man. 'Could it be that yours is the same family?' He waved the piece of paper towards me. 'She lives in...' He looked at the paper again closely. 'Bristol. Is that near you?'

'It's about an hour and a half on the train, I think.' I held my hand out for the paper.

'It's not far, then.' Ajay took the piece of paper over to the bureau. 'Yasmin Lal. I will copy out her name, address, and telephone number for you.' He sat down, took out a pen and notebook and wrote it down. He tore the piece of paper out and folded it in half then gave it to me.

I looked at the paper. I could feel the excitement rising in my chest. I wondered how she would respond to me getting in touch.

'No, I'm afraid I don't remember you at all, young man,' announced the old man, rubbing his chin.

RONNIE: LUCAS

The hard trill of the alarm intruded like a knife in the dark and I reached out a hand from under the blankets, slamming the top of the clock. The impact sent my morning nemesis skimming across the surface of the bedside table and clattering to the floor, where it carried on loudly ringing and vibrating across the linoleum. I let out a long sigh as I bent down to catch and silence the clock. This would result in another complaint from Joan across the hall. Any noise I made in the morning, even the gentlest opening and closing of the wardrobe door, would earn an injured stare, a verbal rebuke or, as seemed to occur more and more often, a complaint to Mrs Dangerfield, the landlady.

I often met Joan as I slipped across to the shared toilet down the hall. She always managed to come out of her room just as I emerged from mine, to claim the toilet first, as 'her room was closest.' This morning was no different. As usual, I was stopped in my progress to empty my screaming bladder by her lumping forth in the early morning half-light. Her face was fat and pasty, framed by a halo of hair rollers that made her look a right bugger.

'Are you trying to wake the dead again, Ronald?' she asked. This was a favourite of hers. As ever, it was delivered with great satisfaction. She had been expecting a noise and as usual I had not disappointed.

I shrugged, went back into my room for my towel and washbag, and then moved into the bathroom where I started my ablutions by pissing in the bath, running both taps to disguise the drumming of my micturition against the white enamel. As I directed the stream of urine around the bath, I thought about the day ahead. I would see Rose at work. That would be good. Later, I was supposed to meet up with Lenny. That might be more difficult.

I was lodging in a house in Sparkhill. It was cheap and close to the Lucas factory on Formans Road. I had been working for the company for over three years now. Before Formans Road, I had been based at the College Road site in Perry Barr, where I started my apprenticeship. I enjoyed the work and took easily to it. As part of our apprenticeship, we made a full set of our own tools and a metal box to hold them all in, and I've still got that box of tools in the garage now.

Lucas was a large well-respected firm with factories all over Birmingham. It made parts for the motor and aerospace industry. The letter letting me know I had successfully got on the Lucas apprenticeship scheme came through the door the day after my punch-up with Milktooth, but it was quite a few days before I got to read it. It was a big achievement to get to be a Lucas apprentice; a lot of competition meant the exam was really tough and I had to do loads of reviewing for it. But when I did open the letter I couldn't enjoy the success, because father wasn't there to enjoy it with me. He was the one who really encouraged me to go for it, you see.

When mother and I got home from the cinema, after I

had met Milktooth, there was nobody there. I hadn't seen father earlier that night as he was late home from work. I thought he must have gone out for a drink at the pub with some of his work pals, something he did every now and then. Now Lenny had gone too. The house was in darkness and the fire had gone out. Mother stood pondering. I was desperate to have a wash, but I was stopped from heading into the scullery by a sharp rap on the door. It was Mrs Jones, one of the neighbours from the houses that fronted the street.

'Your Bill's been hurt at work. He's at the hospital,' she said, well-satisfied with her news. She looked at mother who was still in her hat and coat, standing there all bewildered.

'What do you mean?' said mother, hand running through her hair. Poor mother must have been at the end of her tether, what with me, all bashed up, and now this.

'He's at the Accident Hospital. The police came and fetched young Lenny.'

The Accident Hospital was on Bath Row, just on the outskirts of the city centre. I made my way to the phone box to call a cab – that was pretty much unheard of, to call a taxi, but we needed to get to the hospital quickly. On the way there, mother was silent. She just sat there picking at her nails. I watched the counters on the meter, wondering how we could afford this.

A porter let us in and took us into Casualty. He spoke low to the nursing sister, who looked up at mother and me, tutted and quickly ushered us into a small office, closing the door. Lenny came in soon after. His face was pale, and he would not look at mother or me.

'Oh my God, Lenny.' Mother grabbed him and pulled him tight against her. 'What has happened?'

Lenny seemed unable to speak. Tears tracked down his cheeks. I couldn't understand what was going on.

'What is it, Lenny? What has happened? How is your father?' Mother was desperate, but Lenny remained silent.

Then this doctor came in and got mother to sit down before he told us what had happened. Father was dead.

He was buried in Witton cemetery on a cold May morning. I remember how mother stood next to me, physically shaking, at the graveside committal. I was worried she might fall down to join father, she was shaking so hard. Lenny stepped closer and held her tight against himself; I wished I had thought to do the same. I looked away, catching glimpses of the other mourners listening as the priest went through his performance. Aunt Betty stood with her family, looking with concern at mother. A couple of the men father had worked with were staring into the naked grave, heads down. There was no-one else.

Afterwards, when we went to the Devonshire Arms for a drink and dried-up sandwiches, one of the men came up to speak to Lenny and me. He had bought us both pints, though I was too young to drink alcohol, and I had to make sure the landlord didn't see me.

'I'm sorry about your old man. He was a good 'un. I

was with him when it happened.' The man held his pint against his chest, against a grubby white shirt with black tie under an old worn suit jacket. His trousers hung down onto boots which, it seemed, he had tried to clean and shine for the occasion.

'What happened?' asked Lenny.

I looked down. I didn't want to know any details. Our father was dead. That was enough for me.

'It should never have happened.' He took a long drink from his pint and gave a long blow. 'We was replacing rails down at the Lifford curve. We had stood back for the one train and then went back on to the line. Your old man was keeping watch, but the smoke from the previous train meant he didn't see the other one, which wasn't scheduled, coming on the opposite track.' He looked away, shaking his head. 'We called the ambulance and tried to keep him as comfortable as we could. He didn't know what was going on a lot of the time.' The man paused for a while, looking down at his shoes and then at us both. 'Which one of you is Lenny?'

Lenny nodded.

'He kept saying he had something to say to you...'

But we didn't get to hear what had been said as mother came over. I quickly placed my beer to one side while the man talked more to her about the accident. There was no further mention of any message from our father before the men left.

I recalled all of this as I finished shaving in my Sparkhill lodgings. Lenny had written, and I think this had rekindled memories. He wanted to meet. As I wondered what he wanted I felt the razor nick. I cursed as a bleb of blood bloomed on my chin. I had planned to ask Rose out for a date today and now I would be sporting a cut. Rose was one of the tracers in the drawing office, she had been doing some drawings for a piece I was working on. I didn't want to leave asking her out too long or one of the other men would snap her up. The problem was I had that letter from Lenny: Meet me at the Brown Lion in the Jewellery Quarter at 8pm on Thursday, it said. That was tonight and it would cost money. After I had paid for my lodgings and put some away in the Municipal Bank, there wasn't enough to go out two nights in a week. But I hadn't seen Lenny for a long time and I wondered what he wanted, so, I would ask Rose out today, but the date itself would have to wait until Saturday, when I had my new wage packet.

I would have preferred to go out to the pictures with Rose tonight, but the tone of Lenny's letter implied it was important. We only had each other now. Mother died within months of father and, after that, Lenny and me just drifted apart. Lenny was off playing with his band in Germany a lot of the time. He rarely wrote and there was never a permanent address for me to write back to, even if I'd felt inspired to.

I packed my shaving things away slowly, excited at the thought of seeing Rose, yet anxious at what the meeting with Lenny was all about.

THE RED LION

When I got back home after our India trip, one of the first things I did was go and see Lenny and tell him about Yasmin. I was supposed to have a guitar lesson, but that took a back seat, at least for the first part of my visit. In truth, I had not been practising my guitar anywhere near as much as I should have been, and I was not making any progress.

When I first arrived, Lenny was not bothered about guitar either. He was too keen to hear about India. He had given me a list of places to see and photograph: old schools, his favourite cinema, the Catholic Church in Shimla. I had the film developed using the Boots' express service, so there were plenty of photos to show him, but what Lenny was most excited about was hearing of Yasmin. We hadn't discussed her before, and I hadn't shown him the pieces my dad had written. I suppose I was still not sure, not ready to share all of that with him.

'I'll give her a call,' said Lenny. 'Yasmin was like a sister to your dad and me.'

He picked up one of the photographs from the pile scattered across the chest cum coffee table. It was of the church in Shimla. 'That's what I don't understand.' He traced the outline of the church with his finger, then didn't say anything more for a while. He just sat there looking at the photo, lost in his thoughts.

'I tried to contact your dad a long time ago. We were supposed to meet up in this pub but then he never showed up.' He flicked through the photos then he started up again. 'There was this watch, you see. It caused us a lot of trouble, did that watch.'

I thought about what dad had written. It seemed that Chandra Das had that watch. Lenny must know that.

'Mum had it,' he continued. 'I never knew where it came from. But then on one of my visits back to Birmingham, after your grandma died, something happened that made me wonder about that watch.'

'Yes?' I prompted.

'I was working in Hamburg then, you see. Playing in the band. There were loads of British bands there.' He looked up at me. 'The Beatles were there.'

'Did you know them?' I was incredulous.

'We used to see them around,' he said casually. 'I didn't think much of them at the time. They were just another one of the bands that were there. I spoke to them a few times. They were a good laugh.' He shrugged. 'Anyway, I was talking about a visit back to Brum.'

Lenny picked up a photo I had taken of the flats where he told me they lived in Shimla. 'I think life kills people,' he said suddenly. 'The stress of life and how we react to it, literally traumatises the cells and our organs just wear out. Take your grandma for instance.'

It seemed weird him referring to her as my grandma. I had never even known her.

'Your grandad died in this awful accident on the railway.' He looked at me. 'Did you know about that?'

I knew there had been some kind of accident from

what dad had written, but I just acted dumb.

Lenny shook his head. 'Your dad didn't tell you anything though, did he?'

I carried on acting dumb.

Lenny shook his head. 'So, a year later your grandma is dead too. Massive heart attack.' He stopped speaking again then and I sat there feeling awkward, not knowing what to say but desperate to fill the silence. Eventually he started up again.

'While your grandma was alive, I would go back to Birmingham every now and then to see her, but then after she died there wasn't much point. Once she had gone, your dad gave up the Winson Green house and took lodgings closer to where he worked. I came back to Brum less often then, and when I did, I kipped on a sofa at a friend's in Moseley, I hardly ever saw your dad. But then I went to this pub in Digbeth called The Anchor and bumped into one of your grandad's old railway pals, Mick. He recognised me straight away from the funeral and asked if we could sit down and talk.'

I was willing him to go on.

'We sat down and then he lowered his voice and looked around, as if he was giving me a map to buried treasure or something. "I'm glad I've seen you mate," Mick said. "I didn't get chance to speak to you properly at the funeral. I wanted to tell you something." He took a cigarette out at that point, offered me one and then made a big play of slowly lighting up. That irritated me.' Lenny gave a dry laugh. 'This Mick was about to tell me some key fact regarding your grandad's death and then turning it all into some kind of dramatic reveal. Well, eventually the cigarettes were lit and Mick blew a few smoke rings to add to the tension and then started up again. "While we were waiting for the ambulance on that day, your dad was trying to tell me something," he said. "He was saying something about a watch. Something about giving the watch back and he mentioned a girl's name, Jasmine–'

'Yasmin? The same Yasmin?' I couldn't help interrupt.

Lenny nodded. 'Mick went on a bit. He said, "I remember the name because my late wife, God rest her, always loved having jasmine growing in the garden. Yes, Jasmine. Do you know her? Only, your dad was saying something about a watch and Jasmine." Then he kept telling me to tell Lenny.'

'Did he say anything else?'

'I asked Mick that,' Lenny said. 'But Mick said, "Not much. Your dad just kept going on about a watch, this Jasmine and Lenny. He weren't quite with it. He was in a bad way. I don't know if it means anything. I meant to tell you at the funeral but then I remember your ma came over and I didn't want to say anything. But seeing you here tonight, I reckon it's best if I tell you".'

Lenny stopped for a bit, then the rest started to pour out of him.

'I bought the man a couple more pints but didn't get any more useful information out of him. He kept on going back through all the gory details of what happened with the accident and how British Rail were to blame, but I didn't want to know about that. What was done was done. Digging into it all wasn't going to bring the old man back. Eventually, I managed to get away. But I wondered about the pocket watch. It seemed it had something to do with Yasmin. And so I decided I needed to speak to your dad about it.

'I didn't get chance to catch up with him on that visit. Very few people had telephones in those days. It was easier to write. So the next time I was coming back to visit I wrote and suggested a time to meet him at the Red Lion in the Jewellery Quarter. He wrote back and all seemed tickety-boo.

'But then when I went to meet him, he never showed up. I wrote to him again, in case there was a mistake or something but he didn't reply. Seemed like he'd got the hump with me. I even heard later that he got married and he didn't even let me know.

'So anyway, after a while I found out that he'd bought the house in Hall Green where you are now and I decided to go and pay a visit. When I got there it was pouring down with rain and there was no one in. I was getting soaked. I thought, this is ridiculous, and so I took a look under the door mat and there was a key. I let myself in and decided to wait for him to come home. I made myself a cup of tea.

'It was a long wait and I ended up making another cuppa and then I needed the toilet. That was when your dad came home. I was just walking down the stairs. He saw me and went mad. Accused me of trying to rob him and all sorts of stuff. I quickly made my way out of the house and out of his way. I thought I would let him calm down. Then I wrote to him, letting him know I needed to talk about an old family heirloom, but he didn't respond, and I have never been able to get in touch with him again since. And that's it all, son.'

I didn't get any more out of Lenny after that. He changed the subject and got me to get the guitar out, but once he realised that I hadn't been practising, he lost interest and sat silent, impervious to any of my attempts to find out more. I decided to go home. I tried to leave the guitar behind, but he made me pack it up and take it, and so I had to lug the useless thing all the way home.

WHITEY

I sat out on the kitchen step, head between my knees. A rushing sound filled my ears, muffling the sound of the party. Dots of sweat were breaking out on my forehead and back. I could sense them getting bigger until my forehead was soaked, and rivulets of fluid ran down between my shoulder blades and soaked my t-shirt. People stepped around me as they moved in and out of the garden, some carefully, others drunkenly, clumsily knocking me against the door frame as they pushed past me and into the garden. Regardless, I continued to sit there gulping in the fresh outside air, trying to keep the nausea, that intermittently threatened to overwhelm me, at bay.

After a while I was aware of Jay kneeling before me. 'Steve, are you alright, mate?'

Then there was another voice and a hand stroking mine. A female voice. 'Stephen, just keep your head between your knees and breathe.' It was Jenny. That was nice of her. Especially after what had happened earlier.

I heard an unfamiliar voice next. 'Just let him sit it out. He'll be OK in a bit. Was he smoking?' I heard Jay reply in assent and the voice continued. 'He's having a whitey. Smoke too much draw and you get a whitey. Especially if you've been drinking. Let him sit it out. He'll be OK.'

I sat it out. I could do nothing else. My head remained clamped between my knees, and I listened to Jenny's soothing voice. I inwardly groaned. It had been a bad day.

I had drunk and smoked too much. Now I just wanted to go home to bed, but I couldn't work out how I was ever going to get away from this kitchen step. And as I sat there, I reflected grimly how this sense of immobility, the sense of wanting to get somewhere with no will or strength to act on it, now applied to my whole life.

The day had started with me trudging up Wake Green Road to get my 'A' level results, the Victorian gothic tower of Brookfields School looming ominously. That a state comprehensive school, rather than an independent fee-charging establishment, occupied this impressive building with its grand tower was a wonderful thing, but I was not in the mood to appreciate that as I met Jay beside the elaborate stonework of the main entrance. I had just seen Sue Boyd coming out of the school gate. She had smiled at me in a way that seemed sympathetic, feeding into my fears regarding my results.

Later, I would wonder how I could ever have imagined I might pass my 'A' levels. Throughout my time in sixth form, I had little enthusiasm for the subjects I was studying. Once my father became ill, my efforts to study and revise dropped considerably, and being drawn into the world of CND, Moseley and the lure of Mimi, further efforts were cursory and of zero value. Any time I set aside to review my books was spent looking out of the window and mooning after Mimi. So, as we looked at the results pinned to the noticeboard, I was surprised to receive an enthusiastic hug from Jay – he was congratulating me? However, as I scanned down the page and found my own name and saw my dismal results, followed by Jay's straight A's, I realised he was celebrating his own success.

'I'm sorry, mate,' said Jay as he found my results. He said nothing more and slowly walked out of the room and back to the main entrance to go outside. I followed him, considering the implications. What would I do? How would I tell my mum? She would be so disappointed. But I was disappointed too. My dream of gaining a new life away from home at Leeds University had continued in spite of both the loss of my overbearing father and the greater freedoms and experiences that loss had opened up. Now I had no idea what I was going to do. Even the new world I had been introduced to in Birmingham was going to change, because Jay would be going off to Bristol. I would be left behind, living with my mum. Involuntarily, I groaned loudly.

'Are you alright?' asked Jay.

'Yeah. Well, there's nothing I can do about it,' I said.

'Let's go to the pub,' said Jay.

'It's only 11 o'clock in the morning.'

'They'll be open.'

I had no cause to celebrate, but the pub seemed about the best option. Going home would mean facing mum.

We headed for The College Arms on the Stratford Road, and had already had a couple of pints when Spooner came in.

'Hello, lads.' Spooner spoke as if we were old mates, sitting down beside us. 'What are you up to?'

I smiled nervously, wondering how quickly we could politely get away.

'Fuck off,' said Jay. 'We don't want to speak with you.'

Spooner put his hand on Jay's arm. 'It's OK, mate. There's no need for that. I was just being friendly.'

Jay pulled his arm away. 'Keep your dirty hands off me, Spooner. I said I don't want to speak to you.'

The pub had gone quiet now, the raised voices attracting the attention of the lunchtime drinkers. But they had also attracted the attention of the landlord who slowly started walking over to us.

Spooner noticed him. 'It's alright, Bill. I'm going anyway.' Spooner slowly walked over to the door and then turned around, looking straight at Jay and me. 'Wankers,' he shouted loudly and then slammed the doors shut after him.

There was a ripple of nervous laughter around the room and then the drinkers went back to their conversations, but the landlord, still standing over Jay and me was not smiling.

'Listen, lads. I know he's a bad 'un, so I'll let you both stay for now, but I don't put up with trouble in here, so any more of that,' he pointed his thumb at the doors Spooner had just slammed out of, 'and you'll be following him.' He wiped the table and then fixed us both with a stare. 'Alright?'

I quickly nodded assent, but Jay remained silent.

'I said, alright?' The landlord continued to look down at Jay.

Jay slowly nodded. 'We didn't start it, but there won't be any trouble from us.'

We had another drink and then walked up the Stratford Road towards Jay's house. As soon as Jay's mum let us in, I started to regret the decision to accompany him back to the family home.

'Well?' Jay's mum stood beside the front door. It seemed she was not going to let us into the house until she knew Jay's results. Jay told her and she opened the door wide enough for us to get in, throwing her arms around her son as he moved past her.

'Get off, Mum!' Jay struggled to pull himself away from his mother's embrace.

'And how did you do, Stephen?' Jay's mum was still beaming.

'I didn't do so well,' I replied.

Jay's mum's face darkened, 'What did you get?'

I told her my results, wishing I'd gone home instead. Telling my own mother would have been easier. Much easier than seeing the pleasure Jay's mum had taken in her son's results tempered by my disastrous outcome.

She slowly and tentatively tapped me on the back. 'Sit down in the kitchen, Stephen, I'll give you something to eat.'

I had to go through it all over again with Jay's grandfather: the enthusiastic reaction to Jay's success and the celebration-muting reveal of my dismal failure. However, the old man was philosophical.

'Don't be downhearted, Stephen,' he said. 'Consider

this a blip. It may seem a big thing now, but in years to come it will be nothing. You may even find that it leads you in a different, more exciting direction.'

Narinder, Jay's sister came in while her grandfather was speaking. Obviously she had heard the news. 'Who cares about stupid exams anyway?' she added. 'It doesn't mean anything.'

'Excuse me,' said Jay. 'I'm all for commiserating Stephen here, but I'd like to get some credit for what I've achieved.'

Narinder stuck her tongue out at her brother and sat down with us at the table.

'How's your family, Stephen?' asked the grandfather, changing the subject. 'How is your mother?'

Glad to leave behind exam results, I spoke about mum and, because I thought the old man would be interested, started telling him about my discoveries regarding my roots in India.

'Oh my God, he's going on about that again,' Jay moaned to a grinning Narinder. 'Trying to claim some bond with us brown people. I think it's because we're becoming trendy.'

'Shut up,' said his grandfather. He turned back to me. 'Your father's family is Anglo-Indian? Not a lot of Indian people here will know about them, but of course being in the Army I got to meet quite a few. I always felt they seemed a bit lost. It was like they didn't know whether they were Indian or British, and the trouble was, the British only wanted them to help them run India and the

Indians were not interested in them at all.'

I nodded, glad of the old man's interest but embarrassed to speak further on the subject in front of Jay and his sister.

'Anyway, it's all a bit boring,' said Jay. 'Shall we eat?'

I normally enjoyed eating at Jay's, but today I could not work up an appetite. The results and their consequences sat so heavy in my throat and chest, I could barely swallow. Jay's mum tutted as she looked at my plate of half-eaten food. Added to my dismay at the exam results was Jay's reaction to my family history discoveries. I had discussed this with Jay before and Jay had not seemed interested then either, though he had not been so dismissive previously. I had thought this was something, an affinity I could share with my friend, but Jay did not seem to be able to relate to it at all.

I hung around at Jay's all day, not wanting to go home. But my annoyance continued even as, later, Jay and I walked down to Moseley where we had planned to visit the Prince of Wales. He prattled on about his plans for going to Bristol, which made me more annoyed. Why couldn't he change the subject. He had passed. I had failed. But he just had to keep rubbing it all in my face.

When we got to the pub it seemed fuller than usual with a younger clientele, which I soon realised was because it was full of 'A' level students celebrating their results. Mimi and Jenny were there with several girls from Mimi's school.

'How did you get on, Stephen?' asked Jenny.

I told her, watching the smile on Jenny's face fade away.

Mimi was close by and overheard. 'Too bad, Stephen,' she said.

'How did you get on?' I asked.

'3 A's,' replied Mimi carelessly, 'I didn't even do any work for them. But I don't think I'm bothered to go to university anyway. I don't want to end up working for the man.'

'What are you going to do, then?' I wondered who the man was.

'I'm going on the dole. I'm going to carry on working in politics, that's the priority for me. We need to work towards the revolution. Who cares about exams?'

'We're going to a party,' interrupted Jenny. 'It's at Sherry's.' She pointed to a tall blonde-haired girl standing talking to another group of youths. 'She wouldn't mind these two coming, would she, Mimi?'

Mimi looked doubtful. 'I don't know, She's very particular.'

Jenny looked annoyed. 'I'll ask her.' Jenny went over to Sherry, and I watched them talking, Jenny pointed over to Jay and me. I smiled at Sherry as she quickly glanced in our direction, nodding to Jenny and then returning to her conversation.

Jenny returned. 'That was easy, you can both come.'

Mimi shrugged and nodded noncommittally but I didn't care anymore what she thought. I was no longer obsessed with her. I had come back from India with a new perspective on Mimi and stopped chasing around after her. Maybe that was fuelling her apparent indifference to me now.

The party was at Sherry's parents' house near Cannon Hill Park, on a road lined with large 1930s houses. As we walked over, I heard Sherry talking about how her parents had gone to their holiday home in the Dordogne, hence her opportunity to hold a party to celebrate 'A' level results. I reflected that organising a party to celebrate anticipated successful results had been presumptuous, however people like Mimi and Sherry seemed to have a self-assurance that I felt I could never hope to attain. They seemed to sail through life without mishaps, a safety net of wealth behind them, that seemed to mean that good exam results, though desirable, were not essential milestones. Yet for people like Jay and me, they were the difference between being a success or a total failure in life.

At the start, we all stood in the hallway, drinking bottles of beer bought as a take-out from the pub. More and more people arrived, and we moved into another room. I steadily drank my way through beers, lost in my own thoughts. Jenny had done well in her exams and was telling me about her plans for an Art degree, but I must admit I was finding it hard to pay attention to what she was saying.

After a while I found we were alone together. That was when I decided Jenny was interested in me. All this time I had been chasing after Mimi, when Jenny had been actually wanting to get together with me, I thought. In my drunken state I made a clumsy attempt to take advantage of my new found knowledge. I tried to gather her in my arms and kiss her, but in doing so I finally lost my centre of gravity and ended up pushing her into a china cabinet, which precariously rocked back against the wall. A sickening clunk of the expensive-looking crockery sounded ominously, but the cabinet righted itself and no damage appeared to have occurred. I heard laughter and whoops from around the room. Jenny gently pushed me away and left the room, leaving me standing embarrassed. I sat down in the corner and rolled a joint, but when I lit it, an annoyed Sherry told me to take it outside to smoke.

So, that's how I ended up alone on the kitchen step, humiliated and ashamed, taking tokes on the joint until the normal relaxation and euphoria of the cannabis was overwhelmed by the harder-edged nausea, sweat and oppressive inertia of the whitey. Still Jenny came to help look after me, I guessed she was just a nice person, even if uninterested in me in that way.

Once I recovered a little, Jenny suggested I should go home. She was trying to find money for me to get a taxi but I refused.

'I'll be fine,' I said. 'The walk will sober me up.'

Jenny looked doubtful.

'Look, he can come back to mine.' Jay joined in. 'There's a spare bed. At least we'll know he gets home OK.'

I wondered what my mum would make of me not going home. I'm any case, Jay's house was no nearer than my own, though the advantage would be Jay's company, in spite of how I had found him annoying earlier on. Additionally, I actually did not feel safe to get home by myself.

As it turned out, though, the journey home was far from safe.

It was me who saw Spooner first. I had sobered up a little walking through the night air.

'Spooner.' I hissed the name, feeling dread and panic overwhelm me.

It would have been bad enough on any other occasion, meeting Spooner and his friends in the middle of the night, but after seeing him earlier on that day, this was disastrous. Jay did not respond.

'It's Spooner. Over by the church,' I repeated, more urgently this time.

'I know,' responded Jay. He sounded calm. 'It's OK. I can see him. Just act cool. Carry on walking. I'm not scared of him.'

'Oi.' Spooner's shout of recognition resounded through the night air. The sound of boots slapping on tarmac followed and Jay and me instinctively both ran, cutting up through an entry between shops that led to a car park behind. There was a gate leading into a yard at the rear of one of the shops. We went through, shut the gate softly and hid, crouching behind some large dustbins. I could hear Jay's hard breathing and tried to slow down my own so we wouldn't be heard. The cannabis and alcohol brain soup had cleared and now I was hyper-alert to the smells and sounds around me. We could hear Spooner and his friends in the car park. The youths seemed to have stopped and were looking around, probably guessing we hadn't run further than the car park. The whispering of our pursuers' voices came closer and then the gate of the yard we were in opened.

I could feel my heart beating violently and I was sure whoever was in the yard must be able to hear the thumping going on behind my ribs. But then the footsteps moved away and we heard the sound of other gates opening further off. Suddenly there was the sound of a window opening and a voice yelling, 'Clear off out of here. I can see you. I'm calling the police.'

At first, I thought the voice was aimed at Jay and me, but then Spooner's voice cut once more into the night. 'Fuck off.'

Nevertheless, that seemed to signal the end of Spooner's search and footsteps were heard walking away and then the sounds of the youths' voices in the distance.

Jay stood up, motioning for me to stay where I was. There was no need. I had no intention of getting up, despite the acrid smell of the dustbins. I did not want to move away. Not yet. I shook my head at Jay, motioning for him to get back down and wait.

Regardless, he went out into the car park. I remained crouching, realising I was curled up tight like a ball. I saw with horror a rat run across the yard, and then I heard Jay yell in pain followed by the low noise of a near silent beating. Grunts, the noise of boots on gravel, punches and then kicks. Spooner and his cronies must have come back silently and waited. I knew I should go out and join Jay. I would be of no use in the fight, but still I should go and join him. Stand united with him. But I could not.

Instead, I remained curled up tight and shivering uncontrollably as I listened to my friend being beaten.

SHAME

A hard light penetrated my eyelids, causing a sliver of pain to radiate to my brain and lodge there unmoving. My mouth was dry and sand raw. But the physical discomfort was insignificant compared to the overwhelming shame. I pushed my face hard into my pillow, gripping the case edges as if to stifle the memory of last night. I had left Jay. I had left my friend unconscious. I had left him to get beaten. He may not even be alive. I bit into the pillow. Why had I not gone out there and stood side by side with him? The worst that could have happened would be better than what I felt now. What was going to happen? What would I do?

The harsh trill of the telephone in the hall downstairs cut through my thoughts. I heard movement and then my mum's voice as she answered. I confess, I would often lie in bed listening to the one-sided telephone conversations, trying to work out what the other party was saying.

'Yes?' She sounded uncertain. It was not someone she knew. 'I think so. I didn't see him all day. I was quite worried, but then I heard him come in during the early hours. Dirty stop-out!' She gave a hollow laugh. So, it was about me, but who was it? She wouldn't speak like that to the police.

'Oh no! Oh my God!'

It must be about Jay.

'Have you been able to see him?' Mum's voice changed now. The earlier uncertainty and formality was replaced with concern and intimacy.

I got out of bed and opened my bedroom door, standing on the landing, but out of sight, trying to hear the scratching voice emitting from the telephone handset. There was a long pause as mum listened. Despite my efforts, I could not hear what the voice on the other end of the line was saying. What was going on? Mum would ask me what had happened. What would I say? How would I account for what had happened last night and where I had been?

'Oh, I do hope he's alright. I'll go and check on Stephen now and see what he knows.'

Hearing that, I quickly crept back into bed.

'Yes, yes, I'll call you back later. Let me know if there is anything I can do.'

There was the clunk of the receiver and the closing ding from the phone followed by thudding as mum moved swiftly up the stairs. I pulled the covers over my head, pretending to be asleep but that was not enough to thwart her.

'Stephen, are you alright?' Her voice was panicked, and she pulled the cover off me. The light had been turned on and I made a fair effort at blinking deliriously. 'What happened last night? Jay is in the hospital. Were you in a fight?'

I moved up on to my elbows. 'No, Mum... I wasn't with Jay. Is he alright?'

Mum seemed relieved now and her voice softened. 'I think he's in a bad way. It seems he was badly beaten in a fight of some sort.'

I swung my legs over the edge of the bed to sit out, but I was not sure whether to get up or stay in bed.

'I've just spoken to Narinder on the phone. They're obviously really worried about him. They were worried about you too and she wanted to make sure you had got home alright.'

I lay back down on my bed and groaned. 'How is he? What's wrong with him?'

'She says he's in the Intensive Care Unit at the Accident Hospital. He's got a bad head injury.' Mum sat down on the bed. 'So where were you all day? Who were you with if you weren't with Jay?'

My nausea became stronger and I could no longer withstand the urge. I stood up quickly and ran to the toilet. Kneeling in front of it, I vomited violently. The hard retches made my eyes water as I gripped the cold porcelain of the toilet pan.

I heard mum sigh loudly and then go back downstairs. I washed my face, drank from the tap and went back to bed. Lying there I thought back to what had occurred.

Once I heard Spooner and his friends leave, I had gone out to Jay, who was lying on the floor. I knelt down and gently shook him, calling his name, but there was no response. I listened for breathing and, panicking, felt for a pulse, pressing around the wrist until with relief I felt a faint throb and heard the slight breath. Then I moved Jay onto his side, into the recovery position, as I had learnt in Scouts. I didn't want to leave him, but I knew I needed to call for an ambulance. Reluctantly, I ran over to the phone box on St Mary's Row. Then I went and waited with Jay until I heard the siren. I hid back in the yard behind the dustbins, listening to the men from the ambulance as they worked. Finally, when the vehicle's doors slammed and it drove away, I got up and walked home, carefully listening and looking out for any sign of Spooner.

I hid because I was frightened and ashamed. I was frightened I would have to give evidence as a witness to the attack, frightened of the repercussions from Spooner and his gang. And I was ashamed. Firstly, because I had not gone out and stood with my friend and secondly, because now I was too scared to stand witness. I was also ashamed I felt unable to go and see Jay in hospital. I did not want to have to look Jay or his family in the eye.

I stayed in bed all day, partly to avoid mum and partly because I was so hungover. But when the police officer arrived, I had to get up.

As soon as I heard the doorbell I felt it must be to do with the events of the night before. I heard voices and then mum coming up the stairs.

'It's a policeman,' she said in a low but sharp voice as she came into the room. 'Get yourself dressed.'

The officer sat in the front room, at the dining table. He was looking around, as if assessing the furnishings, his peaked cap and notebook laid out neatly on the table. He smiled affably, introduced himself as PC Gordon and invited me to sit down. He was tall and looked just a few years older than me. He affected a matey manner that made me feel even more uncomfortable.

PC Gordon asked me if I knew Jayshree Virdee. I told him I did.

'Did you know he had been apparently attacked last night?' The officer seemed bored with the questions, and he continued looking around at the room as he spoke.

'Yes, my mum told me,' I answered.

The officer asked me what I had done and where I had been with Jay the day before. I told him that we had left the party together but that I had headed the opposite way from Jay along Russell Road.

'Someone called an ambulance after your friend was attacked.' The policeman flicked through his notebook, wearily. 'It was from a call box. It was a young man's voice.' He looked up at Stephen. 'It wasn't you, was it?'

'No.' I tried to stare into the policeman's eyes as if to convince him I was telling the truth. But there was no need, because he didn't seem to care whether I was lying or not. He wrote in his notebook. 'OK, you weren't there. It wasn't you. It was someone else. That's fine.' The policeman looked silently at me for a while and then asked more about what had occurred during the day. I related the events, starting with collecting the exam results, omitting the visit to The College Arms, and once more sticking with the story that Jay and I had separated outside the party on Russell Road.

'How did you get on?'

I looked at him blankly.

'With the exams.'

I told him I hadn't done well.

'Oh dear. So, you had a bad day yesterday.' The constable looked long and hard at me once more. The silence was worse than being questioned. 'You need to be careful, young man.'

I looked away, worried. I thought the officer had believed my story about not being present when Jay was beaten. Perhaps not.

'You need to be careful about who you hang about with.' He stood up and, once more, looked around the room. 'You live in a nice house.' He looked out of the window. 'In a nice area.' He nodded towards the back room. 'Your mum cares about you.' He looked at a family photo, on the mantelpiece, of mum, dad, Susan and me. 'Dad at work?'

'Dad's dead,' I said, wondering where the conversation was going.

'Oh, I'm sorry,' continued PC Gordon. 'But then it makes it more important that you be careful who you hang around with. People like that Jay will just end up getting you into trouble. Stick with your own sort and then you won't end up getting coppers like me knocking on your door.' He smiled, gathered up his cap and notebook and walked over to the door. 'I'll let myself out. No need to get up.'

I continued to sit. I heard the door slam and then watched as PC Gordon walked up the front drive and got into his car.

Mum came in. 'Where's he gone?'

I nodded towards the window, where the officer could be seen sitting in his car.

Mum rushed out and I heard the front door opening. I hoped the officer would drive off before she could get to speak to him, but mum ran up the drive, and I watched her standing next to the police car as the policeman wound down the window. The conversation did not take long and I soon saw mum coming back down the drive. She looked annoyed.

'What's going on Stephen?' she snapped.

I sat down and folded my head in my hands.

'Don't do that. Look at me. What the hell is going on?'

I still said nothing. I could think of nothing to say.

Mum sighed in exasperation. 'That policemen doesn't seem to think you know anything about what happened to poor Jay. But I'm not so sure.' Her voice softened. 'Have you been threatened?' She sat down next to me. 'Are you frightened of the people who did that to Jay?'

I felt a pain in the back of my throat and tears filled my eyes. I tried to stifle the sob that was threatening to break out of me. I did not want to cry and I forced my eyes shut; my head bent down. Mum sensed this and put her arm around me. This action released the emotion and the tears forced through.

She waited a while before speaking. 'Are you going to tell me how did on your exams?'

I told her and she pulled me tight against her. 'It's no

surprise, really, Stephen. You haven't been concentrating properly. You've been going out too much. Too many late nights.'

I sensed her pulling away from me, trying to look at my face, but I kept my head down.

'It's not been easy for you, Stephen. What with your dad and everything.' She stood up. 'But you need to sort yourself out. You need to decide what you want to do and stick at it properly. If you want to do your 'A' levels again, go for it. Otherwise look at doing something else. But right now, you need to do the right thing by your friend. You need to call up Jay's sister, I promised her we would call back. Find out about going to see him and, if you do know something, which I think you do, get in touch with that policeman and let him know.

LENNY

Lenny came the next day. He had called to speak to me, but, of course, Mum had answered. I wondered who it was, if it was news of Jay, but she had spoken in such a low voice, I couldn't catch anything. After a while, I heard Mum treading up the stairs and then I saw her head peering around the door.

'It's Lenny,' she said flatly. 'Do you want to speak?'

I shook my head and mum shrugged and closed the bedroom door shut, going back to the phone. It seemed a long time before I could make out the close of the telephone conversation, but I did not know what they were speaking about.

Later, I heard the doorbell ring and then Lenny's voice as he came into the house. I was surprised that my mum had even spent so long speaking with him on the telephone. Even more so that she seemed to have allowed him to come round to the house. I quickly pulled on some clothes and sat on my bed, waiting for a call to go down. But there was none, and I sat there hearing the deep rumble of his voice permeating indistinctly through the floor from the living room below.

After a while, there was a tentative knock on my bedroom door, and Lenny came in. He opened the curtains, blinding me with the sudden daylight. Then he sat on the bed beside me.

'So, what's going on with you?' Lenny asked, looking out of the window for a second before he turned and looked at me.

In the end I just told him the truth, everything that had occurred with Jay and me. I couldn't help myself. There was something about his look that seemed to unlock a part of me. Telling the truth felt liberating. I was still ashamed but felt the burden had become smaller.

'Look, you just need to go and see your mate and go and tell the police what happened,' said Lenny. 'Stop lying here stinking in your bed and feeling sorry for yourself. Go and do something useful about the situation.'

Then, just like that, he changed the subject.

'Anyway,' he said reaching into his trouser pocket. 'I've got this to show you.'

It was a once-white envelope, folded in half and looking more than a bit dog-eared. He opened it and took out the letter within. I recognised the writing. It looked very similar to the letter my dad had wanted to be posted when he was in the hospice, the one he had not wanted me to take to a letterbox but had given to the nurse. Lenny opened out the letter. Sellotaped to the paper was a small key.

'It's been with the old lady, Gerda, all this time,' said Lenny, 'I think I told you that she takes all our post if we don't get to the letterbox in time? Her niece hadn't been for a while, then she handed me this yesterday.' He showed me the post mark on the envelope. 'It was sent the day your dad died.'

I looked at my dad's normally strident cursive writing, now faltering with the debilitation of his oncoming death.

St Mary's Hospice
Raddlebarn Road
Selly Oak
Birmingham

Dear Lenny,

I am writing to you because I am dying. I would like to see you before I go, but there is not much time now. I should have written to you before, but it has taken me this long to work out what to write.

You and I went through so much together in the past. And now I realise how tragic it is that we have lost touch with each other and become strangers.

I am sorry for my part in all that has happened between us. It should not have been so, and if I had been honest with you from the start, we would not have reached the state where we are now. It is not right that two brothers do not speak to each other. You could have been part of my family. You should have been an uncle to my children.

I went to the Brown Lion on that night, like you asked but you never showed up. I was so mad. And then when I found you in my house that day I was furious. Then I'm afraid I just ripped up the letters you sent without reading them.

But I think I know what you were looking for when

you came to the house on that day. I should have let you have it in the first place. It wasn't worth us falling out over it.

There's a wooden box in my desk drawer at work. You have the key. There is also a false bottom in the drawer with some writing I have been doing. I would like you to have both. I don't think there is much time now for me, so we may not see each other before I go. There is a separate note for Ken at the factory. He will show you where the desk is.
Take care big brother, from your little brother,
Ronnie.

'He went to the Brown Lion and I went to the Red Lion,' said Lenny when he saw I had finished reading. 'Perhaps I made a mistake on my letter to him. Both of those pubs are in the Jewellery Quarter.'

Then he was silent for a while, and I sat there waiting for him to carry on.

'Anyway, I went to see Ken,' continued Lenny, 'But there was nothing in the false desk compartment. He told me that you and Susan had been, so...?'

I reached under my bed, pulled out the wooden box and handed it to Lenny, my hands shaking. Despite everything else, I was excited to see what was inside.

Lenny turned the box in his hands, feeling the smooth inlaid surface. Then he found the sliding section and revealed the keyhole. He gently placed the key in and unlocked the box.

Inside was an old stainless-steel cigarette lighter.

'It's my dad's old Ronson,' Lenny said, smiling. He looked like he was more pleased than if he had found the gold watch.

He clicked the lighter open and I was assailed by the odour of petrol. He pushed his thumb along the wheel within; there was a spark but no flame.

'It needs filling up,' he said absently.

After that, I gave Lenny the pieces that dad had written.

Lenny read through them slowly. Once he had finished, he put the whole sheaf of paper carefully on the bed beside him. 'Stephen...' he said, then stopped, looking around the room.

'Yes,' I answered, willing him to go on. He seemed to have something to tell me.

'Like you, with your friend Jay, I have something to confess. Your dad hasn't told the whole story about what went on when we were on the ship over.'

I sat up.

'In return for him keeping our secret that Peter was a stowaway, Das wanted that gold watch.'

'So Das does have it,' I said.

Lenny held up his hand, a shushing gesture. It was time for me to be quiet and listen. I let him speak.

Lenny took a deep breath and recounted his story.

'We felt we had no choice but to do what Das wanted, so the next day, when our parents were out of the cabin, your dad went and took the watch. It was in that wooden box. Later, in the evening after dinner, Das returned to our cabin to claim what he wanted. Peter was in the top bunk. I opened the wooden box and took out the watch. Das moved closer; he had this really greedy look in his eyes. Peter in the top bunk leant over to get a closer look, and in doing so, overbalanced.'

Lenny stopped speaking for a moment and then took a deep breath. 'The idiot ended up landing on top of us.' He shook his head. 'There was not much space in that cabin, and we were all caught in a confused tangle, with Ronnie, the only one still standing, pushed up against the cabin door. Peter and I got up, but Das was still on the floor. I bent down to look at him.'

Lenny stopped again and got up. He wandered over to the window and looked out. His voice was small now, and I had to listen carefully to make out what he was saying.

'He was lifeless. His face was drained of all colour. We tried to rouse him, but there was no response.' Lenny walked back over towards me and sat down again and then continued in a whisper. 'Das was dead. Peter falling on him must have broken his neck.'

I was getting confused now. 'So if Das was dead, who is...?'

Lenny nodded meaningfully. 'We talked long into the night about what we would do. In the end we wrapped Das in a blanket, and with Ronnie acting as a lookout, dragged the body out on to the deck and tipped him overboard into the sea. We were lucky nobody saw us.'

I was starting to work it out now.

'After that, we used Das's key to get into his cabin. Peter used that cabin that for the rest of the voyage. He got away with it too.'

'So Das is actually Peter?' I checked.

Lenny smiled grimly. 'He managed to get through immigration at Tilbury. He became Chandra Das. He had all of Das's papers and passport. It seems he's been passing himself off as Chandra Das ever since. He went a bit over the top with the accent though.'

Shocked as I ws, I started thinking ahead. 'But what happened with the watch?'

Lenny shrugged. 'We returned it to our parents' room. They didn't even know it was ever taken away. Maybe it was pawned or something?'

But I didn't think it had been pawned. I had a hunch that I knew where the watch was. There was something I needed to do before I could check.

ACCIDENT HOSPITAL

Birmingham Accident Hospital loomed in grimy Victorian splendour. A line of ambulances only served to enhance the drama. If I had been nervous about visiting before, the sight of it in reality did nothing to encourage me to enter now I had arrived. And, even as I worked up the courage to cross over the road and approach the building, I saw Jay's sister Narinder stepping out of the entrance, leaning against a barrier, and taking a deep breath. I ducked down a side street.

After a while spent aimlessly wandering around, wondering what to do, I decided to approach the hospital once more. Narinder was no longer standing outside. Hoping she had left, I entered tentatively through the main doors. But there she was, sitting on one of the long leather benches, eating a sandwich. I thought about walking out again, but she had already seen me. She looked up at me neutrally and I felt I had no option but to go and speak to her.

'Where have you been? Why wouldn't you speak to me when I called?' She looked at her half-eaten sandwich as if she could no longer stomach it, and then carefully and neatly wrapping the cling film covering around it, she put the sandwich down on the smooth leather seat.

I looked away, searching for anything to look at but the cold accusing stare of Jay's little sister. My eyes settled on a man with his arm set in white plaster. He was struggling to use a drinks vending machine.

Narinder was still talking. 'You were with Jay, weren't you? You must have been. You two are inseparable. Why didn't you go with him to the hospital?'

I sat silent, staring at the man at the vending machine. The drink had been dispensed, but he could not get it out. He had to lift the plastic guard up with one hand to get at the beverage, but then the cast would not allow his other hand in to remove the cup. He swapped hands but could not manage to lift the plaster guard.

I turned to Narinder. She deserved a response. 'How is he?' I could not think of anything else to say.

She shook her head. 'Where were you? What sort of friend are you?'

'How is Jay?' I persisted.

She picked up her sandwich and took it to a litter bin and then went over the vending machine, where the man with the plaster cast had started banging his head in frustration against the metal casing, the booms attracting the attention of the people in the waiting area. Narinder got the drink out then led the man over to a vacant section of bench so he could sit down. She gave him his drink, then came and sat back down next to me.

'How long would you have sat watching that man struggling? You're so selfish. You're so immature.'

We were silent for a while.

Narinder's burst of anger seemed to lead to relative calm and she spoke once more. 'Jay is a lot better now. They've moved him onto the normal ward. They're going to get him out of bed today to see if he can walk. He's struggling to use his left side, but they think that will get better.' She knotted a finger into her eye orbit. 'He's had a bad head injury. You'll see that when you go up. He knows who we all are, but he can't remember anything about what happened.' She stopped and looked up. 'What did happen, Stephen?' She shook her head and looked down at the scuffed parquet flooring. 'He's been so worried about you. He keeps asking if you're alright.'

I looked forward and, keeping my eyes away from Narinder, I told her exactly what had occurred. I started with meeting Spooner at The College Arms, then I went on, telling her about running and hiding from the gang in Moseley. I told how Jay had gone out to his beating while I remained hidden. I looked at Narinder. She stared back at me, and I had to look away.

After a while she spoke. 'So, it was you who called the ambulance?'

I nodded, thinking this was a point in my favour. I was wrong.

'But you haven't told the police what happened?'

'I'm going to tell them.'

'Didn't they come to see you?'

'Who?'

She stamped the floor, exasperated, and her voice became louder. 'The police?'

I nodded slowly. Mum must have told her about the policeman dropping by.

'So why didn't you make a statement then?'

I tried to find the words. I didn't know how to explain

myself. In the end I simply said, 'I'm going to make a full statement and tell them exactly what went on.'

Narinder stood up and looked at me with disgust. 'You come round to our house, eat our food and then go on about your dad being from India, trying to claim that you're one of us. But you're not one of us. You look white. You're treated like you're white and you don't have to suffer racism because you are white. And when it comes to Jay, who is supposed to be your friend, being beaten up by racists, you protect the white people who carry it out.' She stopped speaking and turned to leave, adding more quietly. 'He's on Ward 2. I'll give you half an hour.' Then she walked outside.

I walked up and down the ward looking for Jay. A nurse came out from behind some bedside curtains. I asked after him, and she pointed in the direction of a bed I'd already walked past. Jay was unrecognisable. He had black swollen eyes, his lip was badly swollen, dirtied with stitches, and his head had been shaved. Despite all this, I was relieved to see that he was trying to smile.

'You. Didn't. Recognise. Me,' said Jay slowly, as I pulled up a chair. Every word seemed a struggle for him to utter. He must have bitten his tongue. The engorged lip wasn't helping either. Additionally, it seemed the head injury had affected Jay's speech and there was a kind of vacancy in his eyes I had never seen before.

'Look. At. Me.' He ran his hand over his shaven skull. There were dressings on it. 'They. Drilled.'

I looked in horror and shame at Jay's head. 'I should have come before now. I'm so sorry.'

Jay nodded, trying to smile. 'No. Point.'

'I'm sorry. It was just...'

Jay shook his head. 'Here, now.' He pointed to his scalp. 'What happened?'

I took a deep breath and once more went over the events. Jay did not seem to remember anything. 'I'm sorry, Jay. I left you to take that beating on your own.'

Jay grinned. 'You. No. Good. In fight.' He laughed but that seemed to cause him more pain.

The statement was true, obvious and no less than I deserved, but still I felt hurt by it.

'Police?'

I looked down.

Jay looked perplexed. 'Haven't?'

'I'm going to tell them exactly what happened.'

'Scared?'

I looked at Jay's black eyes, battered lip and shaved head. 'Well yes. Look what he's done to you. But I am going to give a full statement.'

Jay shook his head. He held up his arm. 'Wrong colour.'

'I'm going to go and tell them what happened,' I insisted.

Jay shrugged.

As I was leaving, I met Mimi, Jenny and Liz in the entrance hall.

Jenny looked concerned. 'What happened, Stephen? How is Jay. You weren't hurt?'

I didn't know what to tell them. I just mumbled that Jay was OK, on the mend. They were going to see him anyway. I was too ashamed to tell them what had really occurred.

'So how come you didn't get beaten up, Stephen?' asked Mimi flatly.

I felt my face reddening.

'Do you know who did it?' Jenny was looking at me, it seemed, with some suspicion.

I told them about Spooner, trying to avoid going into the details of how I had hid. They didn't ask me anymore details about what had actually occurred, but it was obvious I had abandoned Jay. I felt that Jenny and Mimi, like everyone else, were disgusted with me.

'It was that lot who came to the demo?' asked Mimi.

I nodded.

'I think they're NF bastards,' continued Mimi.

I knew Spooner was a racist, I hadn't imagined he was part of an organised far right group like the National Front.

'We'll find out,' said Mimi, 'And we'll get the bastards.'

'I'm going to speak to the police,' I said.

'What's the point?' replied Mimi simply. 'They're not interested. Jay is Asian. They don't care about him.'

They carried on up to the ward and I headed for the doors out, but I was aware of an elderly Asian man beckoning to me from the leather benches. It was Jay's grandfather, as smartly turned out as usual. I did not want to speak to him. I had felt ashamed at every turn on this hospital visit, but I felt unable to ignore the old man so I went and sat beside him. 'I saw Narinder,' the old man said. 'She told me she spoke to you when you arrived.'

'Yes, I saw her.' I wondered nervously where the conversation was going.

'Are you going to the police?'

'Yes, I must,' I said.

'I overheard your friend, that girl. I don't think it will help trying to get revenge. As Gandhi said, "An eye for an eye makes the whole world blind", but I have little hope that the police will give us justice either.'

I nodded uncertainly.

'Nevertheless, you should go and tell the police what really occurred. There is no better option than to tell the truth.'

'I'm so sorry about what happened.' I could feel the edge in my voice as if it and myself were going to break at any minute. But in spite of this, I felt compelled to confide in the old man. 'Narinder is so angry with me. I've let Jay down, I've let you all down.'

Jay's grandfather put his hand on my arm. 'You were in a difficult position. Narinder knows that, Stephen. Don't be too hard on yourself. What matters is that you go and do what's right now.'

I went round to the police station on my way home. The desk sergeant asked me to sit down and then made a quick phone call. Apparently, PC Gordon was in. I had to wait some time before the familiar figure of the constable who had come round came into view.

He looked impassively at me. 'Come on through' he said, and led me through to an interview room.

I pulled at the chair the officer was inviting me to sit down on. It scraped loudly on the floor.

The officer winced at the noise. 'Don't just drag it. You need to lift it up gently.'

I sat down, even more nervous now.

PC Gordon loudly dragged his chair out, staring at me. 'OK, what have you got to say to me?'

I haltingly went through the story, aware of the officer's gaze. In spite of the intimidation I felt, I managed to include all the details I missed the first time. He sat looking bored, a blank sheet of paper and pen on the table in front of him.

'Why didn't you tell me any of this the first time round?' he asked.

'I don't know...' Then I remembered what Jay's grandfather had said and decided to be completely honest. 'I was scared. I'm frightened of what will happen to me from Shane Spooner.'

PC Gordon stared at me. 'You're frightened. Well, if you followed the advice I gave you when I came round to your house, there would be no need for you to be frightened. So, why don't you just go home to your nice mummy and keep your nose clean. Right? Fuck off home and don't come round here bothering us anymore. We've got better things to be getting on with.'

BURGLARY

I crept past Mimi's bedroom, shining my torch and looking in for a brief moment before I continued to where I guessed her parents' room was. The house was empty, and I had no reason to believe I would be disturbed, but still I tiptoed tentatively and was glad of the luxurious deepness of the Deathridge carpet pile.

I stepped slowly into the master bedroom, my torch picking out what I presumed was her mother's dressing table. There was a box of jewellery on top and I quickly took a look, though I didn't expect to find what I wanted there. It was all sparkles and shines: diamonds and pearls, maybe? Sure enough, the piece I was after wasn't there. I moved over to the wardrobes, two of them, packed full of ladies' clothes and another with a rack of suits and a series of shelves to one side. This was more like it. I felt to the back of a shelf housing balled socks and neatly folded underpants. Nothing there. Then, at the bottom, I spied a thick-walled cardboard box.

I rummaged through it blindly. Just envelopes. Putting back the balled socks, though, one pair felt unusually heavy. I picked it up, and, putting the torch on the bed so I could see better, I carefully unrolled the socks revealing a gold disc with an enamelled top and a polo player painted on it. I clicked it open, the gold chain dripping down over the back of my hand and looked at the watch face within.

I had found Yasmin's gold pocket watch.

I gazed at it for a while and then quickly placed it in my jacket pocket. I moved to go and then stopped, frozen, feeling a sudden icy fear arrest my body. There was a noise downstairs. That wasn't right. Mimi should be at the Youth CND meeting; I had watched her leave earlier on. Her parents should be at the villa in Majorca. But my fears were compounded as I heard an ominous deep rattling cough, a cough I recognised as definitely belonging to Tommy Deathridge.

The decision to enter Mimi's house and take something was not one I had made easily. I had never before entered anyone's house without permission – and I have never done so since. The idea of taking something from someone like Tommy Deathridge was just incredible. But circumstances and events had conspired. The unlocking of the wooden box had opened my mind to something that should have been obvious before. Flashes of gold on the night I had been interrogated by Tommy Deathridge had been nagging away at me like some kind of background noise. The flash of a gold tooth in a drunken smile and a gold pocket watch on the end of a gold chain, that Tommy had taken out to check the time. Slowly, I had come to realise that Tommy Deathridge and Milktooth were the same person.

So, when I heard that Mimi's parents were away that weekend, the thought started to germinate: I could take the watch back and help Lenny return it to Yasmin.

Getting in was easy. The spare key was still there under a piece of limestone in the front garden, where I had seen Mimi get it from when she was locked out. But what about getting out, now I could hear Tommy downstairs. I also heard the voice of Claire Costello.

'Who's there?'

Evidently, I had been heard in return. The question was repeated, and the voice was getting closer, the sound of feet slowly coming up the stairs. 'Is there someone there?'

I looked out of the window. There was a flat roof on the kitchen extension. Quicker than I thought possible, I climbed out the window and on to the roof, then managed to drop down into the darkness of the back garden.

'Oi, you.'

I could see Tommy framed in the bedroom window. There was a side gate which I quickly unbolted before running out onto Chantry Road and then up to Moseley High Street.

I ran across the High Street, breathing heavily. Instinctively I headed for the murk of the canopy over Tesco's. As I did so, I saw Spooner walking up on the other side of the road with his friends beside him. They had not noticed me, and I moved further into the gloom of the store's doorway. But as I did so, there was an angry car horn and the sound of Elvis Presley singing Suspicious Minds from a car stereo. I looked over to see a pink Jaguar come to a stop over the other side of the road. The driver's side window was wound down and there was Das (or Peter, as I was beginning to think I should call him) looking straight at me.

'Stephen,' he shouted, and when I didn't answer, he shouted even louder, 'Stephen.'

Spooner instinctively looked over, spotted me and all three of them came running across the road towards me. Even as they did so, Peter drove off quickly, as if he did not want to get involved.

At that point, I still could have run. How far I would have got I don't know, but I decided to make a stand. Spooner slowed down and, accompanied by the other two, walked towards me.

'Have you been talking to the police about me, Stephen?' he asked, moving closer.

As he came near, I tried to punch him. I knew, as soon as I threw it, that it was weak and ineffective. Spooner caught it with his left hand and launched a right upper cut that smashed my teeth against my tongue and sent me flying backwards with a great bang into the plate glass of Tesco's window. I was surprised I hadn't gone through the glass.

'He tried to hit me.' Spooner laughed with his friends, as all three of them held me back against the shop front. 'He actually tried to fight back.' Then he hit me again, this time in the stomach, and as I doubled up, winded, he asked me, 'Have you got any money, Steve? I'm a little short.'

He went through my pockets, and, of course, found the gold pocket watch. He held it aloft, leaving it to dangle in front of my face.

'This is fancy.' The glint of the gold sparkled with greater intensity as a number 50 bus swung into the stop that was in front of the canopy. I felt a sense of relief. People were getting off.

'It's that NF bastard,' shouted a familiar voice – Mimi. Along with Rick and Jasper.

Spooner turned, the watch still dangling on its chain. 'Fuck off, you slag,' he shouted at Mimi.

'That's mine,' shouted another voice, and the relief I felt at the apparent ending of Spooner's attack, turned to horror as Tommy Deathridge came into view from behind the now pulling-away bus. Spooner's friends used the confusion to run off, but Spooner, still holding the watch, was surrounded.

Tommy pushed through and grabbed the watch off Spooner. 'You took my watch.'

Spooner shook his head. 'It wasn't me.' He pointed at me. 'It was him. He had it.'

Tommy grabbed Spooner and shoved him up against the shop window. 'Do you know who I am?'

Spooner shook his head, his features contorted.

I moved to walk away, but Tommy turned to me quickly. 'You. Stay here.'

Such was the command in Tommy's voice, I didn't think to do anything else but stay.

Tommy stared back at Spooner. 'You might have heard of me. My name is Tommy. Tommy Deathridge.'

Spooner nodded, an involuntary retch contorting his now deathly pale face even further. There was suddenly a strong smell of urine and I saw a large wet patch had emerged at the front of Spooner's Sta Press trousers. Tommy looked down too and instinctively stepped back, the front of Spooner's shirt wrapped tight around his fist 'Oh dear. Couldn't you wait? He turned to Mimi. 'Do you know him?'

'He put our friend in hospital, and he called me a slag,' said Mimi.

Tommy tightened his grip on Spooner's shirt, so that Spooner had to stretch his neck back to breathe. 'You said that to my daughter.'

'I didn't know...' Spooner struggled to speak and looked even more defeated at the news that Mimi was Tommy Deathridge's daughter.

Tommy relaxed his grip. 'I think we all better go back to our house, Mimi, and sort this out. Bring your friends.'

'Please... just call the police,' begged the terrified Spooner.

Tommy shook his head. 'I'm going to sort you out myself.' He pulled Spooner's arm so that it was held behind his back and marched him ahead, instructing Rick and Jasper to walk either side in case Spooner tried to escape. I followed, equally terrified, walking alongside a wordless Mimi. I wondered briefly, once again, whether to cut and run but decided that my best bet was to go along with the situation.

We got to the house and went in to the large kitchen. There was no longer any sign of Claire.

'Get a plastic chair from the garden,' instructed

Tommy to Rick. 'I don't want the smell of piss on our nice furniture.' Tommy himself fetched some cable ties from the garage and Spooner's arms and legs were secured to the chair.

All the while, Spooner protested. 'It wasn't me.' He was crying now. 'It was him that stole the watch.' Spooner jerked his head at me. 'I was just looking at it. He was showing it to me in the street.'

Tommy stood over Spooner, fist raised. 'Will you shut the fuck up, whining away. You're getting on my nerves.'

'He put our friend in hospital. I told you before,' cut in Mimi. She looked at me. 'Ask him.'

'What happened?' asked Tommy.

'Him and a few others beat up our friend Jay. He's in the Accident Hospital.' She looked contemptuously again at me. 'He was there.'

Spooner continued protesting his innocence.

Tommy thrust his fist towards Spooner who immediately shut up. 'I can't think with that racket going on.' Leaving Rick and Jasper to watch Spooner, Tommy ushered Mimi and me out into the lounge.

'So what's going on?'

'Tell him,' said Mimi, looking at me.

Tommy looked at me expectantly.

So, I told the story of what had happened on the night when Jay was attacked. I told the whole truth. I already needed to lie about taking the gold watch. It wouldn't do to try too many lies on Tommy Deathridge.

'And have you told the police?' Tommy asked.

I told him what happened with PC Gordon.

'Yes, that's the trouble,' said Tommy, massaging a clenched fist. 'You can't rely on the normal channels if you want justice.' He relaxed his hand, spreading his fingers. 'But I've handed out enough justice in my time. I have some influence with the police. Perhaps I can use it to help your friend.'

He clenched his fist once more and looked at me. It was a stare that seemed to bore right into the heart of me and I felt a visceral iciness.

'So, what happened with the watch?'

I mouthed at air. My voice had gone.

Tommy turned to Mimi. 'Will you go out. I want to talk to your boyfriend on my own.'

Mimi got up. 'He is not my boyfriend.' She walked out of the room.

Tommy stared at me a while longer and then spoke quietly. 'I know it was you.'

I looked blank. I could speak now but it seemed better to remain silent.

'Don't look at me like that. I know you took the watch. I don't think that idiot took it. It was you. Of course, it would be you.' Tommy stood up. 'So what am I going to do with you? Imagine, someone breaking into the home of Tommy Deathridge and stealing from him? The sheer fucking audacity of that!' He strode over to the shotgun hanging on the wall, staring up at it. 'What should I do with you?'

But then Tommy turned back, his features relaxed.

He walked over and sat down on the sofa next to me. He sat so close his bulk unbalanced me to the point that it was all I could do not to topple against the man.

'Did you notice who I was with when I came into the house.'

I nodded.

His features knotted up again and he looked at me fiercely. 'Are you sure? Did you hear that I was with anyone?' He looked over to a family picture of him, with his wife and Mimi.

I slowly cottoned on. 'No,' I said quietly after a long pause.

'Why did you steal it?'

'I didn't...'

'Don't lie. Do not insult me by lying.' Tommy moved on the sofa to face me, almost causing me to topple once more. 'Tell me the fucking truth.'

I took a deep breath. 'I think that belongs to my family. I think you took it from my dad.'

Tommy smiled briefly, a glint of gold flashing from his tooth. 'You're a good lad. Are you not courting with Mimi anymore?'

I shook my head thinking there had never really been anything between me and Mimi.

'Never mind,' said Tommy. 'She would chew you up and spit you out, mate. I'd steer well clear of her if I were you.' He took the gold watch out of his pocket and held it up, letting it oscillate around on its heavy gold chain, the intricately engraved side interspersing with the enamelled picture of the polo player. I had not had chance to look at it much yet and I desperately wanted to examine it more closely.

'It's a beautiful thing, this watch.' Tommy concentrated intently on the timepiece as it swung around. 'I've always loved it. It's worth loads too. I had it valued once. I could have sold this watch for a fortune, even back in the sixties. God knows what it's worth now.' He twirled the watch round on its gold chain once more and I marvelled at how truly beautiful it was. Then Tommy quickly gathered it up in his hands and placed it in mine. I looked at the watch in my open palm.

'It's yours,' he said.

I looked at the watch, not hearing what Tommy had said.

'It's yours. I'm giving it to you,' said Tommy.

'But...'

'Listen, as you said, it belonged to your dad. I've done bad things in my life and one of them was taking that watch from your old man. I'm starting anew. I have found the Lord and I want to atone for my sins. I am giving back the watch I stole. You coming and taking it today was a sign and I am not going to ignore it.' He put his hand out. 'But give me it back for now. I'll need to show it to the police.'

I reluctantly handed the watch back.

'Don't worry, I'll return it in a few days.' He picked up the receiver of the telephone on the side table and, placing a fat finger in the dial, he started turning numbers.

'Now fuck off home before the police come.' He waved towards the door.

I let myself out of the room. I considered going back into the kitchen where Spooner was bound and guarded. But then I thought better of it. Letting myself out of the front door, I slowly made my way homeward.

COFFEE AT GIGI'S 1984

I considered asking for two coffees while I waited. But then she might want tea, and anyway, if she was late, it would go cold. The lady behind the counter waited patiently. She had a magnificent dusty beehive and thick overloaded makeup, with eyebrows drawn crooked over crusty mascara'd eyes. I finally ordered one coffee. The lady ignored the spectacular faded espresso machine behind her and reached for a large tin of Nescafé.

Like the woman serving, Gigi's was a reminder of times past. With chipped Formica and torn leatherette booths, each with its own jukebox terminal, the cafe hung steadfastly on to the style of its 50s and 60s heyday.

The clientele consisted mostly of the waifs and strays from The Palm Court Hotel, a local hostel for derelicts, alcoholics and the mentally ill. An elderly lady with a shopping trolley, its tartan body precariously tied to the frame with an old pair of tights, sat in the window, drinking tea from a cup and saucer. An old man in a grubby gabardine coat sat in one corner, leafing through a soft porn mag, flashes of flesh drawing my eye, even as I tried to avoid looking. The lady behind the counter tutted. 'I keep asking him to put it away, but he takes no notice.' She slid the cup of steaming coffee over to me, adding, 'The dirty bastard.' She pointed to one of the chrome-topped sugar dispensers, one on each table. 'If you want sugar, help yourself.' Then she took a deep breath before continuing. 'But you look sweet enough already.' Then she giggled shyly and looked down.

I quickly took my coffee over to a table and recounted the events of the evening before.

It was mum who decided to make an occasion of presenting Yasmin with the watch. Lenny and I had planned a visit to Bristol to perform the handover. But when Lenny contacted Yasmin, she had said she was coming to Birmingham anyway for a literary conference. Lenny suggested meeting her in a pub in town.

I told mum about it over breakfast one morning. We didn't often eat breakfast together, but mum had decided to cook bacon and eggs and we had sat down at the dining room table to eat.

'You can't meet her in a pub,' said mum, when she heard. 'I don't think Indian ladies like her are going to go into a pub. Have you asked her where she would like to meet?'

'I don't know, Lenny's arranged it all.'

'That man! How can he expect her to meet you in a pub. I think the best thing is for her to come here for dinner and you give it to her then. It's a special event. And Susan will be back. It will be good for her to be there. You can't meet this Yasmin lady in a pub. Anyway, I want to meet her. Maybe I can start finding out more about your father.'

I felt sorry for mum. She had finally read dad's pieces of writing: the facts he had kept from us all, even his own wife, all of these years. He had been so secretive and yet so domineering.

'How did you put up with him Mum?' I asked.

She stopped and thought. 'He was a difficult man, your father, but he loved us.' She stared at me for a while. 'He thought the world of you. He was so proud of you.'

'It didn't seem like it,' I said. 'I never felt I was good enough for him.'

'He wanted to push you. He wanted you to make something of your life. He wanted you to do better than he did. Not to have the struggles he had.' She stopped again and took a sip from her coffee. 'But then we don't fully know what struggles he had.'

I shook my head. 'It's hard, Mum. It's so hard to find out all these things about him now. He expected so much of me, but he couldn't even give me,' I pointed at mum, 'or you, the truth about who he was when he was alive.'

'He did the best he could, Stephen. He was difficult. I know that more than anyone, but he was a good man, and he did what he thought was best for all of us.'

'I still don't know how you managed to put up with him, Mum.'

She blinked. 'Marriage is all about knowing when to take notice and when to ignore. There was a lot to ignore about your father, but I loved him and I miss him.' She finished her breakfast in silence.

Mum thought long and hard about what to cook for Yasmin. 'She might not eat our meat. She might be religious and just eat special kosher meat like Jewish people.' I had not thought about that. I thought Jay didn't eat beef and sometimes was vegetarian. I knew Muslim people ate halal meat. I wasn't sure about Yasmin. In the end, mum found a recipe for a vegetarian goulash in her Delia Smith recipe book. 'That's the one,' she said, a long painted fingernail marking out the recipe. 'You can't go wrong with Delia. I'll cook some rice and get some nice bread and a bit of salad from Waitrose.' She paused a minute. 'Should I get wine? Do you think she drinks alcohol?'

'I don't know, Mum.' I was irritated by her fussing. 'I've never met her. Why don't you buy a bottle and then we can ask her if she wants wine. I'm sure Lenny will drink wine.'

'Oh, yes.' Mum nodded emphatically. 'Lenny will drink wine. We all know that. He'll probably turn up late too and ruin dinner, knowing him.' But I noticed mum was smiling. The initial animosity with Lenny seemed to have reduced.

As it happens, Lenny was not late at all. In fact, he arrived early, carrying a bag full of Red Stripe lager cans and a bottle of Thunderbird Wine, which he gave to mum with a flourish. He then spent the time pacing around and getting in the way as mum and me prepared for Yasmin's arrival.

Susan intervened then. 'Come into the living room, Lenny. I want to hear more about your Needless Alley days.' She seemed to know more about Needless Alley than me, but, like me, had also been surprised to find out we had an uncle who was in the band.

Jay arrived not long after Lenny. I saw his brother Bal's car draw up outside and watched as Jay was supported by Bal down the drive. He was wearing a turban once more and I don't think it was just to hide the fact his head had been shaved in hospital. Since we had been to India, Jay had got back in touch with the Sikh religion he had been born into.

When they got to the front door, I was shy and unsure what to say, partly because of Bal. I wondered how badly he thought of me, after all that had gone on with Spooner. However, Bal gave a warm thumbs up to me before he carried on back to his car.

'Are you going to let me in or have I got to stand out here all day?' said Jay leaning against the wooden frame of the glass porch.

Mum arrived by then. 'For God's sake let the poor lad in, Stephen.' She held Jay in a tight embrace. Jay silently mouthed "help me" over mum's shoulder, which made me laugh and broke the ice. 'It's so good to see you,' she continued as she held on to Jay. 'I'm so glad you came.'

It was mum's idea to invite Jay and I had been glad of the excuse to reach out to my friend. Since Jay's hospitalisation, I had been embarrassed to go round to his house or even call, worrying about how it would be if I had to see or speak to Narinder or Jay's mum. The last time I saw Narinder was that time at the hospital when she had been so devastatingly direct. The need to invite Jay had meant a nervous call to his house and my fears were confirmed when Narinder answered the phone, but this time she was her old friendly self and reacted as if the hospital conversation had never happened. Jay's mum had also come on to the phone to ask me how I was, so I was finally beginning to feel a lot less anxious about Jay's family's reaction to my role in him being beaten up, though the shame was still very much with me.

Jay sat down and faced a barrage of questions. Since Tommy's intervention, Spooner and his friends had been charged with grievous bodily harm and a court case was imminent in which both Jay and me would be witnesses.

'Has he been charged with stealing that watch?' asked Susan.

'Yes,' I replied. I was ashamed about that, in spite of all Spooner had done. Following the night of the burglary, the story of Spooner breaking in to Mimi's house had circulated. I had not wanted to reveal how I had entered Mimi's house without permission and taken something. Meanwhile, Tommy Deathridge had not wanted it known he had tolerated my uninvited incursion. So the story of Spooner committing the crime stood.

When the doorbell rang, Lenny and me both quickly got up at the same time to answer it.

Mum pointed me back into my chair. 'Let Lenny do it,' she said. 'You stay here.' However, even as Lenny went to the door, mum followed him and I decided I would go into the hallway too.

I was met by the sight of Lenny embracing a small, short-haired Asian lady wearing a Barbour jacket and salwar kameez. She was carrying a brown and battered leather briefcase, which she dropped in order grab Lenny's shoulder. This appeared to be more in order to steady herself than to return Lenny's affections. He released the embrace and held her hands, looking at her face. 'You haven't changed, Yasmin.'

'I should think I have, Lenny.' She looked him up and down. 'We all have.'

The watch was handed over to Yasmin after dinner. Lenny and I had wanted to give it earlier than that, but mum insisted we wait until after the dessert she'd made.

When the watch was finally handed over, Yasmin held it up, her eyes shining as she examined it. Finally, she spoke. 'This is all I have left from my family in India. It means a lot to me to get it back.' She looked at me and then Lenny. 'Thank you.'

She sat silently for a while after that, listening to us all talking. I noticed and moved closer, so I could speak with her. I told her about my failed 'A' levels and then we talked about her work at Bristol University. I was interested and we discussed some of the books I had read.

'Have you considered doing English Lit?' Yasmin asked.

'I would need to do more 'A' levels.'

'Well, do them,' she said. 'You're still young, and you have plenty of time, but still you should make the most of the time you have. I had a health scare recently. Everything is alright, but it has made me more aware than ever of the need to make the most of our lives.' Shortly afterwards she looked at the time and announced it was time for her to leave.

'Before you go,' said Lenny, standing up, 'I have an announcement to make.'

We all stared up at him expectantly. He had come dressed smart in his black suit jacket and Levis, but now after several drinks, his hair was breaking loose from the pony tail he'd neatly tied it back into, and he was looking generally dishevelled. He took another drink from his wine glass. 'I have an announcement to make,' he repeated.

'Yes, you said,' mum replied.

Lenny looked down at her benignly. 'I'm so glad we're friends again, Rosie.'

Mum nodded. 'Yes Lenny, it's good, I'm sorry for all that went on. Is that your announcement?'

'No. I've got something to tell you all.'

'Get on with it,' said Yasmin, smiling.

Lenny poured himself another drink, spilling some on the table. We had finished the bottle of white wine mum bought, a while ago. Since then Lenny had opened the Thunderbird, though nobody but him and me would touch it. Lenny put the bottle down, holding on to it for a few seconds as if he was scared it might topple over. 'So, what I'm going to tell you is...'

'Just tell us...' came a chorus of voices.

Lenny sat down. 'I had a call from Johnny D, the Needless Alley vocalist. He wants to reform the band. The other guys are in too. There's going to be a tour. He said there might even be an album.'

Mum was the first to respond. 'That's great Lenny. I always did like that song you did, "One Night Band".' She sang the chorus a little out of tune. I was surprised mum knew the song. I had only heard it recently.

'Was that you, Lenny?' asked Yasmin, looking impressed. 'I never listened to much pop music, but I liked that one. Very catchy.'

Lenny looked pleased at the recognition, and I was happy and excited for him.

'Now I really must go,' Yasmin said firmly. There was a train leaving Yardley Wood station at 8:30 and she had a hotel booked in the city centre.

Lenny offered to walk her to the station.

'You couldn't walk yourself, Lenny, let alone anyone else, the state you're in,' said mum, laughing. 'Stephen, will take her.'

'I don't need anyone to take me,' said Yasmin. 'I'm perfectly capable of catching a train by myself.' She looked at me. 'Though it would be nice to have some company.'

Yasmin and I walked up the road in silence. I was glad to spend some more time in her company. Like mum, I had hoped to find out more about dad and I thought perhaps this was my last chance. Finally, I picked up the courage. 'What was he like?'

At first Yasmin did not answer and we walked in silence a little more.

After a while, she answered, 'Who?'

'My dad. What was he like when you knew him in India?'

I was aware of Yasmin looking at me. After a while she replied. 'He was quiet and thoughtful. Not like Lenny. Lenny was always easier to get on with. Lenny always had charm, but your dad was a little more difficult. No less likeable, though. You had to scratch below the surface a bit more with your dad. I liked both of them. They were both my friends in different ways.'

'I don't remember seeing that part of him at all,' I said. 'He always seemed so unhappy. I was a disappointment to him.'

'Don't be too hard on him,' said Yasmin. We arrived at the station and walked down on to the platform. 'He had it hard. The Anglo-Indians were a manufactured race. They didn't know who they were. They tried to be British, but the British just laughed at them and didn't really take them seriously. They couldn't be fully Indian, so they had no place. And then, when they came here, they were seen as Indian. It was hard for me, coming here.' She looked down at her salwar kameez. 'I do have a culture to hang on to, but that can be difficult in this country.' She paused for a while before saying, 'We just do the best we can and muddle our way through. That was what your dad was doing. Just the best he could.'

There was a dim vibration coming from the rails and Yasmin looked along the line. The train could be seen approaching in the distance.

As the train drew to a stop, I was unsure how to say

goodbye to Yasmin. But she opened her arms wide and drew me into a hug. 'Thank you, Stephen, for all that you've done.' She let me go and then pressed a card from her handbag into my hand. 'Give me a call sometime. If you're interested in English literature, maybe I can help you.' She got onto the train, and I watched her find a seat and then wave gently to me as the train pulled away.

In Gigi's, my reflections on that night were interrupted when Jenny came in through the door. She sat down at the table and looked around the cafe, at the faded dusty decor and the decrepit waifs and strays sitting around.

'So, you ask me out on a date and then bring me to a place like this.' She looked at me seriously. 'It is a date, isn't it?'

I nodded. 'I think so...' I looked around at the place. 'I'm sorry, shall we go somewhere else.'

Jenny smiled and I thought how beautiful she was. She looked into my eyes. 'It's fine, Stephen. Everything is just fine.'

ACKNOWLEDGMENTS

I should like to thank the following people who have helped me get to the point where I have written and published a novel.

Ann Hamilton, WriteRight Editing Services (writerightediting.co.uk), for her help and support throughout the whole writing, development and editing process.

Kerry Hadley-Pryce for assistance in development.

Claire Morley, My ePublish Book, for her expertise in getting this published.

My niece, Georgia Chapman, for her wonderful talent in designing the cover artwork.

Bharti Patel for assistance in the book launch.

Philip Chapman, Maria Chapman, Dave Lee and Raj Parmar for feedback of early drafts.

Ray Lee, for first helping me develop as a professional writer.

My children, Lewis, Callie and Bella for their love and support.

And my wife Kaye, for her love, feedback, reading, mugs of tea, cakes and belief that I could get this novel completed and in print.